A SLOW, COLD FURY

There is a rare anger that accompanies unwilling separation.

It's an orchid of fury, sprouting in the stinking manure of a once-in-a-lifetime occurrence when normal existence is split in two—the side you loved that is gone and the side you now occupy that is isolated, strange, freakish, and alone.

You wait for the universe to right itself—you wait because you're human and humans are innately optimistic—and then it doesn't, and you feel like a sucker.

You are the original fool, a butt of nature's large, cruel joke.

That's when the flame begins to flicker, low and cold.

You're not mad at the world and you don't want to bluntly attack the innocent—no, it's a sharp, laser-focused anger. The concentrated nucleus is narrowly defined to kick in the teeth and bust the bones of the specific people who did this thing to you.

I did not know for sure who those people were.

I *did* know that I would find him, or her, or them.

OTHER BOOKS YOU MAY ENJOY

Cold Fury

T. M. GOEGLEIN

speak

An Imprint of Penguin Group (USA) Inc.

For Laura, who always has my back.

SPEAK
Published by the Penguin Group
Penguin Group (USA) Inc.
375 Hudson Street
New York, New York 10014, U.S.A.

(Ⓟ)

USA / Canada / UK / Ireland / Australia / New Zealand / India / South Africa / China
Penguin Books Ltd, Registered Offices: 80 Strand, London WC2R 0RL, England

For more information about the Penguin Group visit www.penguin.com

First published in the United States of America by G. P. Putnam's Sons,
a division of Penguin Young Readers Group, 2012
Published by Speak, an imprint of Penguin Group (USA) Inc., 2013

THE LIBRARY OF CONGRESS HAS CATALOGED THE G. P. PUTNAM'S SONS EDITION AS FOLLOWS:
Goeglein, T. M. (Ted M.)
Cold fury / T. M. Goeglein.
p. cm.
Summary: Sixteen-year-old Chicago preparatory school student Sara Jane Rispoli
must unravel a web of complex mysteries after her family goes missing and
she is pursued by unknown enemies.
ISBN 978-0-399-25720-9 (hardcover)
[1. Secret societies—Fiction. 2. Missing persons—Fiction. 3. Violence—Fiction.
4. Chicago (Ill.)—Fiction. 5. Mystery and detective stories.] I. Title.
PZ7.G5533Co 2012
[Fic]—dc23
2011025824

Speak ISBN 978-0-14-242631-9

Printed in the United States of America.

1 3 5 7 9 10 8 6 4 2

ALWAYS LEARNING   PEARSON

PRELUDE

MY NAME IS SARA JANE RISPOLI.

It's not my birthday and I haven't eaten cake since I turned sixteen, but I'm plagued by ice cream.

If anyone offers me a cone, I'll break his nose.

I've been chased for the past month by a creepy black truck that sells frozen treats, and just when I've shaken it, the little nightmare comes tinkling around the corner again.

I have a movie-obsessed sidekick with a roller-coaster weight problem, and an ill-tempered Italian greyhound that's not really my dog but I love him anyway, sort of.

I have a classic 1965 Lincoln Continental convertible in dire need of bodywork and a badass 2000 Ferrari 360 Spider that's like driving a fuel-injected comet.

I have a boyfriend who's finally, actually my boyfriend and who accommodates this decidedly non-petite nose and these braces, but has no idea who he's really dating.

I also have an ancient, worn leather notebook that chronicles a century of Chicago's most valuable criminal secrets but refuses to yield the secret I desire most—ultimate power—holding it mute and indecipherable within its last chapter,

"Volta." The whole thing is held together by rubber bands and masking tape, while my last measure of sanity is held together by an unyielding determination to track down my missing parents and little brother. Every breath I take is fueled by a cold flame of fury that burns in my gut with a need for vengeance and revenge.

I'm alive because I have the notebook.

What I don't have is a real clue where my family is.

They're not dead, but there are ways of being alive that are worse than death.

I hold no mercy for my enemies because mercy is for suckers.

I don't have any plans for the future other than to continue breathing.

I throw a hundred hard combination punches at a heavy bag every day, and it never feels like enough.

When I'm not being chased, I chase back. And when I'm not studying the notebook, I roam the streets of Chicago, where one day soon I'll either catch the people who have my family or be caught by them—either way I'm ready to fight to the death.

As long as I have the notebook, I have a weapon.

As long as the possibility exists that my family's alive, I'll keep looking.

Every violent, unspeakable step I take to save them makes me into someone else. I remember the other Sara Jane, but it's no longer completely me, and that's okay.

She would've only slowed me down.

1

I WALKED FROM ROOM TO ROOM THROUGH GRAY
midday light, inhaling the odor of stale floor wax and dust,
listening to a grandfather clock tick into the void. A thin
sunbeam shone weakly at the bottom of the staircase, and I
stepped into it, feeling no warmth. The home I grew up in,
stripped of the people I loved, crowded my heart with unbear-
able loneliness.

My family was violently kidnapped four months ago.

Then, slashed photos smiled from shattered frames. Gutted
couches yawned next to splintered chairs, and muddy-bloody
handprints and footprints of strangers smeared the walls and
floor. Today, the living room stood bare before me; I'd had the
remnants hauled away, but the emptiness was even worse than
the torn and battered furniture that had seemed so wounded.
Now the room was plainly dead, and it made me feel dead
inside. With one hand on the banister, I looked into the hall
mirror, seeing my dark hair pulled into a careless ponytail, my
usual attire of worn Cubs T-shirt and beater jeans hanging

limply from my body. An aggressive nose, lip-stretching braces, and high cheekbones—my face looked back, dominated by blue eyes flecked with gold, and I noticed something missing from them. Where there had once been hope, even in the darkest moments, now there was only tired despair. It seemed as if for every true fact I discovered, two lies followed, stoking a hatred that has simmered for months.

It's hard to admit, since it's directed at my parents.

Their disappearance and that of my younger brother, Lou, was a result of the duplicity baked into the Rispoli family history. My mom and dad showed me only one of their two faces, and by omitting the full truth, they lied to mine every day. The despair in my eyes—they put it there, and it isn't fair. And then the idea of fairness reminds me that no matter what they didn't tell me or how much damage it caused, no one deserves their tortured existence. The hatred fades and I love them again, completely.

I looked away from the mirror and creaked upstairs to the second floor.

My unconscious will and heavy feet led me to Lou's room, where I shut the bedroom door. Overcome by a weary sense of desolation, I lay on his bed, flipped on his rocket ship clock, and looked at a green, glowing moon on the ceiling intersected by a faint *1:58 p.m.* My family felt farther away than that cold, distant satellite.

As empty as the house was, it paled next to Rispoli & Sons Fancy Pastries.

Our family business had not churned out a cake, pie, or molasses cookie in months. It occurred to me that regular customers would notice that the place was perpetually dark, so I papered over the windows and hung a sign that read REMODELING! PLEASE PARDON OUR DUST! My greater concern was that the Outfit would grow suspicious—if just one nosy thug linked my dad's absence as counselor-at-large (while I fill in for him, my excuse is that he's ill) to the bakery's closure, every crook in Chicago would start whispering "rat." For my family's survival and the preservation of my own neck, I can't allow anyone to assume that he's become an FBI informant.

Closing my eyes, yawning deeply, I tried to picture my family's faces as a song tinkled outside the house like an off-key kiddie piano, and Frank Sinatra crooned along—

Chicago, Chicago, that toddling town,
Chicago, Chicago, I'll show you around, I love it!

My ex-nanny turned assailant, Elzy Zanzara, used to belt it out when I was small, and it startled me awake. I blinked up at the moon intersected by a flashing *2:15 p.m.*

Outside the door, wooden stairs creaked softly as someone tried not to be heard.

I stared at the doorknob turning slowly, silently, and leaped like an insane linebacker, throwing all of my hundred and five pounds against the door and twisting the lock. Someone on the other side hit the ground hard as I flew to the window and looked down at the Mister Kreamy Kone truck blocking the Lincoln. Moments later, a shoulder assaulted the door like a battering ram. Wood groaned, hinges complained, but the lock held; another shot like that and I wouldn't be so lucky. I yanked open the window and grasped the frame, my hair moving in a humid breeze, filling me with the paralyzing memory

5

of a slow-moving Ferris wheel. But then adrenaline trumped fear and I scrambled out, inching along the narrow ledge toward a maple tree's creeping branches. It was too far away, so I stretched, slipped, grasped at empty air, and then desperately pushed off with my other foot, hoping to reach the tree, which I did. In fact I hit every branch on the way down, kissing earth with a thud, feeling like I'd been tenderized by hockey sticks. The bedroom door split and shattered above me as I rolled to my feet, ignoring waves of nauseating pain, poised to sprint for the car, when something in my gut made me stop. It felt like a mistake to look up at the window but I couldn't help myself.

It was leaning on the ledge with both hands, staring back.

I say "it" because the gender was indistinguishable.

Maybe it should be simple to discern one's sex when he or she is covered in something skintight, but this thing's body was model-thin and androgynous—a life-sized is-it-a-Barbie-or-a-Ken? It wore a weirdly militaristic uniform in the same fathomless shade of black as the ice cream trucks, so taut and glossy it could have been latex, complete with a jaunty cap and elbow-high gloves. A thick leather belt cinched its non-existent waist, and when it perched a foot on the ledge, I saw its pants tucked into tall boots. The only other color in the ensemble was red letters, *MKK,* encircled by the red outline of an ice cream truck, stitched on its breast and shirtsleeve. Even stranger, something silver and shiny hung from its neck. Its rigid face was composed of delicate, sexless features covered in snow-white flesh with a thin blue line for a mouth, giving it the appearance of a death mask.

And then it removed its sunglasses.

Its eyes pulsated like electric cherries.

So shiny, so red, and so sickly wrong.

I was stuck in the ghoulishness of it, my feet magnetized to the ground, when the thing leaped from the window. It fell quickly and landed deftly on both feet, and I turned and sprinted for the Lincoln, jumped inside, and locked the doors. I fumbled keys into the ignition and cranked the engine just as the thing threw itself onto the hood like a vampire-monkey. We were inches apart, its wet breath steaming the glass between us. Fear and injustice flooded my chest as a cold blue flame flickered beneath it; I was calm but furious, seeing the demonic thing for the very first time. It had been chasing me for a month, hidden behind its own impenetrable black windshield. Mister Kreamy Kone trucks were windowless vending machines on wheels with no way to see inside; customers deposited money, made a selection, and out it popped. Until I'd learned that a small fleet of them surrounded my home the night my family disappeared, I'd never noticed them around Chicago; I had no real idea how long they'd been on the streets or where they came from. The truck that pursued me was always in motion, and I'd even wondered if it was unmanned and remote-controlled.

Now I had an answer as my burning blue eyes locked onto its glowing red eyes.

We were face-to-face, and I deployed ghiaccio furioso with a vengeance, searching its psyche for its very worst fear, but—nothing. I blinked again and cold fury bounced back, stinging my brain like a cloud of angry bees. The windshield wasn't the problem—I'd conducted experiments of ghiaccio furioso on (poor) Doug, trying to ascertain its power, and I

7

knew glass was no barrier against my concentrated rage. I still couldn't summon cold fury at will, but when the intense emotion kindled deep in my gut, I'd learned to control it in the same way that a stovetop flame can be turned up or down.

The thing's eyes widened, showing fat clusters of veins pumped full of blood.

Its pupils pulsated in time to its heartbeat, nearly thump-thumping out of its skull.

It drew its head back, hammered it against the windshield, shook it, and did it again even harder.

Broken glass rained down as I leaned on the gas, tearing through a hedge onto Balmoral Avenue. The creature flew up and over the top of the car while I cranked the wheel, hauling ass onto Clark Street and up Lawrence Avenue at eighty miles per hour. I was sure I'd thrown it free. I sat back cautiously listening to the world hum past, which became a violent slitting of fabric, a determined ripping of seams as I was sliced in the neck by a hunk of windshield as sharp as a surgical tool. The creature slashed through the convertible top, swinging at my face, missing, and gashing my shoulder while I swerved crazily, trying to shake it off. Car horns screamed, more glass bit and tore at my neck, and I remembered the loaded .45 in the glove compartment. I scrabbled for it with desperate fingertips, bumping it to the floor, and lunged for the cold metal with one hand on the wheel and the seat belt gagging my neck. The frantic wail of a vehicle brought me upright. I veered out of the oncoming traffic lane just as the creature stuck its alabaster face through the convertible top and I squeezed the trigger, blasting once, twice, three times. The thing shrieked and rolled onto the trunk, trying to grip it with all fours as I accelerated, yanking the steering wheel from side to side. First one black glove slipped, then a boot, and then it disappeared as a moving van veered awkwardly and failed to brake, followed by a sick, wet *thunk!*

In an instant the creature was gone for good.

A couple blocks later I pulled to the curb and gulped air, shocked to be alive. I shouldn't have survived, yet there I sat in (almost) one piece, heart hammering in my chest, blood oozing down my neck and raging in my ears. The creature's demise was good because I was safer, but bad because it was a link to my family, but good because I wasn't dead and could still try to find them, but bad because—

Because a piano began to plunk and a voice began to croon.

Chicago, Chicago, I'll show you around, I love it!

My eyes darted to the rearview mirror as the black truck materialized on the street behind me, slip-sliding through traffic. It wasn't possible—I'd seen the thing get hit by a van with my own eyes, or at least thought I had, or at least I'd *heard* it—and yet it was six cars back, then two, gaining rapidly, and without thinking my foot fell like lead on the gas. The back tires shrieked as I tore across lanes, eyes filling with tears as I saw the sign:

CONSTRUCTION AHEAD—WILSON AVE. CLOSED—NO LOCAL TRAFFIC

I made a lunatic right turn, cars screeching and biting curbs behind me as I squinted into the rearview mirror. There was the truck, on two wheels then bumping onto four, on my tail as I sped past the wooden barriers and hit chewed-up Wilson Avenue, which was waiting for new concrete to be laid. It was like driving through the Grand Canyon, all deep craters and ragged potholes, and just as deserted—there were no other cars, sidewalks were empty, construction equipment was unattended and idle. There was an end-of-the-world quality to it— I was in one of the largest cities on earth rocketing though an uninhabited wasteland, pursued by a relentless creature—and the bleakness of it all made me miss the sign posted at the cross street where the road rose up.

WILSON AVE. BRIDGE RECONSTRUCTION— NO ADMITTANCE!

Or maybe I did see it and just sped up.

Maybe I'd finally had enough of searching for my family, which was as futile as chasing shadows, and enough of that childish emotion, hope. A whispered notion occurred to me then, that today was a fine day for *me* to die too, and that an easy way laid just ahead.

Flying up the incline, knowing the Chicago River lurked on the other side, I realized what a relief death would be. All I had to do was keep rolling! And there it was, my side of the bridge—a steel skeleton with girders wide enough to drive on but nothing underneath except a seventy-foot drop. The other half of the bridge was gone. After a long span of air, Wilson Avenue continued on the opposite side. I looked out at the gap of nothingness and wondered how it would feel to be a part of it—to float for a split second with the wheels spinning and then plummet headfirst into the dark, churning water. Solving my problem in one fell swoop seemed unquestionably correct, like doing myself a favor. My foot wavered between gas and brake; gas won, and I floored it thinking of freedom, of peaceful resolution. Except there would be none without knowing what had happened to my family—no peace, no resolution, only an eternity of unanswered nothingness—and I jammed on the brakes. But the steel was slick, and the car skidded to a slow, slippery stop with the front tires at the very edge of the last girders to nowhere.

In front of me, the summer wind whistled.

Below me, deep brown water swirled.

My heart hammered at my chest, and somewhere far away a duck quacked.

For a moment all I could hear was my own disjointed breathing. And then, quietly, Sinatra began crooning behind me as the truck crept up the bridge, eased to a halt, and the creature slid out from behind the darkened windshield, staring intently. I looked into the rearview mirror, wondering why it wasn't torn and bleeding, when its mouth moved and it ferociously licked at pinkish soft-serve ice cream. When it was done, it flicked its hand like shaking liquid from a cup. Something silvery glinted as the thing climbed back into the truck, and I knew it would come for me now, or, more accurately, my brain. Months earlier, Lou told me the captors had invaded my dad's head. It would be the same for me; besides invaluable gray matter, the rest of me was just gristle.

Some days really are fine to die, I thought, stepping out of the car and onto the bridge. *But maybe it requires some help to do it.* I moved carefully, slipping a bit on the slick steel, regaining my balance as I glanced through the girders beneath my feet. All I could see were construction cables and, farther down, the river, and I stopped only when I was equidistant to the truck and the edge to nowhere behind me. The creature now had a clear shot. Standing perfectly still, I pointed at it and then touched my head with the same finger. "You want this? What's inside?"

The truck revved its engine, dying to burst forward.

I closed and opened my eyes, exhaled, and said, "Well then . . . come and get it."

Back tires squealed as the thing barreled straight for me—fifteen feet, ten—and I smiled, extended a middle finger, and stepped between a gap in the girders. I fell a few feet before grabbing a cable and swinging like a pendulum while the truck roared above me. Its brakes complained, searching for traction, but the slick girders rejected them. I hauled myself up just in time to see the truck slide over the edge of the bridge and come to a precarious, tilting halt. I sprinted for it, determined to shove it into space, as a gentle gust of wind blew past. The truck teetered once and was gone. I heard it hit the river before I saw it, and when I looked over, it was already sinking. Water pressure blew out the windshield as cold brown liquid rushed into the truck. The creature stared up at me, clawing at the seat belt, convulsing like it was an electric chair, trying to scream while its mouth filled with water. Grimly, feeling no joy, I murmured, "Fine day, isn't it?"

The river covered its face, the red eyes flickered once, and it sank slowly away with Frank Sinatra gurgling to silence.

I rose to my feet, watching an eruption of fat belching bubbles and stringy motor oil, experiencing the same conflicted feeling as when I believed the thing had been run over by a moving van; I'd saved my own life but lost a connection to my family. The last trace of the truck swirled away and I turned from the river, seeing something shiny lying nearby. I picked up a small ice cream cone the size of a Dixie cup; it was hewn from silver, its conical shape crisscrossed with a waffle pattern. It must have been the object hanging at the creature's neck from which it lapped up the disgusting soft serve. Looking closer, I saw how the creature had lost it—a broken chain hung from a loop—and an engraving on the inside. After two years of high school Spanish at Casimir Fepinsky Preparatory (known as Fep Prep) I was able to read, "*Soy belleza y belleza es yo.* I am beauty and . . ."

"Beauty is me," a voice whispered.

I jumped back, shocked at the creature nearby, its eyes on the cone in my hand. The ghostly thing moved lithely to the edge, peering at the oil slick on the water's surface. I noticed something different about its face—the shape of its forehead, a smaller nose—and that its sexless model body was bone dry. It was like seeing tiny discrepancies in one-third of identical triplets, and I realized that the creature from my house, the thing at the bottom of the river, and the one standing several feet away were three distinct but eerily similar ice cream creatures. A red line appeared beneath its eye as a bloody tear cut across its snowy cheek. "You killed Beauty," it whispered.

"I didn't . . ."

"You killed *my Beauty!*" it shrieked, and I gagged a little, looking at gray stumps where teeth had been and a tongue as slickly black as the truck. The thing was shaking so violently that the silver ice cream cone at its neck danced across its chest. I looked at another truck parked at the bottom of the bridge—I hadn't heard it approach—and realized that they'd chased me tag-team style throughout the past month, one picking up where another left off. After all, a caravan of speeding black trucks would draw the attention of even the most indifferent Chicago cop.

I also realized that whatever they'd been to one another—siblings, friends, something else—they'd loved one another.

When I looked back, the thing's eyes were glued to mine—I'd already begun to think of it as Teardrop—and what I saw in them was different from its dead partners, who had faced me with the detachment of hunters. On the contrary, Teardrop trembled with malice and revenge. I didn't have time to lift a hand before it deftly sprinted the short length between us and punched me in the face like Mike Tyson at his baddest, sending me onto my butt, scrabbling not to fall through the girders. I got to my feet quickly and carefully, spitting blood and pain, knowing it was too strong and fast for a thing that belonged on a Fashion Week runway; it had to be fueled by insanity, chemicals, or both. Its drowned partner slurped soft serve before trying to run me down, and I wondered only briefly what was in that shit before Teardrop charged me again.

PRELUDE

MY NAME IS SARA JANE RISPOLI.

Several short weeks ago, I turned sixteen.

So far there has been nothing sweet about it.

I have braces, the thick, transparent type—they make my teeth appear too large for my mouth and my lips too small to contain them.

I have good hair and acceptable skin but my nose is Roman, as in it's roamin' all over my face, and I plan to do something about it someday.

I have a learner's permit but no license, but I've been driving my dad's old Lincoln Continental since I was thirteen, so big freaking deal.

I have a boyfriend—well, a boy who treats me like a friend instead of how I want to be treated, so BFD again.

I also have a steel briefcase, and inside that briefcase is ninety-six thousand dollars in cash, an AmEx Black Card in my name, a Sig Sauer .45 conceal-and-carry, and an old leather notebook stuffed full of so many unusual facts, indecipherable notes, and unlisted phone numbers that it's held together with masking tape and rubber bands.

The notebook is why I have the gun.

What I don't have anymore are my parents or little brother.

They're either dead and gone, or just dead, or just gone.

I don't have a Friendbook page.

I don't have space on ISpace.

I threw my cell phone into Lake Michigan weeks ago.

I'm being watched, stalked, tapped, and spied on, and if the opportunity arises, the watchers and stalkers will try to snatch me, and the tappers and spies will try to kill me.

As long as I keep moving, I should be okay.

As long as I keep the notebook with me, I should stay alive.

This is not what I thought life would be like when I turned sweet sixteen.

A REQUIREMENT OF STUDENTS at Casimir Fepinsky Preparatory (Fep Prep, as everyone calls it) is to keep a journal of their high school career.

I just reread the first two pages of mine, and so far it's a doozy.

After all, how many sophomores can record their lives as a fugitive-slash-vigilante?

The truth, though, is that I wouldn't keep a journal if I didn't have to. I'm not naturally compelled to share the details of my life. That's why blogging seems self-centered and tweeting is just, I don't know, borderline insane. Does the world really care that I just ate an onion bagel and now I'm laughing out loud about it? Isn't that something a crazy person would say?

Then again, I keep up with it partly because writing everything down helps me stay sane.

The other, more important reason is that it may help me find my family.

My English lit teacher, Ms. Ishikawa, is one of my favorites. She's wise and tiny, like an energetic hamster wearing glasses. In guiding our journal writing, she quoted William Shakespeare's *The Tempest*, saying, "What's past is prologue"—the present is constructed from the events that preceded it.

That's why I've decided to mine the past for information and use this journal as a storehouse—the place where I put the facts in order right up to the moment my family vanished.

The bloody, broken night marked the beginning of a quest—to find them and to discover who and what we really are. To do that requires patience and concentration, but it also requires context, of which I have very little. Tracking them down without knowing what occurred before that night is as impossible as trying to put a puzzle together with pieces missing—you look at jigsaw fragments and see a pair of piercing blue eyes but no head, and a hand but no arm, and the intelligent smile of a young boy but no boy. No dad, no mom, no little brother. Only chunks and shards that don't fit, since, as Ms. Ishikawa and Shakespeare taught, a human life is not made up only of the present. It's constructed from dead slices of time, fading memories, and long-ago whispered conversations. So now I'm examining times gone by like a forensic pathologist, dissecting it for clues about my home torn apart and family ripped free of the living world.

The terrible thing that happened to them didn't occur in a void.

It wasn't a wayward meteor or supernatural act that destroyed our lives and put me on the run.

It occurred because other terrible things happened before it. I'm determined to understand what they were, and the best way to do it is by taking a hard, honest look at my family.

My grandfather, my dad's dad, was Enzo Rispoli, a tiny, soft-spoken man who was in charge of the family business, Rispoli & Sons Fancy Pastries. Grandpa had many nicknames. "Enzo the Baker," which was self-explanatory, and "Enzo the Biscotto," which was my favorite since *biscotto* is Italian for "little cookie," and that's what he reminded me of—a small, sweet pastry. Now and then, some men who spoke in such low tones that only my grandpa could hear them (or as I thought of them, the "Men Who Mumbled") would call him "Enzo the Boss," which was confusing, since the only people he ever bossed around—gently—were my father, Antonio, whom everyone calls Anthony, and his younger brother Benito, whom everyone calls Buddy.

I really do despise Uncle Buddy.

Funny, because I used to adore him.

I can't deny that my uncle was my best buddy, and my parents' too—or so it seemed. Uncle Buddy was always around since, to be honest, he didn't have much of a life of his own. There's a word I hear in old movies now and then—*schlub*—that fits him perfectly. He was short and blocky where my dad is tall and thin, shambling and awkward where my dad is graceful and funny, and he laughed too loud at inappropriate moments. Uncle Buddy ate like a garbage truck, shoveling pasta and spattering his shirt with red sauce, and smoking was a constant habit, with him puffing on our porch in an intense, desperate way, like he was mad at the cigarettes. Besides my family, he was alone most of the time, with no real friends and no girlfriend ever. In general, my family tends to stick close and socialize mainly among one another, but Uncle Buddy was extreme. He oozed loneliness, but an annoying type of loneliness, like he wanted something in particular more than he wanted just to be wanted.

There's an old familiar story my parents tell—they take turns telling it—about how they met. My mom was working in a department store as a hand model, displaying diamond rings, when my dad noticed her. Very smoothly, he asked to see a ring, inspected it, and then, as he slipped it back on her finger, said, "Will you marry me?" Months later, he took her to Italy to pop the question for real and had a ring made for her there, in a little hilltop village called Ravello. It's a gold signet ring with an *R* raised in tiny, hard, winking diamonds, and at the end of the story she always turns it on her lovely finger and confesses that she would have said yes the first time my dad asked if he hadn't been so full of self-confidence.

Uncle Buddy loved that story a little too much.

I know now that he was viciously jealous of who my dad was and what he had, but hid it beneath a thin layer of false good nature.

He pretended to love us, too, but actually despised us, and buried that as well.

He spent hours telling my mom jokes in the kitchen, making her laugh while she used her delicate thumbs and forefingers to shape delicious little ravioli, and helped my dad reattach the lightning-struck weather vane to the slate roof of our big old house on Balmoral Avenue. My uncle happily packed me into his rusty red convertible and took me wherever I wanted to go—Foster Beach or the Art Institute or even shopping on Michigan Avenue, which bored him senseless. On warm summer weekends, we all rode the El to Wrigley Field and sat in the bleacher seats Uncle Buddy had bought especially so we could cheer on his favorite Cubs center fielder, Dominic Hughes.

In particular, I remember breakfast at Lou Mitchell's.

It was Uncle Buddy's favorite diner in Chicago.

He loved everything about the place, from its neon sign on the outside to its snug booths on the inside. It was in one of them, with him and me sitting side by side sharing blueberry pancakes so big they spilled over the plate, and my mom and dad across from us sharing a secret smile, that she told us she was pregnant and that it was a boy. I remember how my dad, tall and thinly muscular (like me) with a perpetual five o'clock shadow (not like me, thankfully), was grinning widely as he put his arm around my mom and pulled her close. I also recall the look on my mom's face. She's gorgeous, with green, almond-shaped eyes, high cheekbones (got 'em—thanks, Mom), and wavy black hair, and she literally seemed to be glowing. I was just a kid, confused and excited at the same time, so maybe I don't remember correctly what happened next, but I think I do.

What I remember is Uncle Buddy's blank face.

He stared hard at my dad and said, "Another male Rispoli,"

as if it were bad news. And then he shook it off like coming out of a trance, smiled his big Uncle Buddy smile, and said, "Hey, since you told us here, you should name the kid Lou!" My parents must have liked the sound of that because several months later my little brother, Lou Mitchell Rispoli, was born at Northwestern Hospital.

Having a new baby around was weird. Until then I had been the center of everyone's attention, from my parents to my grandparents to Uncle Buddy. Now they all cooed at the baby, held and kissed the baby, and sang him soft Italian lullabies. Don't get me wrong, I enjoyed my share of hugs and cuddles with Lou, too. I loved how he smelled and especially his long eyelashes and chubby fingers. But after a while, enough was enough. In those first two (incredibly long) years of Lou's life, with everyone treating him like a little prince, my mother teaching school, and my dad working late at the bakery, I began to feel forgotten. Even at that young age, I was aware that a Rispoli never made a scene, so whenever I felt sorry for myself, rather than complain or cry, I'd open my favorite book (*Laura Lane, Spygirl*) and stare at the pages. I'd only recently learned to read, but it didn't matter since I wasn't interested in the words. It was just a place to put my eyes while I waited for someone to pay attention to me.

That's when Uncle Buddy introduced me to boxing.

I took to it right away, and gave up ballet to learn how to fight.

To be honest, I'm really proud of my left hook.

Boxing was unusual for a six-year-old girl, I admit, almost as much as it is now for a sixteen-year-old girl. But it's just as graceful as ballet, and when you're taught to do it well, you realize that it's less about hitting than not getting hit. Anyway, even though I was taught to stand up for myself if I was being mistreated, it's not like I'm some kind of brawling maniac. My weapons were the self-confidence I copied from my dad and the power of cool logic instilled in me by my mom.

And then there are parts of me that are just, well . . . me.

I'm not shy, I'm quiet. And I'm not a wallflower, I'm an observer.

Also, in the most tense of situations, I grow calm.

Anyway, Uncle Buddy must have noticed that I felt forgotten, and one afternoon he picked me up in his old red convertible and drove us to the southwest side, to a place called Windy City Gym. It was on the third floor of a soot-covered warehouse. When we entered, the building seemed deserted. We climbed a dark flight of stairs, Uncle Buddy telling me to watch my step, and then he opened a set of double doors and we were flooded with sudden sunshine streaming through glass skylights. The room was deep and tall, with high ceilings crisscrossed by thick wooden beams. From those beams hung heavy bags, several of which were being rhythmically pummeled by guys whose hands were wrapped in tape. There were mirrors and speed bags and jump ropes hanging from the brick walls, along with dozens of old photos and peeling posters of boxers who had trained at Windy City. In the middle of it all, beneath a haze of dusty sunlight, sat a boxing ring—not a ring at all, in fact, but a canvas-covered square. It was taller than me and lined with rope on all four sides. Two guys were inside, circling and dancing, dipping their shoulders and popping their boxing gloves off each other. I smelled chalk and heard the squeak of sneakers, the buzz of a jump rope, and a squealing bell. I was aware of my small size, the thinness of my shoulders and legs, but at that moment it was exactly where I wanted to be.

Uncle Buddy laid a hand on my shoulder and said, "Sara Jane, meet Willy Williams." I turned to a small African American man, almost as small as my grandpa Enzo and a little older. He wore steel-rimmed glasses on his face, a newsboy cap on his head, and a gray fuzzy mustache beneath his nose. He offered a hand for me to shake. When I did, he smiled, and his smile made me feel warm and welcome.

"So this is Anthony and Teresa's little girl. You look just like your mama, you know that? Except your eyes. You got your daddy's eyes."

People said that all the time, so I nodded and smiled back.

"How old are you, Sara Jane?"

"I'm six."

"My, my, big six." He nodded at the boxers in the ring beating up on each other and said, "Don't let those guys scare you, my girl."

"They don't scare me," I said, mesmerized by the fight. "It looks fun."

"Fun?" he said, raising his eyebrows over his glasses and grinning. "Say, did you know that your daddy won a very important championship boxing match once?"

I didn't, and it surprised me. "Really?" I said. "He did?"

"Indeed. I trained him myself. I trained your uncle here, too. 'Course, Anthony had a left hook that Buddy never saw coming," Willy said, with a wink at Uncle Buddy.

Uncle Buddy smiled but didn't look happy as Willy went on to say how my dad's build made him the ideal size for a light middleweight. Uncle Buddy's short thickness made him a little too heavy and a little too slow to be a boxer. Then Willy patted Uncle Buddy's shoulder and said, "But no one ever tried as hard as Buddy. And no one was tougher. You sure could take a punch, kid. You sure had a chin."

Uncle Buddy rubbed his jaw and grinned at me, saying, "I sure took enough of them in the ring from your dad, Sara Jane. I sparred with him day and night. If it wasn't for me, he never would've won that championship."

"That's right," Willy said. "He couldn't have done it without Buddy's help."

This time when Uncle Buddy smiled, he actually looked pleased. He put his hand on my head and said, "Well, Willy. What do you think?"

I would learn later that Willy Williams had one of the sharpest eyes in boxing. He could inspect someone from head to toe, even a skinny six-year-old girl, and instantly decide if she had what it took to be a fighter. Once Willy formed an opinion, whether it was about a person's viability in the ring or politics or baseball or any other issue, he would deliver his judgment in a little rhyme. Willy stared at me while rubbing his chin. Finally, he pointed a finger in my direction and said—

"Sara Jane,
to me, it's plain.
Looking at you,
I see a boxer through and through."

I began to train with Willy that very day and never looked back. I started slowly, moving around the ring, getting used to the rhythm and movement, while he taught me how to use my hands and what to do with my feet—how to pivot and move, and how to get around and below a punch. Soon, my brain and body began to work together, the first half strategically directing mechanics, the other executing orders on command, until the partnership became one homogenous fighter, me. There's an odd, empowering phenomenon that boxers experience when their physical and mental selves begin to merge into a single being, and I could feel it happening. It was as if I was gaining control of something inside myself that I didn't even know existed, and it felt like an upgrade, like new features being added to the original Sara Jane. Sometimes before bed, I'd throw a dozen combination punches at my reflection in the mirror. Faster, faster, faster! I'd think, watching my hands and arms pumping like pistons, obeying my command.

Willy also taught me the difference between a boxing match and a beating.

He explained that intent was everything, and that when an older, larger, and more experienced fighter invited a younger, smaller one into the ring for a "little sparring," the other boxer usually intended to treat the newbie like a heavy bag with legs—or, as Willy called it, "fresh meat." The younger fighter was in there to serve as a moving target for the older one to work out whatever issues he was having with his left jab or right cross, or whatever. When the bell finally rang, if the kid was still standing, he generally looked like his face had lost a violent disagreement with a ketchup bottle. Willy ordered me to never, ever spar with anyone more experienced than me, or without him present.

Now, at age sixteen, I still wonder what the hell eight-year-old me was thinking.

Actually, that's the problem—I wasn't.

Instead, I was buzzing with adrenaline after working thirty minutes of whirlwind combinations with Willy. I stood before a sweat- and spit-flecked wall mirror as he showed me how to throw the punches in a smooth, mellifluous way that was like being taught dance moves with arms and hands instead of legs and feet. He slowed me for corrections, and then sped me up as my body caught a groove, eyes found reflective-me in the mirror as an opponent, and then it was like pulling the rope on an outboard motor—*jab, jab, punch, hook*—Again!—*jab, jab, punch, hook*—Again!—until my arms shook, hips ached, and I was convinced that a bony eight-year-old with her nose projecting from headgear like a caged toucan could go one-on-one with the world heavyweight champion.

Or, at the very least, a Chicago Silver Gloves winner.

Willy removed his glasses, thumbed sweat from his eyebrows, and told me to jump rope for three rounds while he made phone calls, which was code for his daily afternoon catnap. It was after his office door closed that I heard my name. A kid smiled down from the ring, hanging casually on the ropes with his hands in fat padded gloves, and I said, "Uh-Oh."

"Hey, Rispol-ita." He grinned. "You wanna do a little sparring?"

Hector "Uh-Oh" Puño was so nicknamed because when

competitors in the twelve-year-old Silver Gloves division saw his fearsome right fist coming, they thought—well, you get the picture. Despite his reputation, he was always friendly and soft-spoken with me, basically a chubby, huggable teddy bear in satin boxing shorts. At that point, after training for two years, I'd been in the ring with only a handful of opponents whom Willy had deemed safe. I was pumped after my lightning combinations, through with being "safe," and scared of nothing. Willy would be angry if he caught me, but I knew that his drowsy "phone calls" never lasted less than six rounds and I'd be done with Uh-Oh by then. I said, "We're just moving, right, Uh-Oh? Pitty-pat punches at most? You've got me by height and weight like crazy."

"*Come si estě loco*. Yeah, of course. I just wanna work out a few things with my right."

I tugged on sparring gloves, Uh-Oh parted the ropes as I climbed into the ring, and the buzzer sounded. For the first several seconds we faced each other, hands high, sidling in a circle like ice-skating on canvas. And then Uh-Oh's left arm darted like an eel, nipping at my gloves. I turned but he was already there, bouncing before me. Boxing is like ballroom dancing in one respect—who's going to lead? Even with his back against the rope, a leader moves in a way that forces his opponent to follow, controlling the ebb and flow of a fight. Uh-Oh was in front of me now, and I went after him with a left of my own, which he ducked, smiling. I took a step, jabbed and missed, and trailed him toward the rope. That was when he spun, I pivoted, and now my back was in the corner, and it was only at the last second, hearing the whoosh of an incoming missile, eyes flicking through the headgear, that I saw his right barreling for my face.

It was no pitty-pat punch tossed by a teddy bear.

It was a sledgehammer thrown by a circus strongman.

Being hit squarely like that felt like all of the injustice that has ever existed throughout the history of mankind, in my nose. Red pain spread into my jaws and teeth, clawing my eyes, gnawing my ears, creating a sensation that the entire world was against me. Somehow I stayed on my feet and was about to quit when I saw the animal pinpoints in Uh-Oh's eyes telling me he'd done it on purpose. I was fresh meat, and something deep in my gut popped and flashed as a tiny, internal flame began to burn cold and blue. Fear, self-pity, outrage—all of those debilitating things faded away, replaced by anger and ice.

Now I realize that moment marked the very first time I experienced the powerful internal phenomenon. At the time, though, all that I felt was a pure sense of invincibility.

A shadow of it must've crossed my eyes because Uh-Oh quit grinning and blinked heavily, and in that second of stasis, my outboard motor kicked in—*jab, jab, punch, hook!*—as he grunted, too late to protect his own nose. My hands were high and I was set to unleash another combination when the blue flame puffed out like a weak birthday candle, the frozen rage going with it. Its sudden appearance and departure was confusing and unnerving, leaving me off balance, and Uh-Oh must've seen that, too. He popped his gloves and advanced, and although I felt like plain Sara Jane, there was no way I would run, no way I'd quit, and stood my ground as he unleashed a barrage of punches that felt like a building collapsing on top of me, one cement block at a time.

"Knock it off, right now! Right now, goddamn it!"

We separated and turned to Willy, Uh-Oh bouncing guiltily, me swaying woozily. Willy had sharp words for my opponent but we both knew whose fault it really was. When Uh-Oh was doing his penance of a hundred push-ups, Willy pulled off my headgear, looked at my rapidly swelling nose, and made a *tsk* noise with his tongue. "Everything I've taught you," he said, handing me an ice pack, "and you still got into the ring with a bigger, better fighter?"

"He's not that much better," I pouted.

"Yeah he is. Much."

"I got my shots in. It was weird, Willy. For a second, something inside calmed me down but made me really mad at the same time," I said, trying to recapture the feeling of a phenomenon that I'm only now beginning to comprehend.

"Adrenaline or something." He shrugged. "That's not the point. The point is, as a fighter, you failed."

I moved the ice pack from my nose. "I failed because I stuck it out? Because I was brave and didn't give up and run away? That's crazy."

"No, what's crazy is catching a beating like the one I just saw, and standing there and taking it."

I shrugged defensively, saying, "I bet my dad wouldn't have quit when he was boxing."

Willy huffed out a derisive little laugh. "I'll tell you one thing about your daddy. Anthony Rispoli was a *smart* fighter.

14

He ever found himself in a tight corner, he got himself the hell out of there, fast." He leveled an unblinking gaze at me and said, "Ever happens again, girl, you better run, too."

"But Willy . . ."

"But nothing. Know what they said about Muhammad Ali, the greatest heavyweight of all time? That he could sting like a bee, but first they said something else . . . 'floats like a butterfly.' Think about it. A butterfly doesn't punch, doesn't stand there like a statue getting its brains beat out. That wise little bug flaps its wings and hurries out of trouble. And that's what a good boxer does, too . . . learns to get far away without getting hit. That's what those brains are for, girl."

As the years passed and I continued under Willy's tutelage, he stressed it to me over and over again, along with the other important points of pugilism—that it's a thinking person's game rather than a punching person's, its tried and true rules must be followed at all times, and that respect for one's opponent lies at the heart of the sport. His opinion was that fighting belonged only in the ring, while using violence to settle a real-life dispute was wrong except in rare circumstances like self-defense. In those cases, where an opponent follows no rules and therefore deserves no respect, it's every man—or girl—for himself.

It became my opinion too, and he and I became friends. Actually, more than friends—Willy became family. It's ironic, then, that he taught me what would become the most important skill I possess in trying to find my actual family.

Not just how to fight, but to run for my life, so that I could live to fight another day.

WHEN IT COMES TO A THRILLER, whether it's a book, movie, or TV show, it always starts with a big, wild action scene—think of a frenetic car chase with blinding sunlight flashing from a pair of Lamborghinis as they soar high in the air and then hurtle down the type of street that exists only in San Francisco or the Alps, the incline as steep as driving off the face of a mountain—and then segues into a familiar tale of uncovering clues. The hero, dogged by a shady past or personal demons, turns out to be an intrepid latter-day Sherlock Holmes, as the gun he discovers in a drawer leads to a footprint in the garden which leads to a safety deposit box in Zurich, where the villain is discovered counting cash or cuddling diamonds or something.

What that type of fiction never shows is a hero with a really sedate, boring past who knows absolutely nothing about anything that's happened.

Also, that some of the most important clues are wedged inside of her own head.

Now that I've began to sift the past for any signal or sign of what happened to my family, I've begun to remember things not only about them but me, too—especially about a cold blue flame that now seems ubiquitous, as though it has always been with me. I remembered its first, brief appearance in the beatdown with Uh-Oh, which walked me forward to an equally odd situation that occurred only a couple years later, when I was ten.

My best friend (actually, my only friend; more on that pathetic situation soon) was Gina Pettagola. One afternoon following school, as we strolled home together, a trio of older girls who lived in the neighborhood cornered us; Gina called them the "Three Muskaterribles" because they were always together and, well, because they were terrifying bullies. They were lumpy, smelled like cigarettes, two of them had red hair, and the last one, the leader, sported a single black eyebrow; it joined in the middle like an angry, fat caterpillar. She particularly disliked Gina, because even then Gina was the most gossipy person I (or perhaps all of Chicago) knew. She was also the most perfectly put-together ten-year-old—clothes, hair, shoes, and so on—which I think annoyed Caterpillar Girl even more, who tended toward black concert T-shirts and jeans with safety pins in weird places. As the Three Muskaterribles surrounded us, Caterpillar Girl popped a fist against an open hand and said, "You got a big mouth, you know that, hairdo?"

"Who, me? Why, what . . . what did I say?" Gina stammered.

"She knows," the first redhead said.

"Yeah, look at her. She's full of shit," the other redhead said.

Caterpillar Girl moved closer. "You want to act like you don't know, fine with me. All that matters is I'm gonna shut that yap of yours once and for all."

I could see Gina was being honest, that in her constant stream of gossip she had no idea what Caterpillar Girl was referring to. That's when I realized it didn't matter, and that she probably hadn't said anything at all—the Three Muska-terribles just wanted to pick on a pair of little girls, and who better than a petite, perfectly coiffed chatterbox and her skinny shadow friend. And then Gina did what she does best—started talking. It was a friendly, nervous chatter that I think was de-signed to lighten the moment, except it came off as, well, gos-sip, and before she could finish her sentence—"Besides, we wouldn't want this to get around"—Caterpillar Girl punched her in the mouth. Gina grunted and lost her balance, stum-bling toward one of the redheads, who grabbed her and spun her to the other one, who pushed her at Caterpillar Girl. She yanked Gina into a headlock, and I saw tears mixing with a line of blood at her lip.

I knew that from a purely visible standpoint, I posed no threat.

I was in a stage of growth where things were a little out of whack—arms long and skinny, hair thick and bushy, and the first hints that my nose would soon begin to bloom like a weed in a flower garden. Plus, I'd begun to perfect the art of fading into the background, chameleon style. But now Caterpillar Girl turned to me, leering with waxy teeth, jerking Gina around while saying, "What about you, toothpick? For having such a loudmouth friend, you don't seem to say much." She was so close that I could see pinpoints in her eyes, dark and feral, brimming with the joy of imminent violence.

"Uh-Oh," I muttered, thinking of a past sparring match gone wrong. Willy's rule about fleeing an impending beat-down was precisely what I wanted to do, realizing with a shudder just how large, mean, and broken these girls were. They intended to do real harm to Gina and me. I didn't want to desert her, but I was growing more and more jittery with a need to run for it.

"Check it, the mute can talk," Caterpillar Girl said, squeezing Gina's neck tighter as she produced a cigarette and tucked it between flabby lips. "Uh-oh is right, princess," she spat, smacking Gina hard, and then, "Uh-oh!"—*smack!*— "Uh-oh!"—*smack!*—until my friend's face was sweaty-pink and tears jumped quietly. Her eyes found mine as she clawed feebly at Caterpillar Girl's headlock grip, and it was that look—choking terror at being trapped—that caused the cold blue flame to flicker in my gut.

It was stronger than it had been two years earlier, more encompassing of my body and brain, as if it had grown along with me. It didn't leap so high as to infiltrate my eyes as it does now, but it leaped high enough, calming me down while pissing me off.

Before I could stop, I cleared my throat and said, "Let her go or I'm going to kick your ass. I mean it."

Caterpillar Girl looked up with the kind of grin that creases a face when a person is happily surprised. She shoved Gina to the ground, hitched up her jeans, and lit the cigarette. Coming close, she blew foul smoke into my face, and then held the tip of the cigarette inches from me. I felt the heat of it on my cheek as she hissed, "What are *you* gonna do, hard-ass? Spit it out before I burn my initials into your—" And it was her turn not to finish a sentence since my left fist cracked her nose twice, and my right once more. She staggered and fell on her butt, and when the bigger of the redheads made a move, I pivoted so quickly, fists raised, that she stopped in her tracks.

"Sara Jane . . . ," Gina said quietly, her voice tight with alarm.

I turned to Caterpillar Girl, her nose gushing red, her right hand holding a small knife as sharp as a steel icicle.

She touched her face, looked at her sticky hand, and said, "You little bitch. I'm bleeding."

I heard the truth in my voice and felt it in my gaze when I said, "That's just the beginning. Take a step with that knife and I'll hit you so fast and so hard that one eyebrow will become two. I don't want to, but I will." My fists were curling and my body was relaxed because I was a good boxer—maybe better than good, a natural like Willy predicted. If she made a move, I was ready. It became sort of a weird staring contest until Caterpillar Girl swallowed thickly, averting her eyes, and put away the knife.

"Aw, screw these two. They're not worth it," she said, her voice shaking, and marched away with the redheads in tow.

Gina and I were quiet, watching them go, until she said, "What just happened?"

"I guess they changed their minds," I said, checking myself for the chilly flame, which had blown out without my notice.

She looked at me with her particular Gina-smirk. "You mean *you* changed their minds. You're a weird kid, Sara Jane. You know that? In an okay way."

"Thanks, I guess."

"God, I can't *wait* to tell people about this!" she exclaimed, spitting blood.

"No, Gina," I said, my other natural inclination kicking in—never, ever being the center of attention. "It . . . it could get back to my parents. They'd be really mad if they knew I was fighting on the street. Please? Just keep it between us?"

She sighed, touching her purple lip. "Okay. I guess I owe you one for saving me like some kind of supergirl."

"It's not like that," I said, shaking my head, thinking of the lesson I'd learned the hard way (thanks, Uh-Oh) that there was a time to run and a time to fight. "I just . . . happen to know how to box."

It was true, and I had Uncle Buddy to thank for it, since he was the one who introduced me to the sport. In fact, at one time, I had a lot to thank Uncle Buddy for. He was always there for me and always listened closely.

Sometimes he paid even more attention than my parents.

My mom is a schoolteacher and her philosophy is that knowledge, in all its forms, whether academic or life lessons, is power. Uncle Buddy adopted that philosophy and perverted it, trying to draw information from me. He listened sneakily, between the lines, hoping to learn things about my mom and dad that I didn't know I was telling him; sometimes I wonder if I ever unknowingly gave something away that contributed to their disappearance. I have—correction, *had*—much to thank Uncle Buddy for, but now gratitude has been blotted out by deceit.

God, I really do hate him.

Actually, *hate* is not a big enough word.

I hate-fear-for-my-life-tremble-in-my-boots at the mention of his name.

I'm sure, or almost sure, or sure enough, that he viciously betrayed my family. Whether or not they're alive, one thing is certain—everything changed forever on a recent rainy night, and so did I. Before my mom, dad, and little brother disappeared, I was someone who faded into the background—at school, with other kids, in the neighborhood—trying strenuously not to draw attention to myself. It's who I was and how I was raised, which are basically the same thing.

Now it's different.

Now I kick ass first and ask questions later. And if the tables turn and I'm the one getting her ass kicked, I find a place to hide, or way to escape. I have a lot of things to be grateful to Uncle Buddy for, but probably the last thing he taught me is the most valuable: when it comes to staying alive, I can trust only myself.

All forms of betrayal are poison.

Whether it's being used as fresh meat in a boxing ring or violating the code of decency that dictates sidewalk behavior, it creates a bitter protective crust over a person's soul. Having my secret fears and self-doubt used as currency against me as Uncle Buddy did was a transgression so deep that it has infested me with a true, pure hatred. It has sparked a flame of desire for vengeance that's stronger than any silly, lingering feelings of affection I once felt for him.

That flame is lit in me now, and it's burning blue and cold.

THERE WAS NO DOUBT in my mind who I wanted to talk to after the earthquake of my first real kiss in the seventh grade.

It was exciting, traumatic, and so, so weird, all at the same time.

I knew Uncle Buddy would give me his undivided attention.

That milestone smooch was applied by Walter J. Thurber, who was known for his yo-dude-floppy-hair-skater-boy look. It should've occurred to me that any kid who dressed like that but never actually rode a skateboard might have issues. Then again, we were thirteen, and he was the most popular kid in school, and I was not. Even then, I sensed something inside myself that made me feel disconnected from the cliques inhabited by my classmates. I knew that if I put myself out there more, I could probably have just as wide a social circle as anyone else. But the overwhelming desire to be included and liked that operated the motors of most kids just wasn't in me. I was content to sit back and let the world come to me; if it did, great, and if not, well, that was okay too.

Later, when I realized who my family really was, and what that cold blue flame in my gut really meant, I would begin to understand why I was so different.

My parents didn't help the situation.

They were overprotective in a way that made me feel like I was made of glass.

They were so family oriented that chatting with neighbors over the picket fence was regarded as a waste of time.

We spent every holiday with my grandparents and Uncle Buddy . . . and every non-holiday, and every weekend, and most weeknights. And the thing is, I loved being with my family because they were funnier and smarter and more interesting than most other kids' families. It's true that if I talked about a classmate's parents—for example, what a kid's dad did for a living—my own parents showed little interest, even wondering aloud why I cared about someone else's personal business. But they weren't being dismissive or rude. They were just being themselves, which was extremely private, and they encouraged Lou and me to be private, too. My dad was strict when it came to us talking about what *he* did for a living, which never made sense to me, since he and Grandpa Enzo and Uncle Buddy were bakers—there wasn't much to tell about cookies, cakes, and pies. But my dad would just shrug and say, "You never know what means something to other people." The result was that most of my time outside school was spent almost exclusively with my family.

In other words, a kiss from Walter J. Thurber was not to be taken lightly.

It happened at Gina's thirteenth birthday party.

Gina was my best friend, but is much less of a friend now. Part of the reason for that is we simply drifted apart, and part of it was due to her inborn nature as a supergossip. One afternoon, shortly before that momentous first kiss, my mom overheard Gina reporting to me the loves, losses, and general scandals sweeping the neighborhood. After Gina left, my mom sat me down and gently explained why it was best that I put some distance between me and her—that if Gina so easily talked about other people, then she'd just as easily talk about me. She opened her arms and said, "This is our home, Sara Jane, and we all have to respect it. We don't want it violated by idle chatter." Of course I understood how my parents felt about our family's privacy. But I have to admit, even though I'd never been friend-centric, the idea of not hanging around Gina bothered me. It was nice to be with someone who was bubbly and outgoing (my opposite), and besides, a challenge was part of the basis of our relationship—she knew I cared nothing about gossip and was determined to feed me that one golden nugget that would actually intrigue me. It was almost like a contest and it was fun. Still, my life was built around my family and their opinions mattered more than anything else. So, little by little, I drew away from Gina.

In the intervening years, she went on to achieve gossip superstardom, which equals popularity (kids love to talk about other kids), while I've retreated into the shadows, not talking much to anyone. She and I are still sort of friends, but I don't tell her much. Gina trades classified information like a double agent, just like she did when she was thirteen.

Just like she did when I told her that Walter J. Thurber had just kissed me.

We were celebrating her birthday in a basement with streamers and balloons, a half-eaten cake and twenty other kids. A sugary pop song was playing with a guy half-whining, half-yodeling, "You're Beautiful" over and over. It was all very seventh grade.

Walter materialized next to me and said, "You are, too."

I had no idea what he was talking about, and said, "What?"

"You. You're beautiful."

With my nose definitely taking on a life (and zip code) of its own, I'd begun to feel the complete opposite of beautiful. Also, although I'd forgone my usual attire of jeans and T-shirt (worn denim and anything soft bearing a Cubs or Bears logo; my mom told me I looked like a model in a secondhand sports store) for a new skirt and top, I was aware that I wasn't exactly the best-dressed girl at the party. That's why his praise was such a surprise, but also seemed suspicious. It just wasn't in my nature to trust a compliment, and I leaned over and said, "What's your point, Walter?"

"No point. You're so quiet and I never see you at any parties or anywhere, and I always wanted to do this," he said, and pressed his lips against mine. There was no mashing or movement like in a movie. It just sort of *was*—a long moment of moist facial proximity that smelled like spearmint gum—and then it was over. Instead of seeing stars or fireworks or whatever was supposed to happen, my truest feeling was gratitude.

Walter had given me a small but important gift, opening the door just a crack to what it would someday be like to actually *want* to kiss someone and be kissed. I smiled and said, "Thanks, Walter."

He smiled back, showing naturally straight teeth, and said, "You're welcome. So, uh . . . later," and walked back to his friends like he'd conquered Mars single-handedly.

I made a beeline for Gina and told her what had happened.

Five minutes later, the room had broken into small groups of whispering kids.

Ten minutes later, everyone at the party knew Walter had kissed me.

The problem was that the information changed as it moved kid-to-kid, like that game at camp where a story travels around a bonfire and at the end it's completely different from the beginning. Some crucial fact about the kiss had been altered in that whispering merry-go-round, because the next thing I knew, Mandi Fishbaum and her little gang of look-alikes— each a variation on the theme of perfect hair plus expensive clothes equals bad attitude—were marching toward me. Mandi was well known for having rich parents, a body that was a decade ahead of every other girl in seventh grade, and being the perennial girlfriend/ex-girlfriend of Walter J. Thurber. Although they'd broken up a month earlier, Mandi acted as if she owned not only Walter but the air he breathed and the ground he walked on, and woe to any girl who trespassed.

She stopped in front of me with her look-alikes fanned out behind her.

Mandi crossed her arms and spit a single word in my direction.

"Slut."

The terrible word echoed around the basement until it hit me with stinging precision, igniting something low and chilly in my gut—I was furious but completely in control as a small blue flame flickered and leapt. It had been three years since I'd experienced the cool, sizzling internal phenomenon while doing sidewalk battle with Caterpillar Girl, and I'd nearly forgotten about it. But when it reappeared, I registered it as natural as breathing or fighting, while the idea of doing something violent to Mandi filled my brain and crept behind my eyes.

As the blue fire roared in my belly, I realized how different it was than at age eight and ten. This time, it was as if I could command her to do absolutely anything through the power of my gaze.

She must have seen it on my face, because her own face filled with fear—in fact, I felt like I could *feel* what she was feeling, which to her was terrible but to me was, well, pleasant. But then, just as quickly as that cold fury rose, it faded, and the only things my eyes projected were tears. When Mandi saw them, she smiled and turned away with her look-alikes in tow, mission accomplished. As a thousand needles pierced my heart and voices whispered around me, I felt a tap on my elbow. I wiped my eyes and looked down at a small boy— much shorter than me, and even skinnier. He had curly hair, metal braces as huge as a bear trap, and warm brown eyes behind a pair of glasses.

"Ignore her. You can't argue with knuckleheads," he said, looking at me closely and smiling. "And Mandi and her friends are world-class knuckleheads."

That was the first time I met Max Kissberg.

I wouldn't see or talk to him again until high school.

In fact, I didn't talk to Max then, just nodded, trying not to cry any harder. I hadn't done anything, certainly hadn't made a move on Walter, and what made it worse was that I was the center of terrible, unwanted attention. I'd been encoded from birth never to make precisely the type of scene that I was starring in now, and the weight of the stares and glares crumpled my heart. By then the room was blurred by tears, so I rushed from the basement and ran all the way to the bakery. The reason I wanted to talk to Uncle Buddy instead of my mom or dad was because they had something else on their minds rather than me. It was an odd chapter in our lives, not unlike when Lou was born, except that instead of a baby, they were preoccupied by a secret.

I came to think of this period as the beginning of the "whispered conversations."

My parents stopped talking abruptly whenever I entered the room and would mutter in the kitchen or in their bedroom late at night.

It would not end until my family disappeared.

One of the first times I eavesdropped on them, the subject seemed to be money.

Only days before Gina's birthday party, I'd listened at their door as my dad spoke in low tones about having "enough to live on," which had never been an issue at our house. My mother wondered how we would make ends meet "when we go through with it."

"*If* we go through with it," my dad said.

"Anthony. We have to eventually. We can't go on like this forever."

"You're right, Teresa. The time is coming. Besides, it's the right thing to do."

I wouldn't understand what they were talking about for a long time. But once I did, it would be plain how hard their decision had been, and what it had cost our family.

At the time, though, with Walter's fresh spearmint flavor on my lips and Mandi's bitter epithet ringing in my ears, I couldn't stand the thought of not having a family member's complete attention. I pushed through the bakery door, the bell jingling madly, and rushed past my grandma, who was cleaning the display case. Lou sat on the marble counter eating a *melassa biscotto*—a rich molasses cookie. Next to him was his perpetual sidekick and best friend, Harry, glaring at me with hatred.

Harry was an Italian greyhound.

To me, he looked like a sleek, oversized rat.

Harry disliked me intensely and I felt the same way about him, but we both loved Lou with all of our hearts, so we tolerated each other, barely.

As I think back now, it's plain that our mutual revulsion was based on simple jealousy. Lou is one of the coolest kids I know (and cutest, with my mom's jet-black hair and a lighter version of the Rispoli blue eyes) with an intellect that surpasses his age. Not only is he incredibly smart, but he can rip through and absorb massive amounts of material—books, maps, journals, essays, DVDs, you name it—and synthesize it so he can put the knowledge to actual, practical use. What I mean is that when he researches a subject and then thoroughly analyzes the result, Lou can be good at—well, anything. Something nudges his attention, then captures it, and then he masters it. For a while it was photography (he built his own camera) and then abstract expressionism (he painted his bedroom magenta, black, green, and orange a la Mark Rothko) and then physics (he constructed a mini-volcano to test Galileo's law of falling bodies) and on and on. With his analytical and deductive abilities, we all knew he was destined for something great. My parents' attitude was to let him try as many things as he wanted until he found it for himself.

That's how Harry came into the house.

Lou developed an irrepressible interest in studying animal behavior.

He was obsessed with the idea of training the untrainable.

His research showed that the most effective way was an obscure method called "salutary discipline." It was created on the premise that animals had shared the earth with people for so long that they had a much deeper comprehension of human language than they were given credit for. Lou believed that if he spoke to them politely and with empathy, as equals, they would respond in kind. When he was ready for a real challenge, we went to the rescue shelter and requested the meanest dog with the lousiest attitude and nastiest disposition. Harry was brought out, scarred and snarling, straining on a leash. Maybe Lou was right, animals really do understand human language, because Harry has hated my guts since I looked at him and said, "You're not bringing *that* horrible thing home, are you, Lou?"

My little brother ignored me, smiling at Harry and offering a hand. "And how are you today, my fine fellow?"

Harry responded by biting him.

Lou didn't wince, just smiled again, but sadly, and said, "Life can be tough and weird, huh, pal? But then things change. Things always change."

There was something so true in the statement that Harry's growl lowered to a rumble, then a whimper, then his ears folded back and he looked like he was going to weep. Lou patted his pate. Love was in the air.

At least, love between the two of them.

For me it was a daily snarlfest, Harry at me and me right back at him.

I once asked Lou why he didn't just train the dog to like me.

My brother shrugged. "He is who he is. I can teach behavior but I can't change how he's made. It's the same reason you box well, but I never will."

"What are you talking about?"

"According to my studies, all the best boxers have something burning at their essential core. They use it to dominate their opponent in the ring. You have that thing and I don't."

"Wait . . . are you saying I have, like, hidden anger or something?"

"I didn't say it was hidden and I didn't say anger. I said core, and it could be anything strong enough to fuel a boxer in the ring. Yeah, maybe anger, but also maybe fear, or insecurity, or a need for revenge. Whatever it is, it burns like a nuclear reactor deep down in a fighter's gut."

I looked at Lou, thinking about his theory. "Are you saying I'm insecure?"

"I'm not going there," he sighed, doing that Italian "discussion over" thing, patting his hands together just like my grandpa.

We never discussed my "essential core" again, but Lou and I talked about everything else. My little brother has an informed opinion on a multitude of subjects, combined with an uncanny ability to figure out what a person is thinking just by studying her expression. That's why I tried to hurry past him into the kitchen that afternoon. I knew that if I paused, Lou would see Walter J. Thurber and Mandi Fishbaum all over my face. I was almost through the swinging door when my grandma said, "Sara Jane! *Non bacio per tua nonna e tuo fratello?*"

My Italian was, and is, pretty mediocre, but any kid who's even slightly Italian knows the word for kiss—*bacio*. The irony that I'd just run ten blocks because of an ill-placed bacio was not lost on me, and I struggled to hold back tears. When I was sure I wouldn't weep, I leaned over and kissed my grandma's soft cheek, and Lou's too, who smelled like molasses. He stared at me with bits of cookie on his lips and frowned. "You look weird," he said, pointing the cookie at me. "Weirder than usual, I mean."

"Thanks a lot," I said, thumbing crumbs from his mouth.

"Sara Jane," he said as I moved toward the kitchen. I turned, and Lou extended a pinkie toward me. "All or nothing. Right?"

I'd taught Lou that move on his first day of pre-K, when he seemed a little iffy about venturing into a classroom full of hyperactive hurricane kids. I took him aside, lifted my pinkie, and said, "Remember, Lou, you and I are Rispolis. We stick together even when we're not together. All or nothing." He'd smiled then, hooked his little finger through mine, and it had been our thing ever since; whenever one of us needs a boost, the other reminds us that we always have each other's backs. I hooked his pinkie, then turned and pushed through a set of double doors.

My dad, uncle, and grandpa spent every day working together in the kitchen of Rispoli & Sons making the fancy pastries the neon sign advertised. They seemed to live with flour and frosting all over their aprons, all over their hands and shoes. It was clear that they had been boxers (Grandpa Enzo too, in the 1950s) by watching them move like ballroom dancers, completely aware of one another and completely in sync. My uncle mixed gallons of batter and kneaded buckets of dough. My grandpa built intricate cakes, towering cakes, wedding and everyday cakes, all baked in pans with a distinctive R stamped on the bottom, so that every cake top bore our family initial. My dad's job was patting, shaping, and rolling cookies of all varieties. Together they swirled whipped cream on top of tiny fruit pies, squeezed smiles onto the faces of gingerbread men, and slid fat slabs of cocoa brownies into the enormous fire-breathing oven. It was built into the wall, lined with white glazed bricks, and dominated by an enormous iron door stamped with the word VULCAN in capital letters. The oven was so large that if I bent over, I could easily fit inside. As I entered the kitchen, my dad was sliding in trays of molasses cookies. I wanted everyone to know how victimized I felt, and sighed dramatically, saying, "Lucky cookies. Can I climb in, too?"

"What?" my father said, clanging shut the heavy door.

"*Cosa?*" my grandpa said.

"Never, ever go inside that oven!" my father said.

"*Non mai!* Never!" my grandpa echoed, pounding his little fist on the long steel rolling table, sending a puff of flour into the air.

I stepped back, shocked at their overreaction. "I was kidding. I'm just . . . I'm having a bad day."

"Of course she was kidding," Uncle Buddy said, wiping his hands on his apron and placing them on my shoulders. He put on his big trademark smile. "You think she's dumb enough to climb inside that thing?"

My dad stared at me, and what I remember specifically is how sad he looked. He and I share a similar trait—blue eyes decorated with little flecks of shimmering gold—and his seemed to be seeing something far beyond the here and now. Softly, he said, "No, Buddy. I think she's the smartest girl I know."

"*Nostra ragazza intelligente!* Our smart girl!" my grandpa agreed.

Uncle Buddy looked at Grandpa and then at my dad, as confused as I was by the outburst. He was still smiling but there was a trace of suspicion in his voice when he said, "Is it just me or is there something weird going on here?"

"Sara Jane, I'm sorry. I didn't mean to yell . . . ," my dad said, ignoring the question. But my feelings were hurt, and I turned to Uncle Buddy.

"Can I talk to you?" I said. "Just the two of us?"

Uncle Buddy looked over me at my dad, who sighed and shrugged. My uncle took off his apron and said, "Okay, sure. Let's go outside." It was early evening and the summer sky was warm and orange as I told him about Walter's kiss and Mandi's word. He sat on the hood of his convertible puffing a "Sick-a-Rette," a non-cancerous concoction of organic herbs prescribed by his doctor to help him quit smoking. The good news was that it was working; the bad news was that it smelled as sickly sweet as a Dumpster full of garbage on a hot day. At the end, I told him what little Max Kissberg had said about ignoring knuckleheads.

"Smart kid," Uncle Buddy said, flicking away the stinking Sick-a-Rette. He produced car keys and said, "Get in. I want to show you something." We didn't talk much as he drove through the Loop and parked off Michigan Avenue. We climbed steps past the lions guarding the entrance to the Art Institute, walked inside the cool, quiet building, and went directly to a gallery where a handful of people loitered silently. One wall was dominated by an enormous painting. Uncle Buddy nodded at it and said, "It's called *A Sunday on La Grande Jatte*." I'd seen it before, shuffling past with other kids on field trips, but now my uncle urged me to inspect it closely. I stepped forward and stared, and slowly my eyes divided a picture of people relaxing on a small island into millions of tiny painted dots. He explained that one of its meanings is that life is made up of an endless series of events and incidents—painful, joyful, and all connected in a way that makes a person who she is. "Just like this painting, Sara Jane," Uncle Buddy said, "point by point, you're in the process of being made. Just keep moving forward and you'll be all right. Trust me."

I did. I trusted my uncle, and it was a mistake.

I would remember his advice later, when I was trying to find out what had happened to my parents and Lou, trying desperately to see the big picture.

Once I began to connect the dots, they were as big as the famous Rispoli & Sons molasses cookies.

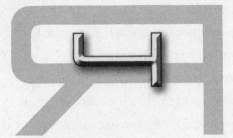

SOMETIMES THINGS CHANGE in a family as slowly as a melting glacier, so you don't notice them until they've begun to rearrange the landscape.

For us, that glacier was named Greta Kushchenko.

It was only about a year ago, when I was fifteen, that Uncle Buddy casually mentioned he was dating someone, which surprised us all. That someone became Greta, and then she was around, not always, just sometimes, at a birthday party or dinner at my grandparents' home—shy, quiet, plain, and, in her own words, humble, based on her upbringing by poor Russian immigrants. And then as the months fell away she was there all the time, at every event and holiday, growing louder and flashier and more opinionated by drips and inches. Her manner of talking crept from mousy to brassy, her views on the world from whispered to blared, and her style of dress from nun to showgirl. She was all bright-red lipstick, huge fake eyelashes, and hair that bloomed from a dull mushroom into a cascade of white-blond curls and ringlets. Even a casual observer could see that she had become an unofficial member of the Rispoli family.

To a noncasual observer (me) it was glaringly obvious that "unofficial" wouldn't cut it with Greta.

Her goal was to fully infiltrate the family by strong-arm tactics, her favorite being to mock and humiliate Uncle Buddy into submission and then kissy-face him until he'd do anything she asked. I once overheard her whisper to him how as the second son, he was regarded as only second best, igniting suspicions that already existed within his insecure psyche, and then tell him how much *she* loved him—that to "Gweta" (yes, nauseatingly, she used baby talk) he was just as smart and capable as his big brother Anthony. She'd perfected the art of driving a wedge between a close-knit group of people (us) and one of its own (my stupid uncle) until we were forced to share her company at the risk of alienating him. To Uncle Buddy, she could say and do no wrong. To me, she was incapable of taking no or even maybe for an answer without firebombing the room. One Sunday afternoon after a long family meal, I was passing by Lou's bedroom when I heard her talking to my brother. I stood outside and listened to her coo, "Come on, Lou, say it once, just for me. It's a very nice offer I'm making. You should be honored."

In his usual polite tone, my brother said, "No, thanks."

And then Greta's tone was anything but polite, it was pushy and mocking as she said, *"No, thanks.* Okay, fine, but you better get used to it, egghead. 'Cause it's *gonna* happen. So *say* it!"

"Say what?" I said, stepping inside. Greta turned and shot

a look she reserved just for me, much like a cornered garden snake eyeing a ferret.

Lou said, "She wants me to call her aunt. Aunt Greta."

"That's what you're pressuring him about?" I moved forward, Greta bumped into Lou's desk, and I locked my gaze onto hers. "How about if he calls you what I call you, a stupid bi—"

"Sara Jane," Lou said, cutting me off. "Forget it. It's silly."

"Aw, to hell with the both of you," Greta said, stomping out of the room.

When she was gone, Lou patted his bed and I sat next to him, and he nodded at the poster of Albert Einstein on the wall. "*E* equals *mc* squared. That's his most famous quote. But there's another one I understand a lot better."

"What's that?"

"'Intellectual growth should commence at birth and cease only at death,'" he said, with a twinkle in his eyes. "In Greta's case, it ceased at about age four. Don't waste your time on her. It's like debating a chipmunk."

"You can't argue with knuckleheads," I said. "Someone told me that once."

"Exactly. On the other hand, you have to admit, she's goal oriented."

Lou was right, as usual.

A couple of months before my sixteenth birthday, Greta became an official member of the Rispoli family when she and Uncle Buddy got married in Las Vegas.

He called my dad from the airport with the news, and when

my dad told my mom, she sighed and said, "Like it or not, we have to welcome her into the family."

"Welcome her?" my dad said. "She acts like she *owns* the family!"

My dad was referring to how Greta was always hanging around the bakery, sticking her nose where it didn't belong and offering opinions whether anyone wanted them or not. She stood over Grandpa Enzo's shoulder while he worked, then questioned the curve of a frosted curlicue he had applied to a wedding cake. She flipped through the receipts Grandma Donatella placed on a metal stickpin next to the cash register, or nibbled one of my dad's freshly baked gingerbread men, wondering aloud why it was so sweet. But worst of all was how she used her femininity like a whip to subdue Uncle Buddy. One minute she was a damsel in distress he had to rescue from the rest of us cruel, spiteful Rispolis, the next a hapless baby doll in need of a sugar daddy, and finally, the angry mother severely disappointed by her naughty boy. My uncle responded to this charade like a dog on a leash, begging to obey Greta's commands. Watching it happen over and over, I thought with certainty, There is the type of woman I will never be.

One day, shortly after Uncle Buddy was married, I came home early from school and overheard my parents talking in the living room. My dad was speaking in the low, measured tone he used when the subject was something he wanted to share only with my mom. I knew they would stop talking if I entered the room, so I stood around the corner and listened to him explain an odd scene that had unfolded that afternoon at the bakery. Apparently, Uncle Buddy told my dad and grandpa that it was Greta's opinion that he ought to have a title. My grandpa had raised his eyebrows and said, *"Cosa? Un titolo?* What kind of title?"

Uncle Buddy cleared his throat. "Vice President and Director of Batter and Dough Amalgamation."

Grandpa Enzo scratched his head, leaving a fingertip trail of white flour on his forehead. "Amalaga-what?"

"It means mixture," my dad said.

"Then why didn't he just say mixture?"

"I don't know, Pop. Why didn't you just say mixture, Buddy?"

Uncle Buddy shrugged. "Greta thinks it sounds more professional."

"Titles, *beh!"* my grandpa said. "We already have titles! I'm a baker, you're a baker, he's a baker! *Tre panettieri,* Rispoli & Sons!" He did the Italian thing with his hands, patting his palms together, wiping them clean of the subject. Before he could say another word, my grandmother opened the kitchen door to tell him that some men were politely asking for Enzo the Baker. He turned to Uncle Buddy and smiled, saying, "See! I'm a baker!"

After he had gone, my dad said, "Why does Greta think you need a title, Buddy?"

Uncle Buddy didn't shrug this time, but said plainly, "We have to plan for the future. That's all."

"How does a title help plan for the future?"

"I don't have to tell you that pop is getting old. Not old-old, but he's not a young man anymore. Plus, with that bad ticker of his, you just never know."

"So?" my dad said, crossing his arms.

"So, Greta says I have to protect my half of the business. That maybe if I have a title, it will be harder for you to . . . well, what I mean is, you couldn't just . . . take over."

"Come on, Buddy," my dad said. "If something happens, of course you'll get half of the business. You have a third of it now. Why would that change?"

Uncle Buddy thumbed at his nose like a boxer protecting his face. "Greta reminded me that you're the older brother, which means you're the senior partner. And also, you got Lou . . ."

"I have Sara Jane *and* Lou," my dad said, trying to keep the anger out of his voice. "Get this straight . . . my kids will *never* have anything to do with the family business, now or ever."

Uncle Buddy produced a Sick-a-Rette from behind his ear, stuck it between his teeth, and stared back at my dad. "How do I know you're telling the truth?"

"Because I'm your brother, Buddy. And I'm not a liar."

"Everybody's a liar sometime," Uncle Buddy said, emitting a garbage-stinking puff of air. "If the situation calls for it."

"Is that what Greta says?"

"That's what *I* say. I'm not dumb, Anthony."

"I don't think you're dumb."

"Everyone thinks I'm dumb. Well, I might not be some kind of book genius like *Lou*, or the perfect family man like *you*," he spat. "But I'll tell you one thing. I'm a very good listener, and I've heard things whispered between you and Pop that you've kept from me for a long, long time. Interesting things I wasn't supposed to hear."

My dad paused, then said, "What things, Buddy?"

"Wouldn't you like to know?" he said, blowing disgusting smoke at my dad.

"Buddy . . . ," my dad said, taking a step toward him.

"Don't stare at me like that! I've had it with those . . . looks of yours, always making me do what *you* want me to do! This time I'm doing what *I* want to do!" Uncle Buddy jammed the Sick-a-Rette into a bowl of cookie dough. He turned his back on my dad, pushed through the kitchen door, and said, "This time it's all about me!"

My dad finished telling my mom about the disturbing conversation with a sigh, and she patted his shoulder. I moved silently away from the living room, more than a little troubled by what I'd overheard. My parents themselves had taught me that listening quietly was the best way to gather information, and although I didn't like what I'd learned, I realized that it was important. So, as the days passed, I took other covert opportunities to eavesdrop on them, listening to my dad explain sadly to my mom how he and Uncle Buddy continued to work side by side every day like usual, except now their conversation was pure business. There was no more teasing, no more joking, and gone was the shorthand conversation that brothers share—phrases that meant something to them but were meaningless to others, punch lines that cracked them up based on a collective memory, small Italian phrases and silly little sound effects. Now they went about their day like two pastry-making robots, one tall and thin, the other small and thick, snapping questions and spitting answers.

Soon, Uncle Buddy stopped coming by our house on Balmoral Avenue.

Even after he married Greta he always found time to swoop to the curb in his convertible, slam the door, and hustle into the house wearing a big smile.

After his confrontation with my dad, that old red car was not seen in the neighborhood again.

For me, it wasn't Uncle Buddy's absence at home that hurt as much as it was from Windy City. At the time, Willy was helping me fine-tune my left hook, which, if thrown correctly, landed just outside the other fighter's field of vision, so it's almost impossible to defend against. According to Willy it had been my dad's signature move, one that my uncle, an impatient, brawling boxer, never saw coming. As I worked with Willy, I kept an eye on the door, hoping to see Uncle Buddy smiling up at me as I circled the ring to find my rhythm, but he was never there. One afternoon as I listlessly poked at the heavy bag, lost in thought, Willy stopped its lazy swing and asked where my head had been lately. I couldn't hold back—I was sad and angry at the same time—and I told him how Uncle Buddy's stupid marriage had ruined the relationship between him and my dad, and by extension the whole family. When I was done I had tears in my eyes. Willy had to unlace my gloves and free my hands so I could wipe at them.

"Sara Jane," he said as he pulled the strings loose, "it might seem simple to blame Buddy's wife. But I've known your dad and uncle a long time, and the real problem is between the two of them."

"What problem?" I said, blowing my nose.

"A rivalry problem. Now, in boxing, a rivalry can be a good thing. It keeps the competition sharp and lively, as long as both sides participate. But when one side ignores the rivalry altogether, well, that's a problem. The guy being ignored realizes the other one doesn't consider him a worthy opponent, and he gets angry and insulted."

I was quiet, thinking about my dad and Uncle Buddy, what I knew about them as boxers, bakers, and brothers. "My dad refused to participate?"

Willy nodded. "Twenty some years ago, when Buddy was helping your dad train for the championship bout, I leaned on these ropes and watched something I never forgot. Your dad was sparring—practicing, moving, stretching—but Buddy was *fighting*."

"But . . . my dad thought Buddy was his friend. His best friend."

"But Buddy thought—and still seems to think—that your dad is his opponent."

The idea of my dad and Uncle Buddy as opponents, or worse, enemies, was ridiculous. It was impossible to believe that my uncle would cut ties with all of us over who owned more or less of the bakery. Thinking about it made my chest ache, like I was going to cry again. I sighed and said, "I guess it's none of my business."

"On the contrary," Willy said. "It's your responsibility to figure out what this business is all about."

"Why me?"

"Because . . . they're your people. You only got one dad and one uncle."

"I can hear my dad now if I try to discuss Uncle Buddy . . . 'It's nothing for a fifteen-year-old kid to worry about.' My dad's not a big one for sharing info."

"You're gonna be sixteen soon. That's no kid," Willy said. "My opinion? You have a right to know what's going on."

I shook my head. "I'd better stay out of it."

Willy leaned in closely and raised his eyebrows. "Are you sure? In a situation like this? In a family like yours?"

The way he looked at me and the phrase he used—"in a family like yours"—sent a tingle marching down my spine like a line of cold ants. Even now I'm unsure if he knew something I didn't, or suspected something that was true, or maybe just meant in a family as (formerly) close as ours. As I look back on it, all I know for sure is that I wanted to blame someone other than Uncle Buddy. I cleared my throat and returned to the subject of Greta—her pushiness and creepiness and general habit of being everywhere all the time. Before I could finish, he raised a hand and said, "I don't know what you should *do*, but I know what you should *know*—

> *She surely is poison,*
> *but ol' Greta don't mean squat.*
> *This is about what one man wants,*
> *and the other man's got."*

Without saying a word, I rose and went to the heavy bag.

With only tape covering my knuckles, I threw a left hook, surprising the leather with a loud, sharp *pop!*

I threw another and another, trying to beat back Willy's words, scared that they might be true.

A MELTING GLACIER is one thing—it meanders, trudges, and settles, taking its time—but lightning is impulsive. Despite its pinpoint precision, it's a crazed and maniacal event—an instant flash followed by a thunderous *ka-boom!* with the deadly power to remove something that was there only seconds earlier. There's no way to prevent it. If you're unlucky enough to be unprepared, there's nowhere to hide.

As my sixteenth birthday approached, I was in a very "un-" phase.

Unlucky and unprepared for the loss of someone I loved with my whole heart.

But also unmotivated and unattached in ways that made going to school not only a drudge, but also depressing.

My unmotivated issue was centered on the Classic Movie Club, which I'd formed at Fep Prep in order to seem more "well-rounded" (total membership including me is two, the other member being Doug Stuffins; more on him later) and which the school was threatening to cancel unless I drummed up the required third member. Frankly, I just didn't have the enthusiasm to beg kids to join who weren't interested in the first place. Each time I approached someone to talk about it and saw a flash of confusion in his or her eyes as to who I even was, I'd give up before I started. My unattached issue was even more of a downer—Fep Prep's annual spring dance (theme: "It's Spring, Yo") was also a little over a month away, falling (depressingly) on my birthday. In my case, unattached translated into unhappily, undeniably dateless.

I was so obsessed with all of those "uns" one day after school that I failed to notice how dark green and angry the clouds were growing as I walked home from the train station. It was pouring by the time I reached Balmoral Avenue, the rain falling in such thick sheets that at first I didn't notice the convertible parked in front of our house.

My heart leapt a little when I spotted it.

Uncle Buddy was back!

I ran up the steps and pulled at the door but it was stuck, and as I yanked harder, a bolt of lightning cut the air and struck a tree in our front yard.

There was no thunder, just a jarring *crack*, like a truck rolling over walnuts, and then a split-peeling sound as a branch fell to the ground with its leaves sizzled and gone.

When I turned around, my dad was standing in the open door looking at me instead of the tree.

He laid a hand on my wet shoulder and said, "Sara Jane, come inside. Grandpa Enzo died today."

I walked into the living room with my shoes squeaking on

marble, pushing strands of dripping hair from my face, my dad following slowly behind. Uncle Buddy and Greta sat on a small love seat. My uncle's face was pale while Greta's too-red lips twisted in a way that made her look sour and inconvenienced. My mom held Lou against her on the leather couch; when she looked up, I saw that she had been crying. Grief had already begun to fill my lungs like bronchitis; seeing the room crowded with despair and anger only made it harder to breathe. Through the fog in my head, all I could think to ask was "Where's Grandma?"

"Lying down, sweetheart," my mother said, reaching for me. "Come here."

I did, and burrowed into her shoulder weeping. She explained in a soft voice how Grandpa Enzo had a heart attack while making a *buccellato*, the circular, sugary cake given by godparents to their godchild's family on the baby's christening day. Someone on Taylor Street was always asking Grandpa to be their kid's godfather and he usually agreed with a warm smile. He had just taken the cake out of the Vulcan before he died, flipping it out of the hot pan that bore our family initial. The distinctive baked *R* was probably the last thing that he saw.

No one said anything until Greta sighed impatiently. When I looked up, she was on her feet.

"Decisions *have* to be made," she said, pacing the room like a four-star general.

"He just died a couple of hours ago," my dad murmured, lowering into the nearest chair and massaging his forehead.

"Nevertheless," Greta continued, "after an unexpected

death, who gets what and how much has to be hammered out immediately!"

"Greta . . . ," Uncle Buddy said in a low voice, staring at his hands.

"Greta *nothing*, Benito! If you don't stake your position *this instant*, you'll get the short end of the stick, as usual!" she cried, waving her arms wildly. Her elbow bumped a shelf and everyone but Greta saw Frank Sinatra tip and fall into the air.

Uncle Buddy leaped to his feet, arms extended, and caught the statue head like a football, just inches before it shattered on the ground. He sheepishly handed it to my dad and they looked at each other for the first time since I got home. My dad paused, then turned and put it back on the shelf, where the bust continued to stare at the room. It was the tackiest thing we owned—a white plaster Frank Sinatra head with a garland of leaves in its hair, like Julius Caesar, and eyes tinted blue. Although my mom hated it on an artistic level, she insisted that it never move from its honored place on the shelf.

The bust suddenly took on the significance of people I loved who were dead.

It had been a gift to my parents from my nanny.

She gave it to them as a good-bye gift, only days before she died.

Lucretia Zanzara—Elzy, as we called her (for her initials, L.Z.)—was petite, tough as nails, and always perfectly dressed in a retro-mod sixties style, complete with jet-black beehive hairdo and cat's-eye glasses. She was an organizational Einstein who ran our household from breakfast to bedtime with a gentle iron fist. Elzy knew someone who could do anything at any hour, from delivering a perfectly crispy *pizza margherita* at eight a.m. to fixing a refrigerator at midnight, to scoring a badly desired Tickle Me Elmo for three-year-old me the day before Christmas. Her contacts were limitless, ability to get things done, genius, and devotion to my family, seemingly inexhaustible.

Elzy had come to our family via the bakery. Long before I was born, Grandpa Enzo employed her father, Bobo Zanzara, as a baker or pie maker or something. Grandpa and Bobo worked closely until, according to my dad, Bobo took a vacation and never came back. When I asked my dad what kind of vacation lasted forever, he smirked and said, "The federally funded kind," and nothing else. If I asked for more details, he shrugged and changed the subject. Later, Elzy's older brother came to work for my grandpa at the bakery, too. Elzy always referred to him as "Poor Kevin," before shaking her head and *tsk-tsk*ing. Apparently, Poor Kevin had been a lethal combination of knucklehead and hothead. There had been an incident at the bakery, but again, no one ever explained exactly what had happened. If my dad or Uncle Buddy began to discuss it, Elzy would hold up a hand with perfectly polished nails and say, "The past is the past. Poor Kevin made a mistake. Only the strong survive." Her voice was solemn in an Italian way that made further words on the subject indulgent and unnecessary.

Elzy had two unmistakable characteristics. One was her voice—a nasal combination of West Side Chicago and a lion suffering from strep throat—and the other was an undying love for Frank Sinatra. Her gargle-growl took on a terrifying tenor when she sang "Fly Me to the Moon" or "Witchcraft," making dogs howl up and down Balmoral Avenue. The more the cancer spread and the sicker she got, the less she sang. After a final visit to her doctor, Elzy knew that she was going to die. It was right before Lou was born that she gave my parents the Sinatra bust, touched my mom's belly tenderly, and told them that Frank would watch over them when she was gone.

He has sat on the shelf in the same spot ever since.

I was thinking of them both, Grandpa Enzo and Elzy, hoping they died happy, and it was only the fingernails-on-a-chalkboard tone of Greta's rant that brought me back.

She had her fists on her hips and was wagging her head from side to side, speaking her piece about "unfair to Buddy" this and "our share of the pie" that.

When she paused to take a breath, my father said, "Calm down, Greta. Buddy knows full well that he's going to get half the business."

"Yeah?" she said, crossing her arms and arching an eyebrow. "*Which* business?"

Then it was my mom's turn on her feet. I was surprised at how fast she crossed the room, right into Greta's face. In a tone that was quiet but full of nails, she said, "We don't discuss *that* business in front of the children. Not in *this* family."

"I'm just as much a part of this family as you are, Teresa! And don't you dare think that you're entitled to more than Buddy and me just because you have them . . . with their blue eyes . . . especially him . . . ," Greta huffed, pointing at Lou.

Her words drifted around the room like balloons broken free of their strings.

I should have stood and demanded to know what they were talking about, just like Willy had advised me. But I didn't because Grandpa Enzo had just died, and Lou was burrowing into me like I had burrowed into my mom, and—and because I was scared to know. Even though I'd held it at bay, even trying to punch it away, I'd been frightened since I was a little kid of my parents' whispered conversations about money, and "doing the right thing," and especially Uncle Buddy's increasing anger and steady withdrawal from our lives. I wanted everything to go back to how it had been when I was little, one big, tight-knit, happy family; I wanted Uncle Buddy to rise up and stand between Greta's accusatory finger and us. But he just sat there inspecting his hands, satisfied to let her do the dirty work she was so good at.

My mother cleared her throat and said simply, "Get out."

They left without a word and without looking back.

I heard Uncle Buddy's convertible cough to life and squeal from the curb.

I didn't see them again until Grandpa Enzo's funeral at Our Lady of Pompeii, which was so packed with mourners that people stood in the aisles and outside the doors. Our family was on one side of the first row of pews and Buddy and Greta sat on the other. While my grandma wept quietly and touched her nose with a white lace handkerchief, Greta attempted to set the hysterical-crying-at-a-funeral record. Each time the priest murmured Grandpa's name, Greta shrieked with tears like she'd been touched with a cattle prod and buried her face in a bright-red handkerchief. After one explosive outburst, I couldn't help but glance over. Greta peeked from beneath the red silk square and sneered at me, mouthing some Russian obscenity.

Afterward was a hundred-car procession to Mount Carmel, where Grandpa was laid to rest inside a family mausoleum built from mossy limestone. Our name, RISPOLI, is etched on the green bronze door, while the small building itself is topped by a molasses barrel carved from marble. Waiting inside were my great-grandparents, Nunzio and Ottorina, each of whom died decades before I was born. When the service ended and it was time to leave, Grandma Donatella touched Grandpa Enzo's casket and said, "*A presto, mi amore.* See you soon, my love." I had never witnessed anything so sad in my life. I was still thinking about it later, at Gennaro's on Taylor Street, where the entire neighborhood had come to dinner to honor my grandpa.

As I pushed fettuccine around a plate, I felt a small elbow in my ribs.

Lou wiped red sauce from his mouth and said, "Who are all those guys talking to Dad?" I looked up at a line of men of all sizes and ages in dark suits waiting patiently to mumble to him. At first I thought that they were offering condolences, but then I noticed something that froze me a little—Uncle Buddy sat only one table away, but none of the guys paid him the slightest attention, much less spoke to him.

Uncle Buddy, however, was paying attention to my dad.

He was staring at him hard enough to burn holes in the back of his head.

Greta hissed something at my uncle, who nodded, straightened his tie, stood up, and forcefully tapped my dad's shoulder.

After exchanging a few muttered words, they cut through the crowd and headed toward the kitchen, passing Lou and me. My dad smiled at us but didn't look happy, while Uncle Buddy didn't look at us at all. They pushed through the double doors, and then I saw my mom across the room, watching the scene unfold. She hurried after them, and I rose to follow.

"Wait," Lou said, grabbing my hand. "Can I come too?"

"I think it's better if you stay here," I said.

He hooked a pinkie at me and said, "But I thought it was all or nothing?"

Lou was just as suspicious as I was, but suddenly he seemed like such a little kid. I wasn't sure he could handle what was going on between my dad and Uncle Buddy, and I didn't want him to worry. So I hooked his pinkie and said, "We are, even if we're not together. Wait here, okay? I'll be back." Without another word I hurried across the room and through the kitchen, past busboys and line cooks, and stopped in my tracks, ducking behind a tall shelf crowded with canned tomatoes. My mom and dad were talking hurriedly and quietly just on the other side, heads close together.

My dad said, "He's out there in the parking lot, waiting for me."

"What does he want?" my mom asked, trying to stay calm. "Does he know, Anthony? Does he know about . . . the plan?"

My dad paused. "He dropped some hints but I'm not sure. It could just be Buddy being Buddy."

"Buddy's being a jealous asshole," my mom said tersely, surprising me, since she rarely, if ever, cursed. "You have to get him to back off . . . he could ruin everything. Your dad's death, sweetheart, it's a tragedy. You know that I loved him like he was my own father. I wish he could've lived forever, but . . ."

"But it's the chance we've been waiting for, for a long time," my dad said. "Go back inside, Teresa, pretend like everything's fine. I'll take care of Buddy." They embraced, and then my mom hurried past without seeing me, and my dad stepped out the back door, into the parking lot.

I followed him carefully, looking left and right, and spotted them next to Uncle Buddy's convertible. It was like watching TV on mute, my dad with the palms of his hands extended, mouthing silent words while Uncle Buddy talked back, his jaw snapping and head shaking violently. My dad crossed his arms and listened, and then it was his turn to shake his head. He looked so tired, so worn down, and finally he fluttered a hand in the air and turned to walk away.

In slow motion, I watched Uncle Buddy yank his shoulder and spin him around.

I saw Uncle Buddy make a fist and go into an uppercut crouch to hit my dad.

I watched my dad bob and weave, and then lean inside with a gorgeous left hook that found its target on Uncle Buddy's big jaw.

It was the only noise I heard across the parking lot—a hard, sharp *pop* of knuckle on bone—as Uncle Buddy disappeared from sight, and I realized that he had gone down. And then my dad was helping him up, my uncle wobbly on his feet but pushing him away, hard. My dad spoke to him again with his palms out, silently apologizing, but Uncle Buddy stormed away without looking back.

Greta was a slowly moving glacier, but Grandpa Enzo's death was a lightning bolt from the blue.

And my dad knocking down Uncle Buddy was a tremor before the earthquake that would split the Rispoli family apart.

EVERYONE LIVES A SELF-CENTERED LIFE.

From the world's greatest humanitarian to those incredible nuns who work in slums, everyone wakes up each morning thinking about herself.

Whether it's trivial, like what's for breakfast, or more ambitious, like achieving some lofty goal, a person is constantly on her own mind.

How else can I explain the fact that, despite what was happening in my family, I was still focused on myself? My grandpa had died only a week earlier, my parents whispered something about a mysterious plan, my frustrated dad punched my rotten uncle in his stupid face, and I was genuinely worried about all of it. Yet, when I opened my eyes each morning, what did I immediately obsess over?

Not having a date for the spring dance, which was one lousy month away.

Graduating with honors, which meant a trip to Italy as a reward from my parents.

Studying Italian so I could speak like a native, or at least not embarrass myself.

Me, me, me.

There wasn't much I could do about being dateless—no one had asked me and there was no one I wanted to ask—so, even though it was two years until graduation, I focused on school even more. Honors required not just good grades but also the elusive "well-roundedness" on the part of a student. That's why I was a member of the Environmental Club (we planted trees—yawn) and Red Cross Club (we gave blood— ouch) and eventually decided that I should shake things up and make my own mark on Fep Prep.

What better way than forming an organization and naming myself president?

I considered a boxing club, but it felt too personal— something I didn't want to share with the whole school. It was my mom who suggested a movie club, leaning over and whispering it while she, my dad, Lou, and I watched *The Third Man* for the millionth time. We were jammed, as usual, on the big leather couch, with Lou the keeper of the popcorn. He shushed my mom since it was his favorite scene—Holly Martins (yep, a guy named Holly) meets Harry Lime (yep, Harry's namesake) on a Ferris wheel, seeing but not quite believing that his friend, whom he thought was dead, is in fact alive. Each time we watched the scene, Lou hugged his knees and said the same thing.

"Meeting on a Ferris wheel, high in the sky, where no one

can see them," he said quietly. "Private *and* dangerous . . . perfect."

Like I mentioned before, *The Third Man* is Lou's favorite movie, and my dad's too. My mom loves Bette Davis's self-confidence in *All About Eve*, while I can't get enough of *Pulp Fiction*, especially the character Butch, a boxer who fights off some very icky guys in a basement. All in all, the best way to say it is that we're a family of movie geeks, and based on that, I started the Classic Movie Club.

The Fep Prep student body was less than enthusiastic, to say the least.

The only other member was Fep Prep's (maybe the world's) most unpopular sophomore, Doug Stuffins.

His name, by a twist of fate, perfectly defines what he looks like and who he is—incredibly puffy, his three-hundred-pound body stuffed full of junk food, and incredibly smart, his giant brain stuffed full of movie information.

I met Doug during our freshman year in homeroom—my *R* last name seated near his *S* last name—when he turned to me as the teacher droned on about something, and whispered, "You look like an Italian film actress from the sixties."

"I do?" I whispered back. "Which one?"

"All of them," he said with a wink of his piggy eye.

When I sat across from him the next day, he waved and said, "Ciao, bella"—"Hi, beautiful" in Italian—not in a flirty way, but appreciatively. He'd paid me two nice compliments in two days, and for a girl with a very real issue with her very Italian nose, there are few better ways to start a friendship. We talked every day, covering all of the essential subjects—his lousy home life, my super close relationship with my family, the stunning lack of romance in our lives. The one thing we never discussed, maybe out of sensitivity for each other's feelings, was our unpopularity—his by decree of the student body, mine mostly by choice. I probably wouldn't have had a problem dating; I didn't like how I looked, but some guys seemed to be okay with it. But the insularity of my family had gotten into my bones, and so I never pursued a bunch of friends. Doug was different than other kids because, in his isolation, he was the same as me. We bonded over being outsiders and, of course, over movies.

Doug knows more about movies than any kid in the world—maybe any adult in the world, except for his hero, film critic Roger Ebert. He talks about movies constantly to anyone who will listen, and doesn't seem to know (or care) how to shut it off. Sometimes he quotes movies that most people have never heard of, much less seen, which makes him sound sort of insane. He's constantly, frenetically tapping on his laptop, and when I ask what he's working on, he always says the same thing—it was going to be the greatest screenplay ever written, an epic story about a tortured hero. I asked if I could read it and he said maybe when he was done, but no peeking—Orson Welles and Quentin Tarantino never let anyone see their work in progress, either.

And then there's his obsession with the movie *About Face*.

It's a black-and-white comedy made during World War II starring an obscure comedian called Charlie "Chuckles" Huckleman, who wrote and directed it. Doug has an original

About Face script he "scored" (his word) on eBay that he's continually studying, which he calls "the highest form of the craft" (also his words). To sum it up, Charlie Huckleman plays a guy called Dinwiddy who stinks at being a soldier—too cheerful to be disciplined, too uncoordinated to march in a straight line, and too timid to shoot a gun. Through it all, he's harassed by a bulldog sergeant who's frustrated by his lack of military ability. The big joke of the movie is that when the sergeant orders "about face," which means turn around, Dinwiddy always turns the wrong way and bumps into another soldier. Doug explained that Dinwiddy's failure to turn correctly *seemed* like a B-movie gag but was actually an unspoken antiwar statement. That, in fact, the entire movie was a metaphor for why civilized people should *turn away* from violence.

Unfortunately, Fep Prep, too, has its share of uncivilized people.

Doubly unfortunate, Doug's ever-ballooning weight and nonstop movie chatter make him a constant target of teasing and harassment.

Since the beginning of our sophomore year, he's been picked on mercilessly by Billy Shniper, a.k.a. "Bully the Kid."

Billy-slash-Bully has blond, spiky hair, eyes set too close together, and balloonlike biceps, and he is as relentless as a starving shark when it comes to baiting, circling, and cornering a victim. Once he finds his torture groove, he gets jacked up and jumpy, his skin flushes red, and he begins to giggle—a creepy, choking laugh, like a hyena being strangled, which echoes through school. Every time I hear it, I know some poor kid is being teased to death. More often than not, that kid is Doug Stuffins.

But Doug is kind of amazing.

He takes it like a statue, showing no emotion whatsoever.

Even while Billy calls him names (fat ass, freak, effing loser) or pokes his belly ("It's like vanilla pudding!") or yanks away his laptop, Doug stands perfectly still with a look on his face like he's elsewhere. This cool calmness makes Bully meaner, which is when he zeros in on Doug's movie obsession. The insults are weak and stupid, but they hit Doug where it hurts, which is the genius of a bully—to locate a person's most sensitive feelings and then exploit them in a public way. Bully spews his idiotic commentary and chokes on his hyena laugh while Doug remains motionless, waiting for it to end.

Finally, when Billy loses interest and drifts away, Doug picks up his laptop and finds a quiet place to write.

A few weeks ago, I found him under the old oak tree on the south side of Fep Prep, his chubby fingers a tapping blur.

I sat next to him in silence, and then put a hand on his shoulder, and he squinted into the sun without turning to me.

"Sara Jane," he said quietly. "Do you want to go to the spring dance with me?"

Other than being forced to climb the knotted rope in gym class, there was probably nothing in the world Doug considered as torturous as attending a high school dance. He knew I wanted to go and was willing to make the ultimate sacrifice for me—tight dress pants, tucked-in shirt, and hours of hip-hop in the school gymnasium. I gave his arm a gentle punch and told him that I knew he didn't really want to go. He blushed and grinned, saying, "Well, nobody's perfect."

I thought for a second. "*Sunset Boulevard*?"

"*Some Like it Hot*," he said, pleased with the obscurity of his movie quote as he huffed to his feet and waddled away, whistling.

I watched him go, impressed that even after being persecuted by Bully the Kid, Doug could find it in himself to whistle about, well . . . anything.

In my bleak, dateless state, I never whistled anymore.

Also, I never hummed or sang to myself.

My iPod currently moaned with only the saddest, most self-indulgent songs.

The wicked irony is that, in general, I roll my eyes at books, TV, and movies that depict people my age stuck in some moody teenage dilemma. If they're rich kids, they're *moody* rich kids, if they're vampire kids, they're *moody* vampire kids, if they're postapocalyptic kids . . . you get the picture. The thing that bugs me most is that very few people my age even have time to be moody. We're busting our butts doing tons of homework, or forming classic movie clubs, or working part time, or just, I don't know—dealing with an existence thick with expectations. According to Doug, there are three or four kids at Fep Prep so worried about their futures that they worked themselves into a state of exhaustion and weirdness and had to be prescription medicated to deal with it.

Our lives are not the ones our parents lived when they were our ages.

Theirs were simpler, slower, and analog.

Ours are complicated, competitive, and digital.

My generation is the smartest, hardest working, most wired and interconnected ever. It's not easy, but it's exciting, because we're in training to take over the world.

And yet—

And yet, for maybe the first time in my life, what I wanted most was to luxuriate in my own moodiness, to listen to sad songs and think about how tragic it was that I didn't have a date. I considered it pathetic that I could count on one hand the number of times I had been kissed, or kissed someone, since Walter J. Thurber pressed his lips against mine three years ago. I was mortified by the realization that I was three weeks from turning sixteen and had never had a real boyfriend. Despite what was happening in my family, or maybe because of it, I was experiencing a profound sense of aloneness—an overwhelming feeling that I would never find a person who had been made especially for me. It was an isolating sensation, as if I were the only girl in the history of the universe who had ever felt this way. What I wanted was to connect with someone who was *not* a family member, *not* a Doug-type friend, but instead a person who was similar to me in good ways and completely different in other ways. And also someone who would just sort of, well— adore me.

I was so me-centric that I sometimes found myself staring into space.

Other times I floated in a warm pool of self-pity, absolutely sure that I was destined to be alone forever.

And then I re-met Max Kissberg.

TO SHAKE OFF MY FUNK over the upcoming dance that I would positively, absolutely not be attending, I decided to focus my energy on recruiting that coveted third member for the Classic Movie Club. My big brainstorm was a pathetic sign-up sheet and pencil-on-a-string that I taped next to the office, labeled with the optimistic headline "JOIN THE CLASSIC MOVIE CLUB AND DISCOVER WORLDS UNKNOWN!"

It hung there for a couple of days.

Every time I checked it, the page was depressingly blank.

Finally, someone stole the pencil.

My literature teacher, Ms. Ishikawa, is also the Fep Prep activities coordinator. She pulled me aside, wrinkled her little hamster nose, and warned that unless I fulfilled the three-member rule for all clubs, funding for movie rentals and use of the theater room would be canceled. All I could think of was how bad it would reflect on my well-roundedness if I couldn't successfully organize a club where all someone had to do was sit in a dark room, stare at a screen, and eat snacks. Finally, facing the inevitable, I trudged past the office, glanced at the sign-up sheet—and there it was.

MAX KISSBERG, printed in red ink.

At first, the name didn't ring a bell.

After all, it had been three years since Gina's thirteenth birthday party, when he told me not to pay attention to world-class knuckleheads.

And then, rolling the name around in my mind, I vaguely recalled a tiny kid with monster braces who had moved to the suburbs. If he hadn't spoken to me at Gina's birthday party, I wouldn't have remembered him at all, except for an extra blip of memory that came out of nowhere. We were even younger than at the party, maybe nine or ten, and there had been a school talent show where Max played a part in a scene with some other kids. I remembered his little body swallowed up in a huge pinstripe suit, his hair slicked back, and a little mustache drawn in black pencil under his nose. He was onstage, and I remembered that I knew his lines as he uttered them—they were from a movie I had watched with my parents countless times, with my dad's running commentary of what, in the film, seemed "legit" and what was "phony." Max had been playing Vito Corleone from *The Godfather*; he displayed a sly sense of danger that hushed the audience. As I stared at Max's name on the sign-up sheet, I recited his lines from memory—

"I'm going to make him an offer he can't refuse," I murmured.

"What kind of offer?" a voice said.

I turned and looked up at a face smiling down at me that I found a little familiar and very attractive, and then looked closer at the curly hair and imagined thick glasses covering the warm brown eyes. What threw me off was how tall he was—at least half a foot taller than me—but there was no denying it was him.

"Max?" I said.

"Sara Jane, right? I remember you."

"I remember you, too," I said, my throat going dry.

I was suddenly hyperaware of how I looked (or didn't look), wearing distressed (in a real way, not in a fashionable way) jeans, one of my dad's beat-up Cubs T-shirts, and a pair of ratty Chuck Taylors. I couldn't for the life of me remember when I'd last brushed my hair, and I licked my glossless lips trying to think of something cool to say. Max, on the other hand, looked like he could star on a TV show as the hot new guy in school—tan, just muscular enough not to be annoying, wearing a vintage motorcycle T-shirt and jeans that were not distressed, faded, or ripped, but normal and blue. It wasn't exactly love at first sight since I'd seen him before. Maybe it was love at second look, since we were both older now and I was seeing a different Max, a Max who wasn't a little boy anymore but with the same confident smile. Finally I said the stupidest, most obvious thing that popped into my brain. "Um, well . . . you grew."

Max laughed a little. "You too."

"You had glasses," I said, realizing that I was examining his face as if it were a fascinating work of art. "And braces . . ."

"Contacts," he said, overblinking, and then tapped an index

finger on his teeth. "My braces came off last year, finally. It feels like my teeth got out of prison."

"I'm so jealous," I said, squeezing my lips over my mouth, hiding my supposedly-but-not-really-invisible braces. "I feel like I was born with these things."

"It sucks but it's worth it," he said, and then I felt him inspecting my face, traveling from my mouth to my nose (how could he miss it?) to my eyes, where he paused and smiled, nodding at the sign-up sheet. "So are you in this thing?"

"The Classic Movie Club? Yeah, well . . . I guess so."

"It's a cool idea," he said.

"It was my idea!" I said, hearing my words fly out too fast and too loud. I cleared my throat and held back a blush. "I'm, uh . . . I'm the president."

"You are?" he said, looking at me in a way that gave me good goose bumps. "Hey, have you watched any gangster flicks? I'm into film noir . . . the old black-and-white stuff. The dialogue is fast and smart, and there's always a wiseguy who you know is dead from the first time you see him. He either likes being a criminal too much and wants to be the boss or can't outrun his criminal past no matter how hard he tries."

I told him that the club (i.e., Doug and I) had seen several gangster movies, the most recent being *The Public Enemy*, and how I'd felt that the main character was doomed from the first scene. Max was surprised I even knew about the movie. He told me it was one of his favorites and that it was based on an actual guy, a bad-to-the-bone thug who ran a big criminal operation in Chicago during Prohibition.

I said, "That was the no-alcohol law, right?"

Max nodded, saying how criminal gangs raked in enormous amounts of cash by making and selling illegal alcohol, and then paused, grinning. "You can tell me to shut up anytime you want."

"What?" I said, staring into his eyes, and then realized I was staring. "No, no! It's really interesting. How do you know so much about it?"

He shrugged. "I like history. My mom always says, if you don't understand what happened in the past, how can you understand what's happening now?" Max was right, and it reminded me of what Willy said about my dad and Uncle Buddy, about their history and making it my business. Before I could reply, his phone buzzed. "My mom," he said, glancing at the screen. "Since we moved back to the city, she thinks I'm going to be randomly shot or kidnapped."

"What does your dad think?"

"Hard to tell. I haven't spoken to him in a while. My parents got divorced a couple of months ago and he took off for California with his girlfriend."

"Geez . . . that . . . sucks," I said, and blushed. The lameness of my reply made me feel like one of the world-class knuckleheads he'd referred to so long ago.

"It does, worse than braces. My mom was determined to move back to the city, even if it meant me transferring to another school with what, only two months left until summer break? But hey, at least I got to escape the suburbs," he said cheerfully, but fake cheerfully, like he was trying too hard. He put on a half smile and said, "So, when are we getting together?"

"Together?" I tried and failed to get a wild strand of hair behind my ear, and asked, "For what?"

Max's half smile became a real one. "A classic movie?"

"Oh, right, of course! Uh . . . soon," I said. "Tomorrow?"

"Awesome. What are we watching?"

"Oh, um, well, we're watching . . . we're watching . . ." I scanned my brain for the title of any movie I'd ever seen, and came up blank until Doug's chubby grin filled my mind. "We're watching *About Face*," I said. "It's genius. You'll love it."

Max nodded and said, "I trust you," and walked down the hallway. At the exit, he turned and waved.

I waved back casually, like I was the coolest chick in the world.

I waited until he disappeared.

When I was absolutely sure he was gone, I did an excited little Muhammad Ali shuffle move and threw a one-two left hook combination in the air.

Talking to my mom and dad about boys I liked (who usually had no idea I even existed) always made me feel weird. I couldn't help bringing up the subject, but then felt shy or silly as soon as I had. My parents seemed to sense my anxiety, and would tiptoe to the edge of a question, asking something decidedly neutral like, "What color is his hair?" I wanted to confess my deepest feelings, to discuss my crush like an adult, but then I'd chicken out and become a kid again, settling for something meaningless like, "Brown. He's got brown hair."

All of that changed with Max.

I found him endlessly fascinating and had an overwhelming need for the people in my life to know all about him. It was impossible to stop talking about him to my parents, or Lou, or Doug, or, frankly, anyone who would listen.

In fact, talking itself was the best thing about Max.

Besides his smile, and how tall he was, and that he liked all of the old movies I did, he and I talked for hours about everything.

We talked at school before Classic Movie Club, then afterward about the movie we'd just seen, and then later, on the phone, about school and our families, about politics and baseball (he's a White Sox fan, ugh!), and about the world in general. There were no uncomfortable pauses or goofy utterances or trying to sound cool—the conversation just flowed. I noticed that we both naturally avoided slang, and we agreed that every kid in the world saying exactly the same thing over and over again sounded idiotic. But the best part of talking to Max was the simplest—he made me feel interesting. As someone who had never opened up to many people outside of her family, it was a wonderful, weird sensation to have such close attention paid to my thoughts and opinions. It was as if, in my years of mental and emotional solitude, I'd warehoused a vast array of exotic information, and I'd finally found someone to share it with. Whether it was sports or movies or yeah, even slang (Max informed me that "hipster" was actually from the 1940s; I countered with "geek," enlightening him on its early-1900s German origins), we usually ended up talking about how something began. In the three weeks leading up to my birthday, if Max didn't think of me as a girlfriend, then I was definitely a friend who was a girl. It wasn't what I wanted, but I had to admit that our constant chatter was a good way, maybe the best way, to get to know each other.

And then, when he asked me to the spring dance—something I had wanted so badly—I couldn't have cared less.

That's because, a few seconds earlier, he said something even better.

He told me I was gorgeous.

Actually, he didn't use the word *gorgeous* and maybe he didn't realize he was paying me a compliment, but he'd said it, and then he asked me to the dance.

Let me clarify—he *kind of* asked me.

We were staring at a flickering screen in the theater room at Fep Prep, just me, Max, and Doug, with Doug grazing from a family-size bag of Munchitos, his junk food of choice. He'd recently been on a "great Italian directors" kick—we watched films by Fellini, Antonioni, and Rossellini—and had developed a minor obsession (he was easily obsessed) with the director Vittorio De Sica. First we watched *The Bicycle Thief*, which was the saddest movie I'd ever seen, and then *Marriage Italian Style*, which was about a guy cheating on one girlfriend with another girlfriend. It starred Sophia Loren, with whom Doug developed another minor obsession, and we moved on to an old Hollywood film she starred in called *Houseboat*.

Sophia Loren was one of the most beautiful women I had ever seen.

On-screen, her face glowed and her body shimmered.

It was at that moment—the greatest of my life—that Max

whispered, "Hey . . . you look like her. Especially your eyes. You have little bits of gold in there."

I thought I heard him wrong. I was scared to move, scared to breathe, and the seconds that followed felt like hours. Finally I said, "Who?"

"Her," he said, nodding at Sophia, whose face filled the screen like a sexy angel. I didn't know what the scene was about and didn't care—all I knew was that Max told me that I looked like *her*. I was about to say something witty (i.e., stupid) when he said that his mom was forcing him to go to the dance and that maybe I should suffer too. I said something back like, "Yeah. Whatever. Maybe," while trying to stifle a smile that, if I'd allowed it to run its course, would've dominated my face.

"I mean, we could meet there," he said, still staring at the screen.

"I guess so."

"Shh!" Doug hissed.

"If you go and we run into each other, you know, well . . . great," Max whispered.

"Great," I said in as casual a tone as I could muster, even though my heart was almost thumping out of my chest. Maybe it wasn't the hearts-and-flowers way that I'd hoped he would ask me, but he'd asked me, and it was enough. I was going with, or meeting, or running into Max at the spring dance!

"My mom keeps telling me that I need to meet other kids, and that, quote, it's not going to happen by spending all of my extracurricular time in a geeky movie club, end quote," he whispered. "I reminded her that every kid with half a brain is a geek about something. With me it's motorcycles. I've got this vintage Triumph Thunderbird and she promised that if I went to the dance, we'd get it out of storage. Have you ever ridden a motorcycle?"

"No, but I can drive a car," I said shyly, and felt a small blush cover my cheeks.

"You can?" Max said, looking at me more closely, giving me the happy shivers.

"Shh . . . for the *second* time!" Doug said.

I leaned in and whispered to Max how I'd sat next to my dad in the Lincoln a thousand times watching him turn the key, put the convertible top down, and drop the long, flat car into drive. One afternoon when I was thirteen, when he was at the bakery and my mom was out with Lou, I grabbed the Lincoln's keys. Ten minutes later I was stuttering down Ashland Avenue—too much gas, too hard on the brakes, squeal of tires, repeat—until a red light came out of nowhere. I jammed both feet on the brakes as the Lincoln shrieked to a halt, rear wheels smoking and my heart punching my chest.

I looked to my right and a guy in a Mustang shook his head.

I looked to my left and it was my mom in her little Fiat, a red-lipstick slash of disapproval on her mouth.

"And then what?" Max whispered.

"She surprised me."

After she followed me home and the Lincoln was safely in the garage, I expected a stern speech and punishment. Instead, she told me that normal society would *expect* her to say that driving at age thirteen was wrong, but that she didn't agree.

She said it was important to play by the rules, but that sometimes it was just as important to know how to break them, too. So the disobeying-the-law part, driving without a license— yeah, obviously that was wrong—but not the learning-to-operate-a-car part. As a teacher, my mom encouraged the accumulation of knowledge. If I wanted to learn to drive, she would teach me.

"That was cool of her," Max whispered.

"So cool."

I didn't tell Max about what happened next because it didn't seem to have much to do with the story. In fact, I wouldn't realize until later that what my mom said at the end of our conversation was the *real* story—that it was best not to tell my dad about my little joyride. I should've been relieved that she encouraged me not to tell my dad about taking the Lincoln for a drive, but it surprised me, and I asked why not.

"It might upset him," she said, looking away. "That old car was presented to your grandpa in 1965 to celebrate the birth of your dad, his first child and oldest son."

"Presented?" I asked. "You mean like a gift? From who?"

"Just . . . friends," she replied vaguely, and for some reason my mind went immediately to the Men Who Mumbled.

"What about Uncle Buddy?" I asked, thinking of his beater convertible. "Was that a gift for Grandpa too? To celebrate the birth of his second kid?"

"No," my mom replied. "Buddy bought that car himself."

Back then, the idea of Uncle Buddy buying a convertible so he could have one just like his older brother made me sad for him. Of course, what I feel now—that he's a twisted, world-class bullshitter who was jealous of my dad when they were kids and hates him now that they're adults—is completely different. However, at the moment, telling Max the story in the darkened theater room, all I could really think was, I'm going to the dance with Max! Or at least going to a dance where he would be.

"Listen," he said, pushing brown curls out of his eyes. "After I get this dance thing out of the way, do you want to go for a ride on my motorcycle? As soon as I get my license, I mean."

"Yeah, sure . . . I guess so," I said breezily, with my heart about to burst.

"People, please," Doug said. "There's rude and there's pathological. For the last time, and with feeling . . . shh!"

I mouthed "sorry" to Doug as he settled back with junk food on the left and a root beer on the right. Watching him, I realized that Max was partly correct. Yeah, most kids with half a brain are geeks about something, but others require no brain at all.

Like Billy Shniper, for example.

Bully the Kid displayed zero evidence of having anything remotely resembling a cerebral cortex, yet he was a geek about teasing Doug.

Over the course of the school year, his bullying had progressed from frequently to constantly in pursuit of the goal he had yet to accomplish—making Doug cry. After Max witnessed one particularly intense display, he told Doug that he was going to intervene the next time it happened, and didn't care what Bully the Kid said or did to him.

Doug smiled sadly and said, "Did you learn nothing from *About Face*? The only way to combat violence is with nonviolence. Aggression begets aggression."

"Yeah?" Max said. "Well, someone needs to beget a fist in Billy's mouth."

Doug shook his head. "Dinwiddy turned away from violence. Bully the Kid or no Bully the Kid, I shall do the same."

I had to admire Doug—his commitment to passivity was rock solid. He had created a set of rules for himself and vowed never to break them. I'd been boxing for years, where physical engagement inside the ring came with a set of hard and fast rules too. You played by them or were disqualified. You respected them or did not compete.

At that point in my life, rules were important to me.

I thought that if I followed them, they would apply order to the universe.

I foolishly believed they kept chaos at bay.

I didn't know yet that the lesson my mother had taught me—knowing how to break or even ignore the rules—would become the only rule I would follow.

THERE'S NOTHING LOUDER or more disruptive to a family than prolonged silence.

Before my grandpa's funeral, my dad and Uncle Buddy spoke only on a functional basis about orders and inventory. In the days that followed, that stilted conversation broke down even further, descending into monosyllabic grunts.

And then something so sad happened that it forced them to speak, at least briefly.

It forced them to make funeral arrangements again.

Grandma Donatella had returned to work almost immediately after Grandpa Enzo died, reclaiming her place behind the front counter. She had always been a tiny bundle of energy, constantly in motion—boxing up cookies and cakes, ringing the cash register, scrubbing display cases—but now she sat motionless on a low metal stool watching customers come and go with her mouth drawn down. Whenever someone from the neighborhood asked her how she was doing, her eyes filled with tears as she silently reached into a display case, removed a heart-shaped cookie, and broke it in half. She began to complain about her own heart, how it ached for my grandpa, and then how it just ached, and then she died too. She had made good on her promise to join my grandpa *a presto*—soon.

After she was placed inside the Rispoli mausoleum, my dad and Uncle Buddy stopped speaking completely.

·The silence between them was so deafening that I had to leave the bakery kitchen if they were both there at the same time.

It was as if my grandma were the last structure standing after an earthquake, and when she died, everything in the family quietly fell to rubble.

In that short period between my grandparents' deaths, Uncle Buddy's work habits had grown erratic; now they were just plain weird. He came in late and left early, mixed batter and dough in a lazy, halfhearted manner or not at all, and barked at customers if they were too slow in making up their minds. Sometimes he just sat in the kitchen smoking a Sick-a-Rette, staring hard at my dad, as if the power of his hateful gaze would force my dad to do or say something. I was unsure of what that something was, but then it didn't matter anymore because Uncle Buddy stopped coming to work altogether. Instead, he used his keys to come in after hours and rummage through the kitchen, storage rooms, and basement, ripping open boxes, splitting sacks of flour, pushing over shelves. My father would find the mess, shake his head, and clean it all up, muttering, "He'll never find it."

"Find what?" I asked, picking up broken dishes.

My father shrugged, answering vaguely, "Whatever he's looking for."

"Dad?"

"Yes, sweetheart?" he said.

His eyes were full of a sad sense of looking beyond the here and now, it rattled me a little, and I lost the nerve to ask more about Uncle Buddy. Then something caught my attention, and I glanced past him at thin lines of smoke seeping from the Vulcan. "Something's burning!" I said.

"Damn it! The *melassa biscotti*!" he cried, dropping the broom and rushing to the oven. A plume of black smoke rolled up to the ceiling as he pulled open the door, yanked out a tray of smoldering cookie lumps, and threw it on the mixing table. The stink of scorched sugar filled the room and I gagged a little. Overhead, fire sprinklers coughed and spurted streams of tepid water. My dad leaned on the table with both hands, hanging his head, and then pounded it with a fist so hard that I jumped. "It's all ruined! Everything!" he shouted into the indoor thunderstorm.

"It's just cookies," I said.

"No, it's everything! Everything," he said, and then moved so quickly across the room that I jumped again. He was staring at me intently, almost like he was going to cry. "Sara Jane, you're the oldest. You're so smart and so . . ." He trailed off, then pursed his lips and bowed his head. When he looked up, the possibility of tears was replaced by something cold and rooted on earth. "Innocence fades for everyone," he said slowly. "If a person has any hope of survival, it must be substituted for plain reality. Listen to me closely, not with innocent ears, but with the ears of an adult. If something happens, you need to know about our family . . ."

"What could happen?" I said, a shudder racking my body.

"Anything," he said in a voice that I'd never heard before. He had made the leap into plain reality and I had to join him. I stopped shaking, or at least tried my best, as he said, "I have to tell you important things about our family business. And about the bakery . . ." He paused as his eyes flicked past me.

"What is it?" I whispered.

"Yeah, what is it?" Uncle Buddy said from the kitchen door, striking a match and lighting a Sick-a-Rette. Its rotten-garbage smell mingled nauseatingly with burned molasses as he came toward us, a little grin on his lips. "Or should I say, *where* is it?"

My dad squared his shoulders and positioned his body sideways, a boxer setting his stance.

Uncle Buddy did the same thing, cautiously.

I moved closer to my dad, determined not to leave his side, mirroring his posture without realizing it.

Uncle Buddy chuckled. "Well, look-it here, a daddy-daughter boxing team. Hey, Sara Jane, before you unleash the stunning power of those spaghetti arms on old Uncle Buddy," he said, his laugh turning to a sneer, "just remember it was *me* who made time to get you into boxing, not *him*."

"But *he's* my dad!" I said, surprised at the acid in my words.

"It doesn't make him right," Uncle Buddy declared. "Remember what I'm teaching you, kid, it's an important life lesson. Just because he's your dad does *not* make him right. In fact, your dad recently made a very *wrong* decision that could be very, very bad for your family." He smirked at my dad, saying, "You're surprised I know about that, huh? Stupid old Buddy? Well, stupid old Buddy has been *hacking* your voice mail and *peeking* at your e-mail . . . techniques just like the *government* uses."

"Buddy," my dad said, his voice full of warning.

"I know, I know . . . not in front of the kiddies, right?"

"Sara Jane can handle anything you can dish out and more," my dad said.

"Oh, please." Uncle Buddy chuckled again. "She's still mooning over a kiss that happened five years ago."

"Three," I mumbled. I'd never heard my uncle's mocking tone directed at me. It crushed my heart a little, but I also realized that I was curling my left hand into a fist.

"Come on, Anthony. Enough of the playacting and bullshit. You know that I know all about that notebook," Uncle Buddy said.

"What notebook?" I said.

"Buddy," my dad said, this time almost growling.

"I'm tired of looking for the damn thing, and besides, it's not like you're going to need it anymore," Uncle Buddy said. "Just give it to me and then you and your little family can go on your merry way to wherever they send your kind of people."

"They who?" I said. "What does he mean, 'your kind of people'?"

Uncle Buddy grinned at my dad, the Sick-a-Rette stink-smoldering between his lips like something scooped from a litter box. "You want to tell her or should I?"

My dad paused, his jaw rippling, and said, "Even if I did give it you, Buddy, you wouldn't know what to do with it. It's too dangerous for someone like you."

Buddy's smart-aleck smile stayed in place, but his voice was ice. "What the hell does *that* mean?"

"It means someone . . . who wants to be like me," my dad said slowly. "And you're not, Buddy. You're not like me."

"Maybe I could be," Uncle Buddy said, in a tone both angry and wishful, "if you give me the notebook."

My dad remained silent, his face full of iron, as he shook his head no.

Uncle Buddy said, "Okay, kid, here's *exactly* what we're talking about—"

My dad cut him off abruptly, saying, "Sara Jane, go wait in the car."

"But Dad . . ."

"Yeah, kid, go wait in the car. Go do your nails or something else just as girly," Uncle Buddy said. "It's a perfect example of one of the important things he was going to tell you about the family business . . . a woman's place is on the outside looking in."

"Yeah?" my dad said. "What about Greta?"

This time Uncle Buddy's smile slipped. "Keep her out of this," he said.

"You're the one who put her in it. Right between us."

"*She's* not between us!" Uncle Buddy said. "*This* is! This family and its secrets! It has always been between us!"

"Not for me," my dad said quietly.

"Of course not for you. You're the older brother," Uncle

Buddy said, pointing the stinking Sick-a-Rette at him. "*You* have a healthy, blue-eyed son."

They stared at each other until they remembered I was there, and then they slowly turned toward me. Their faces were so different, my dad's weary and worried, my uncle's smug and disdainful. Fragments of the past—Uncle Buddy's unhappy response long ago at the announcement of Lou's impending birth, my parents' urgent "doing the right thing" conversations they'd been whispering about for years, the line of men at my grandpa's funeral waiting to talk to my dad, the older son, while ignoring my uncle—appeared like pieces of an unfinished puzzle. My conversation with Willy about the history between them echoed in my mind, especially his ominous words "in a family like yours." Whatever it all meant, I at least understood that the rift between my dad and uncle had shifted from depressing to dangerous. Even more clearly, I saw that danger creeping toward Lou. My entire body was shaking when I said, "What's this about, Dad?"

"Go to the car, Sara Jane."

"No, Dad! You keep talking about brothers, and about Lou! What about him?"

"There's nothing to tell."

"Oh yes there is!" Uncle Buddy said.

"What about me? Does it affect me, too?"

"No," my dad said.

"Oh yes it does!" Uncle Buddy cried.

"Dad!"

"Sara Jane!" he thundered, stripping the air of noise, my lungs of air, and Uncle Buddy's face of confidence. We stepped away from him, me in one direction, my uncle in another. Veins stood out on his forehead, but his eyes were as frigid as two blue ice cubes, the gold flecks glowing brightly. He was vibrating with fury and yet weirdly calm at the same time. The combination was terrifying, and something clicked in my head as a little movie began to play. It was a memory from when I was four or five, when I witnessed a nearly identical phenomenon that scared me just as badly, except it wasn't my dad.

It was Grandpa Enzo.

I toddled through the door of the bakery kitchen looking for a cookie.

I came upon my grandpa hissing like a Sicilian snake.

His back was to me, while before him stood one of the Men Who Mumbled. The man was a foot taller and a hundred pounds heavier than "Enzo the Biscotto," yet he stood quaking with fear in a dark suit and sunglasses while staring at his feet. My grandpa tapped the blunt end of a mixing spoon in time to his words against the man's chest—*mi* (tap) *capisci* (tap) *idiota?* (tap)—while the man's lower lip trembled and his forehead beaded with sweat. I realized that I was witnessing something I shouldn't, so I backed away, bumping a bowl from a shelf. It shattered on the floor. My grandpa spun on his heel, and I looked into two quietly furious blue ice cubes. It was him, but it wasn't—with flaring nostrils and gritted teeth, this was Evil Grandpa from the coldest corner of hell. It terrified me so badly that I began to wail and ran from the kitchen. By the time I was buried in my grandma's apron, the mumbling man had left the bakery.

I felt a soft tap on my shoulder.

With one eye, I peeked up at my grandpa, who was himself again.

His face was warm and regretful.

He crouched on his knees, placed his hands gently on my shoulders, and stared at me with the same blue eyes decorated with bits of glittering gold as mine and my dad's. "*Cara mia . . .* my sweet, that wasn't really Grandpa, oh no-no-no. That was just work . . . part of being a baker." He kissed my forehead, patted my cheek, and with a profoundly sad smile, produced a molasses cookie from behind his back.

It was as if the devil had peeled back his mask to reveal Santa Claus.

I was staring at that same mask now, on my dad, except that the mask seemed much more real than what was underneath. My own worst fears—isolation, abandonment, rejection— flooded my brain and gut, leaving me limp and helpless.

"Go to the car, please," my dad said in a placid tone that made the hairs on the back of my neck stand up.

I opened my mouth to object, but his eyes froze the words in my throat.

I gladly turned for the door and my uncle did too.

Before Uncle Buddy's foot even hit the floor, my dad said, "Stop. Sit," like a stern master training his dog, and my uncle obeyed, quickly finding a chair.

I pushed through the kitchen's swinging door almost as fast as I had when I was a tiny kid escaping my grandpa, but this time was different. Once I was away from my dad, separated by a brick wall, fear was replaced by curiosity. As the door swung back, I heard him mutter "molasses," "Nunzio," and "notebook." Of course I knew about the Rispoli & Sons molasses cookies, and about my dad's own grandpa, Nunzio Rispoli, who founded the bakery in the 1920s. At the time, though, I wasn't yet aware of the notebook—that ancient collection of criminal secrets that would become central to my survival—and it intrigued me.

Carefully, I peeked through the door's porthole window.

My uncle sat trembling in a wooden chair, trying and failing to look defiant.

My dad popped an index finger off of Uncle Buddy's chest as he spoke.

The look on Uncle Buddy's face was almost identical to the mumbling man who had stood before Grandpa Enzo, but this time was different too. That giant thug was afraid to make eye contact, while Uncle Buddy held my dad's gaze. He was scared, that was plain, but not too scared to look at him, and I asked myself why.

I thought, Because he's determined.

I thought, He's determined because he wants that notebook.

"I'm gonna get it, Anthony," my uncle said, his words so soft that they blew past my ears like a breeze. "And no one had better stand in my way. Not you . . . and not your family, either. Or else."

My dad's hands darted like angry eels and suddenly Uncle Buddy's feet were dangling above the floor. His face turned purple along with my dad's hands, which were wrapped around Uncle Buddy's neck, growing tighter every second. My uncle flailed his arms like he was swimming through air and made wet smacking noises with his tongue while his eyes rolled back in his head. There was a slight *crick*, like a twig snapping, and a line of scarlet blood trickled from his nostril.

"Come near my family and I will kill you."

My dad's statement was uttered in a matter-of-fact tone, as if asserting that "water is wet" or "ice is cold." And then he dropped Uncle Buddy and turned for the door in a motion so fluid I only had time to push against the wall. As my dad walked away, Uncle Buddy rolled onto his back, gasping for air, and croaked, "Or *else*, Anthony."

The door stopped moving, half open, with me cowering on the other side.

I could feel the cool electricity of my dad's anger a foot away. He was trying to decide whether to turn and finish with Uncle Buddy, while I silently begged him to leave the kitchen.

A moment later he strode through the bakery and out the front door, the bell jingling behind him. I fled after him without a look back, catching him at the curb where the Lincoln was parked. He must have heard my footsteps and spun quickly, his fist cocked with a car key jutting between the second and third knuckle. I skidded to a stop, my hands going up instinctively to block a punch, and then we were facing off, each in our stance. I could see in his eyes that Evil Dad had retreated to wherever he had come from. Now they filled with alarm as he said, "You were in the bakery?"

I nodded, slowly lowering my fists.

"How much did you hear?" he said. "Tell the truth."

"I heard Uncle Buddy threaten us. I heard you tell him that you'd kill him."

"Oh God," he said, dragging a hand over his face. "Forget it, Sara Jane. Forget what you heard and saw." He put his hands on my shoulders and tried on a weak smile. "None of it matters now, sweetheart."

"Of *course* it matters!" I said, pushing his hands away. It was that word, *sweetheart*, that set me off, like I was some kind of idiot girl. After his soul-rattling transformation from Dad to Evil Dad, and the horrible scene with Uncle Buddy, he was behaving as if a few reassuring words were all I needed to pretend nothing happened. I felt a small blue flame of anger kindle in my gut as I said, "You were about to tell me something important about our family. You can't start a conversation like that, especially after what just happened, and ask me to forget it."

"I'm not asking you," he said, the smile vanishing. "I'm telling you."

"To do what? Erase my brain? I saw what I saw and heard what I heard," I said. "Tell me, Dad, at least about that notebook. Tell me right now."

"Don't speak to me like that," he said, unlocking the old car.

"You said I can handle it and more."

"I know you can handle it," he said. "I just don't want you to *have to* handle it." He gazed at the bakery and set his jaw. "Like I said, none of it matters anymore. We're leaving tomorrow."

"Leaving where?"

He opened the car door. "Leaving Chicago. You, Lou, Mom, and me."

"But . . . since when?"

"Since now, Sara Jane. Things have changed."

It was too much, too fast, and I stammered, "But I have school, and my friends . . . this is insane, Dad. None of it makes sense. There's no way we're leaving tomorrow . . ."

"Get in," he said, starting the engine.

I shook my head. "Not unless you tell me the truth. About everything."

His mouth was a tight line as he shook his head. "We're done talking."

Without another word, I turned and walked down the sidewalk.

He dropped the car into gear and followed me, saying, "Sara Jane, please."

Silence—walking and looking straight ahead.

"Sweetheart, I'm sorry. I just . . . please get in."

No acknowledgment—still walking.

"Okay, fine. Walk if it will make you feel better. But come straight home."

And then I watched him drive away, waving sadly.

He assumed the short walk to our house would put me only twenty minutes behind him. That assumption made me less angry than depressed, since he'd obviously forgotten that it was Friday night, the Fep Prep spring dance, and that he was to drop me off at Gina's house. And that my dress was hanging in the backseat of the Lincoln.

He'd forgotten that I was meeting Max Kissberg.

He'd forgotten that today was my sixteenth birthday, and that the best gift I could've received was a date with Max.

I knew what a supremely terrible afternoon my dad had—
it's not every day that formerly loving brothers threaten each
other's lives. If my dad was at the point where he was prepared
to flee Chicago in twenty-four hours, it was obviously much
worse than I could imagine. Still, it was extremely disturbing
how something so important to me could be so easily pushed
aside. I've never been a person who needs a lot of attention
from the outside world. But I grew up in such a protected way
that my emotional core is centered within my family; I depend
almost fully on them for attention, approval, and support. So
if there's one thing that sets off a flock of just-about-to-cry
butterflies in my stomach, especially when it comes from my
parents, it's disregard—that lonely, empty sensation of not
being thought of, or even considered. Those butterflies were
moving now, and I wiped at my eyes and began the long trek
to Gina's house.

I was angry at my dad for refusing to tell me those important things about my family, but even angrier that he drove
away without a simple "happy birthday."

Much later, I would remember his sad wave.

I would wish that I'd waved back, since it was the last time
I ever saw him.

TEN LONG BLOCKS LATER, all I could think about was how late it was, how Max probably wondered if I would even show up at the dance, and how the dress I'd sweated and fretted over had driven away with my dad.

Also, how weird it was that Gina and I were going to the dance together.

Over the years, as she honed and perfected her gossip skills by knowing and talking to tons of people (and I pointedly didn't), we regressed from hanging out regularly to sometimes to rarely. My mom's warning had kept me away from her, and so did Gina's ever-growing popularity, but even though we'd grown apart, we still had one of those original-friendship connections. We'd been each other's first real friend, which never quite goes away, especially when you attend the same schools. So, whether it was out of nostalgia, curiosity, or the old challenge that lies between us—would she ever whisper to me a morsel of gossip so juicy that I'd actually want to know more?—we decided to go to the dance together. Days before, we'd found ourselves jammed next to each other in a crowded school assembly and chatted aimlessly until we arrived at the subject of the dance. She wasn't currently dating anyone but planned on attending anyway, and I mentioned I was meeting someone there but basically going alone. And then we both sort of shrugged and decided to go together.

When I showed up at her house, sweaty from walk-running the whole way, she took one look at me, raised an eyebrow, and said, "Jeans, Cubs T-shirt, and Chuck Taylors again? For a dance? See, this is why we never hang out anymore. FYI, Sara Jane . . . the general consensus floating around is that you're a very strange kid." She pulled open her closet to lend me whatever she had, except that I'm sort of tall and definitely on the thin side and Gina is genuinely curvy. I tried on a few skirts but they were too short, and a few tops but they were too airy. Her mom, who had been watching our sad little fashion show, left the room, saying, "We're almost the same size, Sara Jane. I think I might have something." She returned pulling plastic from a hanger, smiling ear to ear, saying, "I haven't worn this since college."

Gina looked at the dress, at me, and at her mom, and said, "Where's it been, in a time capsule?" I stared at the dress glittering before me, knowing Gina had a point. The best way to describe it is to say that Farrah Fawcett would've worn it if she were working undercover, posing as a disco instructor on *Charlie's Angels*.

"It's a spring dance, Mom," Gina said. "Not a Halloween party."

"Well, Sara Jane, if you don't want it . . . ," Gina's mom began.

"No, it's great," I said, mainly because it looked like it would fit and because we were more than an hour late. "I'd love to wear it."

Gina's jaw dropped. "You would? Okay, but I'm walking into the gym alone. I mean it. I don't need it getting around that I associate with a disco queen."

Nothing could've kept me from that dance.

I would've gone in a suit of armor.

And then, once I walked into the balloon-filled gym and took a look around, I couldn't get out of there fast enough.

Right in front of me, encircled by a golden spotlight, Max was dancing with Mandi Fishbaum. A swarm of her look-alikes cruised past me, one of them giving me an up-and-down inspection, saying, "Nice dress."

I flashed a look at her and said, "Shut the hell up," as a small, cold flame began to dance in my gut. It was a strange feeling, one that was scary and thrilling at the same time, and I concentrated the sensation behind my eyes. The look-alike froze, her own eyes wide and mouth slightly open, and then I blinked, and she scurried away like a terrified chipmunk. I stared across the dance floor, sure that the right thing to do was exercise my left hook on Mandi's jaw. But then the flame subsided, the feeling passed, and I turned and hurried from the gym.

"Sara Jane! Wait!"

I was through the double doors and hurrying across the parking lot when Max caught me, touching my shoulder and turning me toward him. "Where are you going?" he said, giving me the same appraisal as the look-alike. He grinned and said, "Nice dress," except that he meant it.

Without thinking, I pushed him so hard that it made him take a step back. "You were dancing with Mandi Fishbaum!" was the worst thing I could think to say.

"So?" Max said, coming at me with his arms open and grin in place.

"So? Do you like her?"

"Yeah, I do."

"But you told me she was a *knucklehead*!"

"That was three years ago."

"So three years later, she's not a knucklehead anymore?"

"Oh yeah," Max said, with his TV-star grin, straightening the lapels of the sport coat he wore over a Triumph Motorcycle T-shirt. He moved brown curls from his eyes and said, "Mandi's still a knucklehead all right. World class."

"But you like her?" I said, feeling tears coming, and pushing him away.

"Yeah. Sara Jane . . ."

"And she's a knucklehead?" I said, pushing him again.

"Yeah. Listen, can you stop doing that?"

"You like her *and* she's a knucklehead?" I said, and before I could push him again, Max grabbed my arms and held them tightly.

"You know, this is starting to sound like a scene from that movie Doug just showed us. *Chinatown*, remember?"

"How can you like Mandi Fishbaum, of all people?" I said, trying to yank my arms free while Max held them.

"Because, as I was trying to tell you," he said, "she's my cousin."

"Your . . . cousin?"

"Yeah," he said, with a smaller, more cautious grin. "Everyone has the right to like his cousin and also think she's an idiot."

"Max," I said, the reality of the situation descending on my head like a wet blanket. I had wanted to be so cool, so laid back and funny, but instead I had come off like some type of stalker/maniac. "Max, I'm . . ."

"A knucklehead?" he said, and the warm smile that followed made it okay. "I really do like your dress. It's old school, but not hipster-fake old school. It's real."

"That's for sure."

"Like you," he said matter-of-factly. "You just seem like . . . you. You don't try to be anyone else."

"You mean the look-alikes."

"The who?" he said.

I explained the term and Max nodded. He understood that I didn't hate those girls but just wasn't anything like them—I wasn't embedded in the type of social circle (or any social circle, for that matter) that dictated how I dressed or who I did or didn't speak to. Finally I said, "What about the dance?"

"I told my mom I'd be home by ten. I did my servitude and now I get my motorcycle." He looked at his phone and said, "It's nine thirty. Why are you so late?"

The day's drama between my dad and uncle, combined with the anticipation of meeting Max at the dance, had worn

100

me down. I was suddenly exhausted, and said, "It's a long story. I'm going home, too."

"Red or brown line?" he said.

"Brown to red."

"You want to ride together?"

Max talked excitedly about his motorcycle as we walked, and then apologized for talking so much. I didn't care what he talked about, I was just happy to be together, and then we were at the El stop, swiping our cards and climbing the stairs to the platform.

The train pulled to a silent, breezy halt, sending litter bits cartwheeling in the air.

The doors separated with a *zwoosh*.

The recorded announcement said, "This is Diversey. Exit on the right at Diversey."

Max and I climbed aboard the mostly empty car and sat shoulder to shoulder. As the train pulled away, he cleared his throat and said, "Hey, you want to see a movie? I don't mean a classic one. I mean a go-to-the-theater movie."

"Which one?" I said, thrilled at the prospect of what sounded like a date.

"See if you can figure it out," he said. "I'm talking about exploding helicopters, 3-D natural disasters, guys doing the super slo-mo spinning-in-the-air thing while spraying Uzis at each other. Oh, and also a gigantic bomb that could destroy earth."

"Let me guess . . . *Ten Seconds to Zero*?"

"What gave it away? The gigantic bomb?"

"You like Ashton Willis?"

"He's not a great actor," Max said, "but he gets blown up well."

"Doug would disapprove," I said. "He'd call it 'culturally insignificant.'"

"Actually, I think he'd call it 'cotton candy for little brains.'"

"Doug hates action movies," I said.

"I know. That's why I'm asking you instead of him," Max said, and nodded his head at the Belmont platform that was rumbling into view. "What do you say? *Ten Seconds to Zero* . . . nine, eight, seven . . ."

"Yeah, sure," I said. "You can buy me some birthday popcorn."

Max's grin made my heart flutter like a baby bird. "No kidding. When's your birthday?"

"Today," I said, blushing for some reason. "Which means my family will probably have a cake tomorrow."

"Which means the world will explode Sunday instead of Saturday," he said. "Sunday at the Davis, noon?"

"Yeah, sure," I said as the train eased to a stop. I rose and went to the exit, then looked back. "See you then."

"Get ready for an action-packed birthday weekend," Max said with a wink.

I stepped onto the platform and was enveloped by the mild night air that blankets Chicago in springtime.

The doors sealed, and Max turned in his seat to wave as the train rolled away.

I watched him go, blissfully unaware of how soon his words would come true.

IT'S ONLY LATER, after the fact, that you remember the mental and physical warning signs that twitch and quiver throughout your body and brain, trying to alert you that something is about to happen. It's like when the flu is coming on and you remember the small, intense headache that you ignored, or the bout of shivers you ascribed to a chilly breeze, even though it's eighty-five degrees outside.

Walking up Balmoral Avenue to my house, seeing all of the windows pitch black, a telltale quake ran up my spine. But I was thinking about Max, and didn't pay it the attention it deserved.

I climbed the steps and saw that the screen door was swinging crookedly on one hinge. Behind it, the front door was wide open.

The interior of the house was dark brown with shadows.

Stepping forward, my foot crushed glass, the *grind-crunch*

making me jump. I entered the house cautiously, calling out to my mom first and then my dad.

The answer was nearby.

It was chatter-laughter, high-pitched and looping.

It shrieked, stopped, and shrieked again, punctuating the silent house.

I had been taught in self-defense class that when something feels dangerous or threatening to stop thinking and flee. But this was *my* house. My notion of it as a secure place had not yet been violated. Each time I took a step forward, the laugh would start again, and I'd freeze, unable to move, holding tight to the empty space around me.

Shree-hee-hee! Shree-hee-hee!

It didn't sound human, yet I heard human sounds in it, perverted by speed.

Shree-hee-hee! Shree-hee-hee!

It should have been repelling, but instead drew me forward.

Shree-hee-hee! Shree-hee-hee!

I turned the corner into the living room and the first thing I saw were piles of feathery guts that had been pulled out in chunks from the belly of the leather couch. Bookshelves were overturned, the books' spines stomped flat, and chairs torn apart with legs missing or at odd angles. Our family portrait hung sideways over the mantle, slashed in half, with Lou sitting on my dad's lap on one side and me standing with a hand on my mom's shoulder on the other. Every drawer had been pulled and dumped, and the big Persian rug was yanked back and rolled over on itself, like a huge abandoned crepe.

Anything with an interior or that covered something else—pillows, pictures, cabinets—had been flipped over or kicked in or slashed apart. Seeing the room like that was so unreal that all I could do was gape.

Shree-hee-hee! Shree-hee-hee!

It was next to me, and I toed at the debris until a pair of piercing blue eyes stared up from a face that was cold and stone white.

Shree-hee-hee! Shree-hee-hee!

I picked up the unbroken bust and looked into its face, watching the cornea of the left eye dilate—wide, narrow, wide, narrow.

Shree-hee-hee! Shree-hee-hee!

I noticed for the first time a whisper-thin seam around its hairline and, holding the statue tightly, I unscrewed the head of Frank Sinatra.

Inside, a mini video camera focused and refocused its lens behind the left eye.

The tape was stuck, winding forward and backward, shrieking loudly.

I removed the camera, pressed the Stop button, and the chatter-laughter stopped.

I understood suddenly why my parents had kept the tacky gift from a long-dead nanny. It was Elzy's parting gesture of protection, a nanny cam, hidden inside the head of the only man she had ever loved. The mini camera was charged, with a tape inside, so of course my parents knew about it and had used it. My hands were so clumsy with fear that I almost dropped the camera as I slid it back inside the skull and screwed it shut. And then I was standing in my borrowed disco-queen dress holding Frank Sinatra's head, sweating and trembling at what might lie beyond the living room. If my mom and dad and Lou were in the house, surely they would've appeared by now. They would've heard me calling out to them, would've heard the chatter-laughter of the stuck tape, would've rushed into the room, turned on the lights, and explained it all as a freak occurrence, some kind of bizarre burglary. Or they had done the intelligent thing that I had not—walked in on the scene, followed their primal instincts, and fled.

Or they were still in the house.

They were here, somewhere, unable to come to me.

All of the possibilities contained in that word, *unable*, flooded my brain and guts and got my feet moving.

I thought of the layout of our house—front door to hallway, living room on the right, twisting staircase on the left that climbed to a second and third floor. The oak-paneled dining room lay straight ahead, the white-tiled kitchen behind it, and a hundred-year-old basement beneath it all. I would go room to room if I had to, despite who or what could be waiting behind a door, and I remembered Lou's baseball bat in the closet. The idea of a weapon was reassuring but it meant that I'd have to put down Frank Sinatra. For some reason I felt safer holding him than a club.

I entered the dark hallway, trying a light switch that responded with no light. Our house was built in 1911 and sat among others just as old or older, all guarded by ancient oaks and giant elms. It was a "stained-glass and turrets" neighborhood, as my dad said, which was beautiful with brick, copper, and slate, but which could also be really creepy. In the day-time, when the sun shone through thick green branches and lawn mowers snored reassuringly, it was as idyllic as a movie set. But late at night, when the train did not rumble as often and shadows fell oddly from oversized trees, it became very real that many lives had passed through those old homes. Standing in the hallway, I recalled times when I had been in the house alone, overcome by the feeling of being watched or that someone had passed close by. I longed for that feeling now, hoping that if I turned around my family would be standing there.

When I did, I saw blood.

It was smeared on the wall.

On the floor were fat spattered droplets the size of fifty-cent pieces.

I followed them through the swinging door of the kitchen, where the drawers had been tossed, cabinets cleared, cutlery scattered, dishes and glassware busted and crushed. The refrigerator was tipped on its side, open and leaking, the oven door yawned, and the pantry door was splintered off its hinges. Through the middle of it all, the white tile floor was fouled by a long scarlet line, as if someone had been dragged or had drug himself.

The blood stopped abruptly at the basement door.

Something far below the floorboards rustled and moaned.

Unbidden, one of Doug's many "rules of the movies" came to mind—never, ever, *ever* go into the basement.

Another moan sounded that was an expression of pure suffering. I hesitated, and then pulled open the basement door and stepped into blackness, the old steps creaking below my feet. I called out to my parents and Lou as I descended, but all I could hear was someone breathing heavily, lungs in crisis, and a sort of scratch-shuffling as if pulling himself across the gritty floor.

"Dad?" I said. "Mom?"

"Rooooo . . ."

The nearness of it made me jump, and I squinted into a dark corner where Harry lay curled in a ball, the bloody trail ending beneath his panting mouth. There was something odd about his position; he seemed to be protecting his side and belly. I knelt down and lightly touched him.

"Roooo-ooo!"

It was a scream instead of a moan. He worked his jaws weakly at my hand, mustering up whatever energy he had to try and bite me, trying to protect himself. And then he saw it was me, and the old hatred in his eyes was replaced by something that was, if not happiness, at least relief. Lifting his head, I saw blood streaming from his nose and muzzle, covering his neck and darkening his normally white chest. I looked closely at shadows covering his side, thinking it was dirt until I realized it was boot prints.

Someone had tried to stomp Harry to death.

I felt his ribs and, thankfully, nothing was broken on the inside.

The blood was superficial, from kicks and cuts on his mouth and face, and maybe from whoever had tried to kill him, too.

I never petted Harry before, but now I gently stroked his

neck until he lowered his head. When he did, his body shifted and I noticed that he was lying on Lou's old Etch A Sketch. When my brother was seven, he taught himself to make wavy lines, then circles, and then, twisting the knobs in perfect harmony, tiny, gracefully crafted cursive letters. One afternoon he left it on the couch and I picked it up. Lou was obviously studying the Constitution in school at the time, because it read, "We the People of the United States, in Order to form a more perfect Union, establish Justice, insure domestic Tranquility, provide for the common defense . . ." I hadn't seen the toy in years; my mom must've stored it in the basement. Carefully, I eased it from under Harry and he nosed my hand, letting me take it. The basement was so dark that I had to hold it inches from my face. When I did, I saw Lou's writing, which was not graceful or crafted but scrawled and mostly illegible. Trying to make it out, I realized that Lou had been here, in the basement, and that he had written it in a hurry.

Squinting, I made out, ". . . we are not . . . beware . . . the house . . ."

I read, ". . . ski mask . . . tried to kill . . . high-pitched . . ."

The air moved with a whiff of foul meat, followed by a noise so faint it could have been my own breath, like a mouse moving inside the wall, or a footstep trying not to be heard.

I glanced at the Etch A Sketch and my skin froze, seeing the words, "If you hear . . . then run, Sara Jane . . . Run!"

And then Harry was on his feet, growling low in his belly with blood dripping between his bared teeth, and lunged past me into the blackness. I heard a muffled curse, Harry's jaw snapping at his target, and then something fell and a shelf went over, smashing to the ground. There was a violent, kicking struggle with Harry grunting and his opponent making no noise at all. I squeezed the bust under one arm like a football and was about to sprint up the stairs when everything stopped, all sound and motion sucked out of the basement as a pair of large, rough hands locked around my neck. Two powerful thumbs dug into my larynx—I could feel my throat being crushed—and all I could do was struggle like a rag doll. Within seconds, flashbulbs of orange and purple popped in the darkness as oxygen left my brain. And then there was a jarring impact, a split second where the hands loosened followed by a growling-ripping noise. I was free, on my knees, gasping and hacking up blood.

Harry had done something in the dark and was now being punished for it.

I got to my feet and swung Frank Sinatra's head at the head of the person who was kicking Harry.

There was a crack of plaster against skull, the bust fell to pieces, and Harry's attacker fell to the floor.

I scrambled for the mini camera, cutting my hands on sharp shards until I found it. Overhead, thunder boomed like a Fourth of July finale followed by a flash of lightning against glass-block windows. The unmoving lump of body lay between me and the stairs, and I turned from it, groping toward the cellar doors instead. They had been locked from the outside since forever, but I was running on adrenaline and threw a shoulder like a linebacker, cracking apart the old wood. Cold bursts of rain hit my face, taking my breath away, and I was about to run across the yard when I remembered Harry. He'd saved my life and had taken a deadly beating to protect the Etch A Sketch because Lou commanded him to—because he loved my brother as much as I did. I listened, hearing only my labored breath, and then heard it—a faint whimpering and scratching at the floor.

Out of nowhere, I remembered Max counting backward on the train.

Ten seconds to zero . . . nine, eight, seven . . .

I scrambled back into blackness.

Harry's whimper was my guide and I felt through the air like I was blindfolded until my foot bumped a body. My hands were shaking as I touched tight smooth fur over bruised bones. I lifted the small dog and took a step toward the door when the impact of a fist on my face put me on my back, with Harry rolling like a bloody wheel right out the cellar door.

There's nothing worse than a sucker punch—the gasping explosion of red pain that rearranges reality and your face.

You get lost in its violation of decent human behavior, and then, if you're a boxer, you get pissed. One of Willy's rules is that a fighter who's knocked down should always get right up and right back into the fight—give the other pug what he just gave you, times two. Trying to stand, I was assaulted by a hammering of double fists on my shoulders. I hit the floor again, this time face-first, feeling like my back was broken, but I ignored the pain and rolled as a boot crushed the empty place where I had been. I hooked an arm around an ankle and yanked as hard as I could. There was a bleat of surprise, legs in the air, and I leaped to my feet as the body hit the floor.

Then it was time to give him back what he had given to Harry.

He was trying to lift himself on a shoulder when I teed off on his face.

I couldn't see quite who I was aiming at, but it didn't matter, I drop-kicked his chin like I was going for an extra point.

He grunted and rolled over, and I saw the ski mask clinging to his lumpish head—nightmarish black with red eyeholes—which gave me a chilly pause before I went to work on him, using my foot like a jackhammer. I was bristling with the same sensation that I'd felt when I saw Max dancing with Mandi, a cold, calm fury that burned deep in my gut. Each blow was accounted for—that one for Harry, that for Lou, for my mom, my dad—and it seemed righteous, like a debt being paid. The best way to define it is that, as I kicked Ski Mask Guy into unconsciousness, I felt more like myself than I ever had in my life. Even as I came back to the moment—panting and sweating, my leg aching and the body not moving—it wasn't fear that spiked my gut but caution. My chances of escape were lessening by the second, I knew instinctively, and I sprinted into the rain, scooped up Harry, and ran for the garage. My dad kept an extra set of keys to the Lincoln in an old coffee can. I fished them out and gingerly laid Harry on the backseat. He blinked up at me with something like gratitude, even comradeship—two furious souls who had saved each other's lives, bound by love for my brother. He licked my hand, and it was covered in his own blood.

I jumped inside, clicked the seat belt, and pushed the remote control.

112

The garage door lifted slowly to rapids rushing down the brick alley.

The back tires spit smoke as I flew out of the garage.

And then I was speeding away without knowing where I was going, desperate to get away. My neck was raw and bruised, my forehead bore knuckle prints, and Harry was making a noise that sounded like his lungs were full of motor oil. The mini camera was on the seat next to me, sliding on leather, while my mind raced with the realization that *someone-tried-to-kill-me-someone-tried-to-kill-me-someone-tried-to-kill-me!* I flew through stop signs and bumped over curbs, my body racked with involuntary shivers. I needed to locate the odd inner calmness that had cooled my skin while I was kicking the crap out of the lunatic in my house or I was going to wreck the car. I pulled to the curb and rested my head in my hands, breathing slowly as the windshield wipers clicked at raindrops. All I had was the small purse that had been strapped across me all night holding a CTA card and my phone. When it rang I jumped out of my skin. I scrambled for it, pressed the green button, and said, "Mom?"

There was a pause and then a woman said, "Sara Jane Rispoli." Not a query, but stating my name as a fact.

"Who is this?"

"Detective Dorothy Smelt," she said. "Chicago Police Department. Are you all right, Miss Rispoli?" Her words were muffled and hard to understand, riddled with the static of a bad connection, which only added to the creepiness of the call.

"How did you know?" I asked cautiously.

"Someone called in a disturbance. Where are you?"

I was quiet because I was rattled and because the phone call confused me—how had she gotten my number? But then relief overcame suspicion since it was the police, an entire force dedicated to helping people, and no one needed help like I did. I was about to tell her when an El train rumbled past. It was too loud to answer the question, but that wasn't the problem. The problem was that, bad connection or not, I could hear the same train on her end of the phone. I swallowed hard and asked, "Where are *you?*"

Pause.

Silence.

She cleared her throat, and said, "In my office. At the sixty-third precinct."

An ambulance ripped past with its siren screaming, and I heard that on her phone, too. I looked up at an unmarked car creeping down the street toward me while an anonymous van pulled to a halt around the corner. Glancing into the rearview mirror, I saw a dark police car inching up behind me. I turned the key, popped the headlights, and Detective Smelt said, "Why did you start the car, Miss Rispoli?"

The jittery shakes I'd had minutes ago dissipated.

I was calm again, and also pissed.

I said, "You heard that, huh? Or did you see me do it?"

"I only want to help you, Miss Rispoli. Remain where you are."

"Yeah, sure," I said, dropping the car into drive. "I'll wait right here for you to either kick my ass or kill me." I leaned heavily on the gas as I fishtailed from the curb.

"She's moving!" Detective Smelt shouted, and I realized other ears had been listening, too.

None of that mattered now.

All that mattered was speed and escape.

I flew past the unmarked car and van, both coming to life and going into squealing U-turns. The cop car lit up like a slot machine, its sirens beaming and blaring, and blasted after me. Streets in my neighborhood are thick with stop signs and speed bumps, and I ignored them all, Harry whimpering at each violent jolt while the Lincoln bounced and sparked. The other three vehicles were right behind me with the police car in the lead, so aggressively close to my rear bumper that I was sure he'd hit me at any moment. This was nothing like the countless car chases I'd seen in movies, those slick, choreographed scenes of airborne Chevrolets and slo-mo spinning tires; this was too fast and close and dangerous, the narrow Chicago streets lined with parked cars, the threat of collateral damage happening at any second.

I felt tears of fury stinging my eyes.

I also felt hyper-alive and totally in control.

I knew this old neighborhood better than anyone, and that my chances of escape were better *behind* the big old houses than in front of them.

I yanked the wheel hard to the right, gunning down the nearest alley.

Behind me I heard the squeal of brakes and tires while I sped straight for a dilapidated pickup. Almost every day, before the neighborhood rises or after it's asleep, junk collectors wheel beater trucks from Dumpster to Dumpster, looking for recyclable metal. They perform incredible feats of balance, using bungee cords and rope to strap old bed frames, water heaters, giant bags of tin cans, and rusty hubcaps to the back of the trucks. The one I was bearing down on now at great speed was an acrobatic miracle—a pyramid of rolling junk parked right in the middle of the alley. I heard the scream of the cop car, looked back at it and the two others barreling after me, slowed just enough to encourage them to speed up—and then yanked the wheel hard left. The alley I entered was so tight that the Lincoln's side mirrors sparked the brick walls. I'd made such a fast turn that the cop car never had a chance to brake, and the last thing I saw before speeding away were two guys in the pickup truck leaping out for their lives.

The last thing I heard was the collision.

It was cop car into truck, van into cop car, unmarked car into van.

It sounded like a calliope had exploded.

Almost immediately my phone rang, and I recognized the number as belonging to Detective Smelt. I ignored it, turning toward Lake Shore Drive, and my mind drifted to my family. Part of me wanted to pull over and weep at the horrible uncertainty of it all, but the other part of me, the one now in charge, knew that the time for weeping, if it ever came, would be only when I had answers.

I drove at the speed limit, using my signals, careful not to attract the attention of the cop cars lying in wait for speeders along Lake Shore Drive. I exited at Grand Avenue, passing throngs of people out on the town. The rain had stopped and it had become a beautiful night. After what I'd been through in the last several hours, it was surprising that the world was going on as usual. I proceeded southwest until the glitz of the

Magnificent Mile faded. Streets became residential, then industrial, then mean and impoverished, and then I was parking in front of Windy City Gym.

Willy Williams lived behind it in a small, neat apartment.

I knew he would take me in, listen to my story, and give me shelter.

Now was the time to be around fighters.

THERE IS a rare anger that accompanies unwilling separation.

It's an orchid of fury, sprouting in the stinking manure of a once-in-a-lifetime occurrence when normal existence is split in two—the side you loved that is gone and the side you now occupy that is isolated, strange, freakish, and alone.

You wait for the universe to right itself—you wait because you're human and humans are innately optimistic—and then it doesn't, and you feel like a sucker.

You are the original fool, a butt of nature's large, cruel joke. That's when the flame begins to flicker, low and cold.

You're not mad at the world and you don't want to bluntly attack the innocent—no, it's a sharp, laser-focused anger. The concentrated nucleus is narrowly defined to kick in the teeth and bust the bones of the specific people who did this thing to you.

I did not know for sure who those people were.

I *did* know that I would find him, or her, or them.

I also knew that one of my teeth was loose, Harry was shivering in my arms, and I was so oddly calm as I rang the Windy City Gym buzzer that I was probably in shock.

Footsteps echoed through the empty warehouse, a steel door on wheels unlatched and slid, and I heard Willy's deliberate padding down metal stairs. An eye squinted through a peephole, more locks slid, and he looked me up and down through steel-framed glasses. After an examination of my bloodstained disco dress, fist-marked forehead, and throat decorated with a necklace of purple bruises, he said, "So. How was the dance?"

I dumped Harry in his arms, sprinted upstairs into the shadowy gym, and went directly to the nearest heavy bag. Its bulky form hung from a chain, swaying in a slow, threatening circle, and I began to hit it with bare knuckles. My arms shot from my shoulders as I circled the bag, throwing the oldest combination in the book—left jab, left jab, hard right, left hook—and felt tears mix with sweat until my hands were as bloody as my dress. Willy tried to stop me but I shoved him away, continuing to pummel leather until I couldn't lift my arms anymore, then collapsed to the mat sobbing. Willy counted silently to ten and then said what he always said to a fighter who was down.

"Get up, Sara Jane."

I did, slowly, and went into his arms. Willy patted my back until I was done crying, telling me whatever it was, it would be okay.

I stepped back, wiped at my eyes, and said, "I don't think so. Not this time."

Willy had lived a long, tough life, both in and out of the ring, and knew there were times that required action rather than reassurance. He led me across the gym to his tiny apartment, handed me clean worn sweats and an ancient satin robe that read "Willy 'Chilly' Williams" across its back, and motioned me toward the bathroom. When I emerged, scrubbed clean of blood but suddenly unable to stop shaking, a glass of hot sweet tea waited at a wooden table. Willy set down a slice of buttered toast and a bowl of cold green grapes, saying, "You need it. You've been running on all cylinders and now you're out of gas."

"Where's Harry?"

He nodded at a threadbare couch where the little dog rested on a pile of blankets, his side wrapped perfectly in gauze and tape as only a good corner man could do. Willy nudged my shoulder gently and said, "Go on."

"I'm not hungry."

"Don't trust yourself right now. Eat."

He knew something I didn't know because even though food was the last thing on my mind, I devoured it, along with another slice of toast and two more glasses of tea. When I finished, I quit shaking and started talking. I told him all that had happened, from the scene between my dad and Uncle Buddy to the terrible moment when I walked into my house to the confrontation with Detective Smelt. By the time I was done, the cold flame in my gut was burning brightly again. Willy rose from the table, opened a cabinet, took out a battered tin box, and removed a single cigarette.

"I quit twenty-five years ago," he said. "But I always keep

one on hand for emergencies." He sat down, scratched a match, and lit it.

"What do I do now?" I said.

"You sure can't go to the police," he said. "I've known a lot of cops in my time, some good, some bad, some ten times more crooked than the crooks they're supposed to catch. Whoever this Detective Smelt is, she's not playing by any cop rulebook I ever heard of. She wants something and she's obviously willing to break the law—hell, several laws—to get it. Seems like that thing is *you*." Willy went silent, smoking and thinking, then said, "Thing is, police are a fraternity—they're tight, and they talk about everything. The problem is that the good cops don't know when they're sharing dangerous info with bad cops."

"So I can't speak to any of them."

"Too risky, at least for now," he said, tapping an ash into a chipped coffee cup. "I'm more concerned about the freak in the ski mask."

"Like I said, he was burly and he could take a punch . . . or at least a kick," I said, suddenly recalling the first time I met Willy and how he described my uncle's ability as a boxer to take a beating and keep on going. "Just like Uncle Buddy," I said.

"What?" he said slowly. "Buddy?"

"He threatened our family, Willy. Today, at the bakery. He warned my dad not to get in his way, or else."

"You didn't see his face, Sara Jane. You don't know for sure it was him."

"But . . ."

"But nothing. Before you go accusing your uncle of . . .

whatever . . . you better be damn sure he's guilty. If he's not, there's no one, and I mean no one, you're going to need more than ol' Buddy."

"Need?" I said, incredulous. "What would I need him for?"

"Listen to me, girl. Of course I know about the bad blood between him and your dad . . . but they're still *blood*," he said. "Buddy is your blood, too. The time may come when he's the *only* one you can count on."

"No, never. You're wrong," I said, shaking my head. "You didn't see Uncle Buddy try to hit my dad at my grandpa's funeral. You didn't hear the oaths he swore against our family. Besides you, I'm in this all alone. So I'll ask again . . . now what?"

Willy stared at me with his hands folded on the table like he was praying. A line of smoke snaked toward the ceiling as he said, "The worst thing I ever saw was my own child's dead body. It isn't natural, your baby dead before you. 'Course she wasn't no baby. She was just three years older than you are now, nineteen."

I knew that Willy's daughter had died a long time ago but he never discussed her, at least not with me. Carefully, I asked, "How did she die?"

"Cars and alcohol," he said, clearing his throat and adjusting his glasses. "When you see the body of someone you love who died too soon, you . . . die a little with them. You didn't see any bodies in that house, Sara Jane, and you're alive. So, what you do now is operate on the assumption that there aren't any. You assume they are alive, too."

"Then what?"

He shrugged, stubbing out the cigarette. "Find them."

"How?"

Willy sighed and pulled a hand over his face, and I saw that he was an old man. "Tomorrow, my girl," he said. "We'll talk it out tomorrow."

"Do you really think they're alive?"

"I don't know what to think because I'm confused and tired, and so are you."

"I won't sleep. There's no way."

"You have to, and despite what you think, you will," he said. "The Crow's Nest is clean, empty, and quiet. You have it all to yourself."

The gym had been a factory a hundred years earlier. Back then, as laborers sweated over assembly lines, a boss kept tabs on the operation from a small wooden office suspended from the ceiling high above the activity—the original "eye in the sky." That old office was still bolted to the roof, complete with large glass windows. There had always been a steady procession of boxers at Windy City over the years, pursuing careers as pro fighters—a few made it, most didn't—all of them young and broke. Willy took pity on these up-and-comers and outfitted the office with a couple of old army cots, a floor lamp, and an ancient TV. The steel staircase and catwalk that once led up to it had been ripped down for scrap decades ago; a winch and pulley lifted the furnishings into place. Select fighters were allowed to stay rent free while they trained, as long as they kept the Crow's Nest clean, used no alcohol or drugs, and mopped the gym every night. To reach it required shimmying up a long, knotted rope; once a person was inside, he could see everything, every corner of the gym, just like sailors who occupied a ship's crow's nest; thus the nickname. The boxers who currently occupied it were gone, fighting on an undercard in Granite City, and wouldn't return for a week.

"Try to sleep," Willy said. "We'll figure out our next move in the morning."

"Okay, Willy," I said, rising from the table, suddenly so aching and bone weary that I was unsure I could make it all the way up the rope.

"I'm gonna move the Lincoln around back, out of sight," he said, and I handed him the keys. Harry's ears perked up at the jingle of metal and he whimpered painfully.

"I'd better take him along," I said, lifting and wrapping him around my neck. "He might need me." Willy followed me out to the gym and stood beneath the rope while I made the trip like an inchworm, Harry whining all the way. I pulled open the trapdoor, clambered inside, and looked down at Willy, who waved up.

"Good night," he said, his voice echoing softly around the vast brick room.

"Good night," I said.

"Sara Jane?"

"Yeah?"

He wiped at his nose, sniffled, and said,

> *"Your world seems empty and broken,*
> *but it ain't completely true.*
> *Even though you feel alone right now,*
> *just remember that ol' Willy . . .*

"Well . . . what I mean is . . ."

"I love you too," I said, and waved back before pulling up the rope and closing the trapdoor.

After Willy's footsteps crossed the gym, everything was silent except for Harry's labored breathing. I made him comfortable and scratched between his ears until he fell asleep. It was when I reclined on a cot and noticed the old TV that I remembered the mini camera from Frank Sinatra's head. I took it from my purse and went to the television, which had a green glass screen set into a wooden cabinet, and looked more like furniture than electronics. Its dial spun to change channels, it had push buttons for volume, and a rabbit-ear antenna sat on top. The only nod to the twenty-first century was a DVD player attached to it. The mini camera had no accessories, but Lou taught me that almost all electronics are compatible despite their age, since a simple cable is still the heart of the technology—just find something that plugs into something else and it might work. I tried all of the DVD's plug-ins, first the red, then the yellow, but it was the black that fit.

I turned on the television and its screen yawned and wiggled.

I flipped on the DVD player, and it whirred weirdly, trying to accommodate the camera plugged into its gut.

Finally I pushed Play on the mini camera, stared at the TV screen, and when it stopped wiggling, I watched someone punch my dad in the head.

I gasped, sucking in air around me, and covered my mouth with both hands at the sight of him reeling onto our big leather couch. He tried to stand but was clearly stunned as a thick man in a plaid suit swung his fist again, cracking my dad's nose. I heard my mom scream off camera. I watched the man turn and when he did, my breath caught in my throat—I saw that terrifying ski mask. He left my dad and sprang in the direction of my mom's outburst. My dad struggled to his feet and went after him, and I heard something break, something shatter, and then he came spinning back to the couch, and there was Ski Mask Guy bounding after him, raising a baseball bat high in the air—

And then the screen became a blizzard of pixels.

I was ice from brain to toes.

I could not move or think, breathe, or feel.

All I could do was stare at the tiny crackling black-and-white dots and allow myself to fall into them.

And then, *zap!* The picture was back, and I jumped, and it was my dad again, slumped on the couch with his nose and mouth streaming blood, his hands tied behind his back. Even with the poor picture, I could tell from the weird angle of his left leg that it was broken. Somewhere far away Lou yelled and a door slammed, and then Harry was barking and my mother was screaming, and I saw every sound, every plea for help register horribly on my dad's face. His chin dipped onto his chest, and when it grew momentarily quiet, he lifted his head and looked into the camera.

"Sara Jane," he said in a raspy whisper.

"Dad?" I said. "Daddy?"

"Please . . . I pray to God . . . that you find this tape," he said. "There's no reason you should, I have no hope, except . . . except that you're *you*, Sara Jane. You may not be

aware of it, but there's something in you that's . . . so strong."
He stopped then, trying to hold back tears, swallowing them,
and said, "You were right, I should have told you about the
family, about the bakery, and about me. Especially about me.
But now there's no time . . . " And he jerked his head, hearing
something I couldn't. He grimaced, straining against the ropes
that bound his hands, and freed them, rubbing his wrists and
flexing his fingers. He looked nervously over his shoulder and
then started speaking again, faster and more desperate, saying,
"They might hear me, he might . . . listen carefully, sweetheart. Listen *inside* my words and *behind* my words."

I moved close to the screen.

I touched his face and felt cold glass.

He looked at me and whispered, "Sara Jane . . . go to the
God of Fire. Go to it, go *through* it, and discover all of its se-
crets. The God of Fire, Sara Jane . . . are you listening to me?
Its secrets will save you. The God of Fire . . ."

"God of what? Who were you talking to?" a woman's voice
demanded, high and shrill, asking the question off camera; the
poor quality of the audio allowed only that the voice was feminine. Ski Mask Guy lumbered into the frame, his back to the
camera, as the voice shrieked, "Who you were talking to?
What did you just say?"

Weakly, my father said, "Go to hell."

Ski Mask Guy yanked him upright, my dad grimacing on
broken bones. There was a second or two of imbalance and
my dad seized it, twisting and throwing a perfect left hook, fist
cracking on jaw, and Ski Mask Guy went into a slow *tim-berrr*,
like a redwood about to fall. But then he found his feet, shook

his head, and lunged with both hands. They wrapped around my dad's neck just as they'd wrapped around mine, and I felt them again, watching my dad try vainly to loosen the punishing death grip.

"Repeat it or you're *dead*," the woman hissed. "Who were you *talking* to?"

My dad's face was tightening from lack of oxygen, his eyes wide and bulging, and his fingers dug frantically into Ski Mask Guy's hands as he uttered a few last words before the tape ran out.

I heard what he said but was unsure what he meant.

Was it an answer to the question—"Who were you talking to?"

Nobody! Nobody! No . . . !

Or, so much worse—was it a final plea for mercy?

No, Buddy! No, Buddy! No . . . !

The recesses of a troubled brain at rest are terrible places because they have no boundaries—no backward or forward or beginning or end. They are timeless, bottomless pits where a sleeping soul goes to sort out its worries and woes.

The body's electricity hums at a lower rate while blood flow slackens its pace.

Limbs are immobilized, eyelids flicker.

Whispered clues escape moving lips.

Meanwhile, the subconscious spins like an awful, haunted buzz saw. It turns faster and faster, ripping through the day's events, shredding forgotten memories, and slicing to bits all hope for the future. Among that splintered debris, it searches

for an answer, or if not an answer, resolution, or if not resolution, peace.

Willy was right—somehow I slept.

It was not restful sleep.

I did not wake peacefully or with resolution.

But I did have an answer.

I blinked awake late Saturday afternoon knowing exactly
where I was and what had happened. Gray sunlight leaked
through the glass windows and Harry had somehow made it
to my cot, his head on my chest. I stared at the ceiling, parsing
my dream, which had been less a dream than a search through
the archives of my brain until I stopped on the day long ago
when I rushed into the kitchen of the bakery, excited and
upset over my first kiss, and melodramatically threatened to
climb inside the oven.

I remembered my dad and grandpa overreacting in a way
that seemed silly then, but meaningful now.

I remembered how Uncle Buddy was as confused as I was
over their outburst, having no idea what they were talking
about.

Then my dream switched to my literature teacher, Ms.
Ishikawa.

She was pacing the front of a classroom, relating a subject
that should have been boring except that she was always so
excited, and her excitement was contagious.

Mandi Fishbaum stopped buffing her nails, Walter J.
Thurber moved the hair out of his eyes, Gina stopped whispering, and Doug set aside his laptop as Ms. Ishikawa recounted
with great drama the violent, stormy world of the Roman gods.

Jupiter was the king of the gods, the ruler of sky and thunder.

His wife, Juno, was goddess of the Roman Empire.

Together, they produced a misshapen little boy who eventually developed into civilization's most famous pyromaniac.

Lying on my back, staring at the ceiling, I recalled the name of their son, who would one day become the God of Fire.

It was stamped in capital letters on the door of the bakery oven.

Vulcan.

LIKE A GANG OF ANTS frantically breaking down a molasses cookie, my mind went over and over what I now knew—clawing, chewing, and digesting it.

Sitting across the table from Willy, sipping tea, my eyes darted in time to a jumpy electrical thought process that ended at the oven, and only the oven. By the end of that long Saturday holed up inside Windy City Gym, it was clear that my single option was to go to the bakery alone. I had involved Willy too deeply already, which was why I didn't tell him what I'd seen on the mini-camera tape. If I had, he would have insisted on coming along to help me, and I couldn't bear the thought of something happening to him—the only person I had left.

My plan was to sneak out of the gym before daybreak on Sunday morning.

It wouldn't occur to me until much later that I'd missed my date with Max.

Maybe he waited outside the Davis Theater Sunday afternoon checking his watch or maybe he went inside alone and counted from *Ten Seconds to Zero* until the world blew up.

My own world was so focused on the great iron oven that served as the flaming core of Rispoli & Sons that the idea of Max seemed remote and out of reach, like a luxury I couldn't afford but wanted nonetheless. I understood that I now had no time for him, but my heart disagreed—it thumped disjointedly in time to his name—with the difference between logic and desire equaling me thinking of him numbly.

The majority of my brain function was devoted to Vulcan. Early Sunday, while it was dark outside, I shimmied down from the Crow's Nest. Harry whined insistently as I tried to leave, showing signs of his usual, assertive self, so I wrapped him around my neck and brought him along. He hadn't coughed up blood in twenty-four hours and was on his feet, but wobbly. He padded softly behind me across the gym and when I whispered "Stay" outside Willy's apartment, he did. I crept inside and found the keys to the Lincoln on a brass hook, and as I lifted them, a soft buzzing rose behind me. Willy was snoring on the couch, glasses on his forehead, one hand on his chest and the other dangling loosely with a length of steel pipe on the floor at his fingertips. I knew how tough he was—I'd seen him spar with guys decades younger and teach them hard lessons to the nose and jaw—and knew the steel pipe was a sign that he meant business. If anyone came after me on Willy's turf, he'd deal with them South Side Chicago style. His readiness to beat a thug sideways in my defense warmed my heart and steadied my nerve.

I found the Lincoln parked in the alley behind the gym.

I put Harry on the backseat and buckled him in.

I turned the key, the engine hummed, and I lost that nerve instantly.

The bakery had always been alive to me, with its fresh tastes and familiar warm smells, its singsong soundtrack of spoken Italian, and the rightness of my family in that place. We owned it, and it owned us. When I thought of my grandparents, I thought of the kitchen's powdery white flour and sweet yellow dough, the brass cash register, neon sign in the window, and sparkling cases filled with pastries. The musical *clink* of a wooden spoon as it turned batter around a bowl made me think of Uncle Buddy. In my mind's eye I saw my dad concentrating like a sculptor and whistling an overture as he rolled and shaped cookies. The bell over the door jangled, and I watched my mom enter, chatting and laughing, holding Lou's hand.

What I thought of now was how the bakery would be locked and deserted.

It would be silent, dark, and dusty.

Emptiness can be the most terrifying thing in the world.

I made an impulsive right turn and sped along desolate streets toward the Loop. The sun was rising over the lake, its pink glow reflecting on canyons of glass and steel, while lines of streetlights popped off behind me, one following another. There was a time not so long ago when I would beg my father to take me along on early morning deliveries of doughnuts and croissants. Even in the summertime, it was cool outside at six a.m. as we drove through the city with the delivery truck windows rolled down. The Loop (named for the elevated trains that loop around it) is the busiest area of Chicago during the week, with literally millions of people coming and going to work. Sidewalks are filled with fast-moving pedestrians while impatient cars creep behind jumpy taxis that dart around crawling buses. Commuter trains rumble past in a long, elevated oval, drawbridges clang up and down, airplanes roar overhead leaving white smoky lines, and car horns and construction noise and people shouting and sirens blipping are the orchestra of the city that does not slacken until late at night.

Early in the morning, it's such a different place that it's almost a different planet.

Cabbies, bleary-eyed from working all night or beginning at dawn, drive lazily along deserted boulevards. Maintenance men hose cigarette butts off high-rise sidewalks, Chicago Transit Authority workers in crisp uniforms amble toward subway and El stations, and the random go-getter, yoga-stretched and dressed for success hours before his coworkers, power-walks down empty sidewalks. This was the Loop I crept through in the Lincoln, unwilling or unable to face the tomb-like atmosphere of the bakery, needing something safe and familiar to fortify my soul before I took the leap.

Blocks later, I hung a hard left onto Jackson Boulevard.

There was the old diner and its retro lampposts, Route 66 sign, and curved counter just inside the picture window.

The sign for Lou Mitchell's glows in pinkish-orange neon, and announces humbly that it serves the world's finest coffee.

I parked on Jackson, made sure Harry was comfortable,

and entered the place that was already half full before most Chicagoans had even opened an eye. The old water purifier burbled by the entrance like always, the smell of crisp bacon and Greek toast filled the air like always, the background thrummed with morning conversation like always—these small, reassuring things connected me to my family. I sat at the counter and ordered coffee. The waitress paused when she set down the steaming mug, looking at her watch and then back at me. The coffee reached my nostrils hot and acidic, and I sipped its strength. As I did, I noticed the waitress's gaze drift and her eyebrows raise. Without moving my head, I glanced sideways at a Chicago police officer in blue, also in mid-sip, taking the waitress's cue to inspect me. His face remained blank as his eyes moved over me— the thick, gray walrus mustache twitching thoughtfully under his nose was the only giveaway that he was concerned. I realized what he was seeing was not pretty—a sixteen-year-old girl alone at six in the morning after more than twenty-four hours in the Crow's Nest with no shower following a world-class ass-kicking, wearing ancient sweats, a face full of bruises, and a nose that, just by its disproportionate size, hinted at trouble. Trying to look casual in that situation was impossible—every fidget made me feel guilty of something, which made me behave guiltily, which made me fidget even more. I was scared to look at him, but realized that he was punching a cell phone.

He murmured into it while staring at me.

Suddenly, I felt as if the entire diner were staring at me.

Turning on my stool, the entire place looked like it was stuffed with cops.

Nerves tingled sickly in my stomach as I glanced around the room. Every table and booth held one or two burly guys with close-cropped hair, or a pair of tough-looking women with no-nonsense expressions. All of them wore casual clothing meant to disguise their copness, which only broadcast it instead. I was sure they were looking at me, or just looking away from me, or trying to act as if they weren't looking at me at all. Maybe Detective Smelt had been tailing me all along and these were her people. Maybe they were just waiting for the right time to pounce.

I sipped coffee, trying to calm down, but then listened to my gut.

It said to forget calming down and wise up.

It told me that unless I did something quick, I'd be leaving the diner in handcuffs.

The officer leaned toward me and smoothed his mustache, about to say something, but I jumped to my feet and hurried to the restroom. I entered the last stall, locked the door, and began biting my thumbnail—there were no windows to climb out of, and I doubted that sprinting for the exit would result in anything other than being tackled by cops. I felt like all four walls were pushing in at me, and that my fate rested just outside the door. I held my head in my hands and stared at linoleum, searching for a solution.

There it was, on the floor between my feet.

I picked up a book of matches, despite my parents' warning never to play with fire.

Except that I wasn't playing—I was deadly serious.

I counted to three, then left the stall and began working

quickly, yanking paper towels from one dispenser and the other until both sinks were full. I wet half of them and stuffed them into the bottom of a garbage can. Then I packed the dry paper towels tightly on top, praying that the wet ones would extinguish the others if need be.

I struck a match and smelled sulfur.

It flamed and I realized what a stupid and dangerous thing I was doing.

I didn't care, and dropped it.

Bits of fire attacked the dry paper towels, leaping nimbly from one to another. Just like in Girl Scouts, I blew on the baby flames until they spread and grew, and the trickle of smoke became a black plume filling the restroom. When it was hard to breathe, I counted to three and kicked open the door, shouting, "Fire! Fire!" The room froze until a thick, scary gust of smoke rolled out behind me, and then everything was in motion. People screamed, an alarm was pulled and began to wail, some customers leaped to their feet and ran for the exit while others came toward me. A jittery busboy with a fire extinguisher tripped and dropped it, its contents sliming the floor, a waitress slid and fell, and I jumped over her, headed for the door, when a steely grip attached itself to my arm.

The cop said, "Hang on there! Stop!"

"Let me go!" I said, trying to yank free.

"What's this about?" he said. "Did you . . . ?"

And then someone bellowed for help, and the restaurant manager was tugging desperately on the cop's sleeve. He was torn between me and a real emergency. I saw the choice on his face, and he gritted his teeth, released me, and ran toward the restroom. I turned and shoved through the crowd, elbowing my way onto the sidewalk, desperate to get to the Lincoln, and darted into the street.

That's when I was hit by the fire truck.

I was in such a hurry that I hadn't seen it flying up Jackson Boulevard.

A blast of its horn and squealing brakes were the last thing I heard before everything faded to black.

When I came to, I was lying on a gurney in the back of an ambulance with my head bandaged. I sat up and the world tilted, and I puked on the floor. The pain on the left side of my skull was so intense that I gasped, and I touched at it gingerly, feeling it pound against my fingertips. My ear was still there, which was good, and my face felt like it was in one piece, but barely. Bits of memory came to me then—glancing up at the last minute, seeing the bright steel mirror of the fire truck and feeling it clang against my face as the rest of the enormous red vehicle roared past. I looked at the scene outside through the windows of the ambulance—firemen hustled around Lou Mitchell's, leaky hoses snaked through the street, flashing lights rolled on top of the fire truck and police cars—and I was overcome by a wave of guilt. Like waking from a dream, I realized that I'd caused all of this because I'd been gripped by paranoia.

I knew it was a delusional result of fear and anxiety (thanks, health sciences class) that attacked a person with feelings of a perceived threat.

Maybe, I realized, the diner full of cops hadn't been cops at all.

Maybe they were just normal folks having an early breakfast.

Maybe paranoia had transformed a concerned police officer sipping an innocent cup of coffee—one who could have helped me—into an imaginary enemy in blue.

I moved to the doors—they were locked from the outside—and saw the officer from Lou Mitchell's headed wearily in my direction. He stopped and spoke to an EMT, pointing at the ambulance, and the EMT nodded. Now that I was seeing him with my delusion goggles off, he looked like a nice, normal guy, probably my dad's age, probably even a dad himself. He removed his hat and scratched his gray head, still talking, then patted the EMT's shoulder and continued toward the ambulance. I was so embarrassed to face him that I stood behind the doors practicing an explanation, then an apology, then a combination of the two. And then I heard something ring.

I peeked out and saw him flip open a phone.

He leaned against the ambulance door and answered it.

Tiny hairs on my neck stood up when I heard him lower his voice and say, "Tell Detective Smelt I got the girl."

Detective Smelt.

The girl.

Me.

Something cold and furious flickered in my gut, moving me around the interior of the ambulance until I found what I needed and lifted it carefully. I lay on the gurney, pulled a sheet under my neck, and closed my eyes as he opened the door. He climbed in and stood over me, still on the phone. I cracked an eyelid and watched him twist the end of his mustache between thumb and forefinger, saying, "That's right, five grand, in twenties. Don't try to negotiate with me, moron, I'm the one who caught the prize. You tell Detective Smelt if she wants a discount, try the Dollar Store. If so, I'll drop this little fishy in the Sanitary Canal where no one will *ever* find her."

I squinted, watching him rock on his heels.

He was listening, smiling smugly.

He twisted the finger inside his nostril, inspected it, and put it to work in his ear.

"Way to go, pea brain, now you're talking sense," he said. "Right. One hour, at the Twin Anchors, Smelt's home away from home. And dummy? Don't forget . . . twenties. *Crisp* ones." He snapped the phone shut, chuckling, and said, "Hey, wake up!" When I didn't move, he gave my leg a shake. "Wake up, firebug! You and me are going for a ride in the squad car." I remained still, my eyes squeezed shut, waiting for him to move closer, and he leaned in, saying, "Open your eyes, whatever your name is . . . Mary Jane . . ."

"It's *Sara* Jane, asshole!" I said, sitting up and swinging an oxygen tank the size of a bowling pin. I caught him hard just above the ear, the tank-on-skull making a *gong* noise. He stared at me with a stupid look on his face, his mustache twitched once, and then he crumpled like a Chinese lantern.

I was off the gurney and on my feet before he hit the floor.

I peeked out the door to make sure no one had seen or heard anything.

Everyone was moving—firemen dragging hose, cops barking into shoulder-talkies, gawkers craning their necks—with the Lincoln parked on the other side of Jackson Boulevard, beyond the cordoned-off area. There was no way I would make it through the crowd looking like I did, from the weird old sweats to the bloody bandaged head. My only chance was an extra EMT shirt hanging in plastic, white and starched, and a cap that read "Chicago Fire Department Emergency." I put them on, each a size too large, and then bent down and felt the officer's pulse (thanks, Red Cross Club), which was strong. I'd watched enough crime flicks to know that there's nothing worse for a cop than being disarmed, and no one deserved that humiliation more than this devoted public servant, so I plucked his gun from its holster and was going for the door when I spotted a pen and clipboard with fresh paper. It took seconds to scribble a message and pin it to his shirt—*I'm a dirty cop who charges five grand to kidnap teenagers. Oh hey, where's my gun?*—and then I stepped carefully from the ambulance. There's a movie Doug showed recently from 1970 called *Little Big Man* that takes place in the American West in the 1880s. In a scene toward the end, as soldiers attack a Cheyenne village, an old Indian chief who believes himself to be invisible walks through the chaos, completely unnoticed.

That's how I felt now.

Action swirled around me as step by careful step I moved toward the Lincoln.

Seemingly unseen, I lifted yellow tape and climbed into the car.

It was after I calmed Harry and slid the key into the ignition that I heard someone yell, "Hey!" and turned to another blue cop, this one younger and much more intense. His uniform was tucked tightly over his wiry body and he removed his reflector sunglasses while leaning forward, Terminator style, inspecting me and the car. I pulled the cap low over my bandaged head and reluctantly rolled down the window. He looked inside the Lincoln, looked all around it, and then his concrete face broke into a grin as he said, "What year is this bad boy? 1964?"

"You mean the car?" I said. "Um . . . '65."

"Man, they just don't make 'em like this anymore. Steel, chrome, and an engine powerful enough to fly a helicopter." He crossed his arms and made a face. "Nowadays it's all hybrid-this and electric-that. Sissy stuff. Gimme old-school, American-made every time. You know what I'm saying?"

"Oh, hell yeah," I said, starting the car.

His face turned stony as he said, "Whoa-whoa-whoa, relax. Where do you think you're going?"

"Uh . . . away?"

He grinned again. "Not unless you demonstrate this old monster's horsepower."

"Horsepower?"

"You EMT folks . . . always so damn cautious," he said, shaking his head. "Come on, honey, peel out! Lay some rubber! Spin this thing!"

"Oh. Okay," I said, squealing from the curb and shooting up Jackson Boulevard with the gas pedal on the floor. When I glanced in the rearview mirror, he was giving me a double thumbs-up. I blasted the horn in farewell and bumped through a red light, my heart beating with freedom. As I crossed the Chicago River, I rolled down the window and flung the cop's gun into an eternity of brown water.

Most people consider delusions a bad thing and pop pills until they disappear.

In my case, paranoia saved my butt.

From then on I'd trust it with my life.

AN ELBOW APPLIED carefully to glass is the second best way to enter anywhere.

The best way is a door, unless you're scared of who might be behind it.

There were two doors into Rispoli & Sons Fancy Pastries and I wasn't about to use either one.

I cruised past for the third time, seeing the neon sign hanging unlit and gray, the interior of the place dim in midmorning sunlight. Even though I hadn't spotted anyone—no cops, no Uncle Buddy—it didn't mean they weren't nearby, watching the front door with its jingly bell or the delivery door on the alley. Even worse, they could be lurking inside, waiting for those doors to open.

I pulled to the curb and stared at the place.

It hadn't even been forty-eight hours since I'd discovered my home in shambles and family missing, yet it appeared as if the bakery had been out of business for a decade. I knew it would be closed and locked, but it was worse than that. The only way to say it is that the bakery looked dead.

It made me want to drive away and to keep on driving.

Except, like Willy said, I hadn't seen any bodies.

I had to assume my family was alive, and I had to go in there.

Harry had begun to whine in a way that suggested a desperate need to pee, so I took a deep breath and climbed out. Just as I opened the back door, a haunting, jingling tune cut through the air, like a slow-moving ice cream truck calling kids with its siren song. Harry lifted his head at it, sniffing the sky, and then, forgetting his injuries, bolted from the car. He was so fast that I had time only to yell, "Harry!" as he hit the bricks, running hard, yowling at the top of his lungs. I ran after him, stopping at the crossroads of the alley, but he was gone. Dark clouds bumped into each other overhead, blotting out the sun, and I felt so alone that I couldn't hold back tears. I wiped them away, looking up at the coming rain, and something caught my subconscious eye—a telephone pole with metal footholds. It climbed higher than the roof of Cofanetto's Funeral Home, which sat hard against Lavasecco's Dry Cleaning, which was next door to Rispoli & Sons Fancy Pastries. I climbed a Dumpster, grabbed a foothold, and when I was halfway up the telephone pole, stopped and scanned the alleyways, but no Harry. The idea that I had lost another member of my family was too much to accept, so I pushed it away, resolving to track him down later.

Truthfully, I was unsure there would be a later for him or me.

I pushed away that thought too, and stepped onto the roof of the funeral home.

From somewhere deep in the building I heard a pipe organ, low and sonorous.

I walked lightly over the pebbled roof, crouching as I moved to avoid being seen. I was four stories in the air, equal to or lower than the surrounding apartment buildings in a neighborhood where someone's Italian grandmother was always looking out a window. Anyone on a roof would raise suspicion, but a teenager in a huge EMT shirt with a bloody bandage peeking out from beneath a cap was a 911 jackpot for a local snoop. I hurried across the roof of the dry cleaner, feeling a blast of heat filled with sour starch, and paused, looking over at the bakery's glass skylight. It sat directly on top of the kitchen, which meant directly over the oven.

It was time.

I stepped onto the roof of the bakery.

Peering through glass, I saw only the square white tile floor below.

Just like in a caper movie, I quickly popped my right elbow off of the window. It splintered, shards tinkling to the floor below. I reached inside, unlocked the skylight window, and stuck my head inside, listening to the silence. There was no sound, no movement, only the hum of the big industrial refrigerator. Carefully, I held on to the window ledge, lowered myself down, and kicked my legs to get my body moving. The top of the refrigerator, my target, was about four feet away. When I was swinging like a trapeze artist, I gritted my teeth and let go, and was in midair when I realized that I wouldn't make it.

It was slow-motion desperation, like a baby bird pushed from a nest with no idea how to fly, my legs and arms flailing at empty space until I hit the hard tile floor.

I tried to scream but nothing came out.

The only sound was a wet-cement-bag noise when my body hit the ground.

I groaned and rolled onto my back, feeling like I'd just been hit by a school bus.

There was a limit to the physical punishment that one sixteen-year-old body could take, and I lay there with every muscle, fiber, and tendon in my body aflame, sure that I'd reached it. When I opened my eyes, I stared up at six letters stamped in heavy metal.

Vulcan.

I got to my feet painfully, holding my back like a retiree, while the oven loomed before me, its massive iron door and old-fashioned dials and gauges like something from a World War II submarine. It was really old—my grandpa's father, Great-Grandpa Nunzio, installed it when he started the business in 1922, and it had been hard at work ever since baking cakes, pies, and cookies. Staring at it, I realized that I'd never noticed how massive it actually was—six feet tall, four feet wide, encased in white glazed brick, with the iron letters painted a fiery red. Unconsciously, like before a bout, I cracked all of my knuckles and reached for the door handle. As I pulled it down, the hinges complained loudly in the silent building, making me jump. It was dark inside, with all of its racks removed. I looked into it just as I'd been instructed and saw nothing but empty space, a deep metal cave.

My heart was beating against my chest.

I had no choice—I'd have to climb inside.

I took a breath, pulled myself up and in, and I fit.

It required crouching but I realized that if my lanky frame fit inside the oven, so could my dad's. Tiny Grandpa Enzo would have had no problem, and even Uncle Buddy, if he figured out how to position his gut—but for what purpose? There was nothing to see, nothing hidden or out of the ordinary as far as ovens go. The burners were down there, ventilation up there, sides made of solid iron. There was a small lightbulb inside but it wasn't lit. Quickly, quietly, I pulled it shut, the light popped on, and something clicked solidly into place. I pushed against the door, felt that it was locked, and my skin went cold with panic, flashing me back to being a small kid when I'd turned a delivery crate into a hideout. Once inside, claustrophobia had attacked my little mind and I was screaming by the time my mom pulled me out. Ever since, I've avoided tight, enclosed spaces. I shoved against the door again with no result, and that's when I noticed a tiny red button above it. It had to be the release, so I pushed it.

The door did not open.

Instead, something began to rumble.

A moment later the world fell out from under me.

I screamed as the box of the oven plummeted, quickly and smoothly. The lightbulb dimmed and lit, dimmed and lit, and I was so freaked out by what was happening that I gaped at it like a hypnotized moth as it tracked my rapid descent. Finally I felt the box begin to slow, and when it stopped, the lightbulb popped on brightly. A vacuum of wind rose behind me, and the back of the oven separated top to bottom, like a small set of inverted elevator doors. I slid out into semidarkness, where, a few feet away, a heavy metal door sat in a brick wall. I approached slowly, squinting at words printed in gold paint that were chipped and worn.

CLUB MOLASSES

PASSWORD REQUIRED

Looking closer, I saw that the *O* in "Molasses" was a glass peephole.

I pushed open the door, which swung heavily on old hinges, and stepped inside a high-ceilinged, brick-walled room filled with stale air. A circle of natural light fell from somewhere high above. Squinting up, I saw that I was deep at the bottom of what, to the outside world, appeared to be the bakery's smokestack. I peered through murkiness like a goldfish in dirty water, spotted a switch on the wall and flipped it, and time reversed itself by ninety years. Green sconces lit the walls while brass lamps with green glass shades burned at opposite ends of a long curved bar trimmed in leather. There were no barstools, no bottles or glasses behind the bar, only a long mirror stained with age that bore the words *Club Molasses* in curved golden script and my reflection staring back. Across from the bar was a raised, empty platform that I recognized as a bandstand; in front of it spread a parquet dance floor with a large *CM* set in an intricate pattern. One wall was stacked with dozens of old, empty barrels, one on top of another reaching high into the air like a rounded, wooden pyramid, each stamped with the image of a maple leaf and the words 100% PURE CANADIAN MOLASSES.

I crossed the floor to a line of old-fashioned steel and wooden slot machines. I'd seen ones like them only in movies, and a place like this in one movie in particular.

Doug's favorite, *Some Like It Hot*.

In the opening scene, two musicians play bass and clarinet in a speakeasy.

Secret nightclubs flourished during Prohibition, providing jazz, gambling, illegal booze, and stealthy good times to Chicagoans.

Later in the movie, the musicians witness the Saint Valentine's Day Massacre, a bloody, real-life incident that happened in Chicago in 1929. Gangsters disguised as Chicago cops machine-gunned seven rival gangsters execution-style in a North Side warehouse. Speakeasies like this one, operated by those same violent criminals, were hidden in the most unlikely places.

In barely a whisper, I heard myself say, "Dad . . . what you didn't tell me was a lot."

Then again, I thought, he said I could handle whatever came my way and more.

That was good, because there was more, covered by a tarp.

It was a large, oblong mass, squatting in the shadows. I knocked my fist against it, hearing the report of metal beneath my knuckles. I lifted the edge of the material and saw thick tires, and then rolled the whole thing back, revealing a silver two-door convertible with its top down that looked more like a rocket ship than a car. It was wedge shaped—high in back descending to a pointed hood that bore the silver image of a horse kicking up on its hind legs. Carefully, I opened the driver's side door to an interior of black leather that was thick and tight, punctuated by a five-speed gearshift edged in chrome. When my mom taught me to drive, she insisted that I learn how to operate a manual transmission like this one, her theory being that if I was going to learn to do something, I should learn it completely. I looked from an odometer showing a grand total of four miles to a speedometer showing a maximum speed of two hundred and twenty miles per hour to a box with a silver bow on the passenger seat.

I slid in and slid the top off of the box.

I lifted out an operator's manual that read *2000 FERRARI 360 SPIDER*.

I put it aside and removed a small plain card bearing a message in black ink.

It was in Italian and I inspected it closely, doing my best to decipher both the poor handwriting and the verbs. My lips moved as I read—

Caro Antonio—

Un piccolo simbolo per la nascita di suo figlio, Luigi. Un bambino maschile è il massimo regalo che un uomo può avere!

Fedelmente—
I Ragazzi

I read it again, not completely sure of my translation but sure enough that on the one hand, my head swam, and on the other, my blood boiled. Basically, I read—

Dear Anthony—

A small token for the birth of your son, Lou. A masculine child is the greatest gift a man can have!

Loyally—
The Boys

In the head-swimming column: Who were "The Boys"? Why were they loyal to my dad? And why had they given him a car for Lou? In the blood-boiling column: What did they mean that a masculine child is the greatest gift? Did my dad agree with them? And where the hell was *my* car? I looked at the manual again—2000 Ferrari 360 Spider, the year my brother was born—and remembered my mother saying how the Lincoln had been a gift from some "friends" to Grandpa Enzo for the birth of my dad. I understood now that if my dad had been born a girl, Uncle Buddy would be the one driving the sleek Lincoln convertible instead of the crappy red one. I didn't know much about Ferraris other than that they were fast and expensive, which meant that "The Boys" weren't just loyal, they were *really* loyal. I looked around, trying to figure out how in the world someone had gotten a car down here, and absorbed the forgotten quality of the room. It was like a museum that had been closed for a long time. Everything, including the twelve-year-old sports car that had never been driven, was dusty, unused, or antiquated.

Except, I now noticed, a door.

It was near the bar, in a small, dark alcove.

It looked twenty-first century, and it looked locked.

The shock of the existence of this place—a speakeasy with a Ferrari in middle earth, far below the bakery—had numbed my powers of observation. But I saw the door now, and was drawn to it like a magnet. Whether it was some sort of weak joke or it had been made that way, the door bore a small sign that read EMPLOYEES ONLY. I put my ear against its cool metal and heard nothing, and then turned its handle that didn't move. A keypad of numbers glowed next to the door, mocking me with its endless possibility of combinations. I tried my birthday—4-29-1996—and then Lou's—6-26-2000—my mom's, my dad's, my grandparents', my social security number, phone numbers, and nothing. The keypad remained mute, the door locked. My blood began to boil again over a cold blue flame. I'd come this far, this deep, with every inch of myself bruised and a couple of cracked ribs just to encounter "Employees Only"? Without thinking, my body running on its own electrical circuits, I heard myself murmur, "Son of a bitch!" as I threw a hard right full of frustration at the keypad.

My knuckles popped off plastic and metal.

The keypad cracked and buzzed and squeaked and smoked and sizzled.

The door yawned.

Shaking the punch out of my right hand, pushing open the door with my left, I entered a small room that was nearly empty except for a battered desk with a lightbulb hanging over it. I pulled the cord and it dropped a circle of light, and I heard a gentle scratching at my feet. Looking down, I saw a rat looking up, sniffing the air, sniffing at me. There was nothing threatening about it—it just seemed to be inspecting me—and then it turned and skittered away, and I watched it disappear behind an enormous map of Chicago that covered almost an entire wall, as yellow as parchment, with streets and avenues drafted in perfect lines. It showed dozens of old structures in amazing detail—the Monadnock Building, North Avenue Beach House, the Biograph Theater, even Wrigley Field. I stared at the ballpark, my eye drawn to the accuracy of the main gate sign, and noticed that something circular gleamed around the *C* in "Chicago"—as in "Home of the Chicago Cubs." Looking closer, I saw it was a tarnished but still bright ring hewn from brass. It was odd. But then, everything was odd, including the stickpins with colored heads—red, blue, black, purple, green—stuck into neighborhoods. The head of each pin was also lettered—the blue one carried a *B*, the black one an *S*, and so on, while the red pin, which was stuck directly on the map where the bakery existed, bore a small, sharp *R*.

"*R* for . . . Rispoli?" I murmured.

I leaned back on the desk and touched something cold. Looking down, I saw a steel briefcase covered in a thick layer of dust. A note written in my dad's hand sat on top. I picked it up, blew away the dust, and read, "In case of emergency." It was a link to him, and I turned it over looking for more words, but there were none.

I tried the latch, which was locked.

I lifted the briefcase, feeling its contents shift.

Every instinct in my body tingled with certainty that the notebook was locked inside that briefcase.

I looked at my dad's note again and questions flooded my mind—how long had the briefcase been there, and what sort of emergency? Of course, my entire life was now one big emergency, but if it had sat long enough to collect dust, what had my dad been anticipating? I recalled my parents' mysterious conversations about "the right thing to do." Had they done it, whatever it was, and it led to this—they and Lou disappeared from the face of the earth, and me far below it? My last question—how did he know I'd survive to find the briefcase at all?

I think the answer is that he didn't, but that he had to pin his hope on something.

What I knew for sure, and instantly, was that the briefcase I now held was the object of Uncle Buddy's relentless search of the bakery.

I remembered my dad saying he would never find it, which meant Uncle Buddy had no idea that Club Molasses existed. It meant my grandpa and dad knew, but that they'd never told my uncle. If that was true, then Uncle Buddy was correct—my dad had held information from him. But why? And then in the next instant my newest best friend, paranoia, told me to quit asking questions, take the briefcase, and beat it, and figure out the "whys" when I was safe. I turned for the door and noticed a black-and-white framed photo on the wall. I peered closely at the image of a thick, balding guy in a light summer suit sitting in the front row of a grandstand while a baseball player in an old Cubs uniform autographed a ball. The balding guy was familiar, but it was a small fellow a couple seats to his right whom I recognized.

Actually, it was the Rispoli nose I recognized.

It was Great-Grandpa Nunzio, trying not to look at the camera.

An inscription read, *To N.R.—Thanks for the cookies! Your pal—A.C.*

I considered taking the photo but the whole thing suddenly felt like grave robbery and I was desperate to get topside, back to the sun and sky. I left the office and crossed the dance floor, took one long look back, and then climbed into the oven and pushed the red button. It rumbled and began to levitate quickly, the lightbulb flashing and dimming as it rose. The box shuddered and stopped, the door whooshed open, and I was back in the kitchen.

I was looking at Uncle Buddy.

Greta was facing him.

She glanced over his shoulder and her eyebrows jumped when she saw me.

Uncle Buddy waved a Sick-a-Rette in one hand, saying, "I swear, when I get my hands on her . . ."

"Oh my God," Greta cried, pointing at me. "Your niece! She's . . . she's in the oven, Benito! Behind you!"

"What the hell are you . . . ?" Buddy turned slowly, his jaw falling when he saw me. And then he saw the briefcase. And then he was a bull seeing red, barreling across the kitchen. My hand shot out and hit the button, the door shut, and the box rumbled and fell. Uncle Buddy's voice trailed after me, saying, "That's *mine*, Sara Jane! I'm coming to get it . . . !"

I had no doubt he was telling the truth.

He meant right now, this instant.

My heart was hammering in time to his violent determination.

As soon as I stepped out of the box, the doors closed and it rose away. Uncle Buddy had figured out how to recall it, and would be stuffing himself inside any second. I ran into Club Molasses and slammed the door, but the old lock didn't work. Hiding inside the Ferrari was silly, crouching behind the bar even sillier, so I sprinted into the office and slammed the door, hoping it would seal itself, but I'd destroyed the keypad. My mind went into lockdown as I paced—waiting, waiting—until I heard the elevator arrive. Uncle Buddy's footsteps on the dance floor moved slowly with surprise at what he was seeing for the first time. I knew that there was no way out, and that my only option now was to fight. I might not save myself, but I would at least do damage to my uncle—he would lose an eye or the use of a limb before he did me in.

His footsteps stopped, it was silent, and then they started again.

He'd spotted the door and was moving toward it.

In a mockingly sweet voice, he called out, "Sara Jane! It's your *favorite* uncle!"

His tone was so sickly disappointing that it drained me of resolve. Instead of going forward with a fist cocked, I cowered against the wall, hugging the briefcase.

"Sara Jane! I know you're in there!"

I couldn't stand to see his smug grin, so I turned to the wall, closed my eyes, and leaned my head against the map, with the tiny metal *C* of the Wrigley Field sign raised against my forehead.

"I owe you one, kid. I *never* would've found this place on my own!"

I heard a faint *buzz* and my body tilted forward a few inches. A puff of earthy-smelling wind swirled around my head.

"Oh, Sara *Ja-ane*!"

I can now state with complete authority that the first step through a secret door that opens suddenly in an underground wall is helped mightily by the fact that someone may be about to kill you. I didn't hesitate any longer than it took to hear Uncle Buddy's hand turn the office doorknob, and I leaped through it. As soon as my feet touched a platform, the door hissed shut and I was standing in musty semidarkness. I saw a thin wire running from the back of the Wrigley Field *C* to a spring—the *C* was a hidden button that opened the door. I also discovered that the little drawing of Buckingham Fountain disguised another peephole, and I peered through it just as Uncle Buddy pushed into the office.

"He-e-e-re's . . . ," he announced, looking around the empty room as his fat face fell. "Buddy?"

I would have loved to watch him pull open desk drawers as if I'd shrunk and were hiding inside, or listen to his soliloquy of obscenities when he finally realized that I had vanished. But I couldn't take the chance of being found out, and turned to a staircase that descended deep into shadows. The staircase fell forever, lower and lower, and I stared at it, thinking that every new discovery plunged me deeper into darkness. I touched a cool, crumbling brick wall and squinted at the painted image of a hand pointing downward. On the other side of the map, furniture was kicked and Uncle Buddy's first

F-bomb dropped. I took a hesitant step, then another, using only the screen of my phone for illumination. Light fixtures lined the wall, some holding ancient burned-out bulbs, some none at all, with the pointing hands appearing each time the staircase took a twist or turn. Finally, when it seemed like I was about to arrive on hell's doorstep, a rectangle of light appeared at the bottom of the stairs, glowing above a metal door. I laid a hand against it as a rumble sounded in the distance, quickly growing louder, and wind played at my feet.

The door fought me on rusty hinges, then scraped open.

I pushed through just in time to watch a subway train barrel past.

It shuddered to a stop at the far end of the platform, and I ran for it.

I jumped onto the last car and fell into a seat right before the doors slid shut. It was empty except for a woman seated across from me. She was perfectly coiffed and crisply dressed in a black suit with an elbow resting on a black leather briefcase as she inspected a folded newspaper. I slumped across from her in the extra-large, now-filthy EMT shirt, freaky sweat pants, and crooked bloody head bandage while squeezing the steel briefcase to my chest as if my life depended on it, which it did. I felt her eyes flick up and inspect me, and when I met her gaze, she executed an old-time Chicago move—the polite but defensive small smile and a nod.

I returned the gesture.

She returned to her newspaper.

Just two hardworking ladies making the daily commute.

I DO THIS THING all the time now where I cry in really short, super-explosive bursts that come out of nowhere, happen anywhere and everywhere, and disappear in seconds.

First my face gets itchy and then my eyes feel fat.

And then, *kaboom!* I'm sobbing, shaking, and my nose is running.

And then I blink, and it's over.

If I'm at school and I feel it coming on, I duck into a restroom or empty classroom and clap a hand over my face, muting myself until it's done. If I'm all alone, however, I try to indulge it—I try to keep it going so I can weep deeper and deeper until I'm all cried out. But no matter how hard I try to prolong it, it always passes quickly, like a short but fervent tropical storm. Something inside my emotional core understands that while I need to expel pressure, completely dropping my guard is way too dangerous.

The first time it happened was on the subway after I escaped from Uncle Buddy.

All that I had seen and learned at the bakery was too much to process.

My brain went numb trying to reconcile it with reality, and failed.

When I blinked around the car, I realized that I'd been riding for hours. The train had risen from the tunnel and was clacking on elevated tracks. My nose itched and then I doubled over with tears, crying so intensely that it felt like I was being kicked in the chest. I was outside myself, wondering who I was crying for, and realized it was me. It ended when I accepted the bitter fact that I couldn't afford to pity myself any longer than a couple of sweet seconds. I sat up and looked at a dozing drunk and an iPad-hypnotized geek, relieved that no one had witnessed my mini breakdown. It occurred to me then that I could probably use a good therapist after all I'd been through. And then I thought of kids who spend hours on therapists' couches bemoaning their lives—some of which was legitimate, some that wasn't, some who actually had ADD and some who didn't but were prescribed Ritalin anyway—and thought, Screw therapy. What I need is my family.

I hugged the briefcase like it was my little brother.

At midnight, I stepped off the train at the station nearest the bakery.

The sidewalks were deserted as I darted to the Lincoln.

My internal-anger engine was whirring at full tilt now, and the tears had long receded. I lingered while unlocking the car door, overcome with a strange hope that Uncle Buddy would leap from a shadow so I could beat him with the steel suitcase and then spend a few minutes kicking in his teeth. But no, I was alone on the street—that pleasure would have to wait for the next encounter with my "favorite uncle." I had what he wanted and knew that he would come after me sooner rather than later. After my long day on the train, in which my brain and heart had been turned inside out, I welcomed it.

Despite the knocks I'd taken, despite becoming a serial weeper, fear was slowly calcifying into an undeniable need for revenge.

Flexing and unflexing my fist, I hoped that one of my pursuers would suffer my left hook very damn soon.

The physical anticipation of throwing a punch made me think of Willy and how alarmed he probably was at my prolonged absence. Looking down a dark alley, I also remembered that Harry was gone. My heart ached at his disappearance, but it was now beating to a recalibrated rhythm, one that informed me that there were things I could do and things I could not. To survive, and for the survival of my family, I had to put aside the problems I was unable to affect—like finding Harry. Actions I could take—like opening the briefcase in hopeful anticipation of valuable clues—had to be executed immediately. My lips moved in silent prayer for the little dog as I started the engine, put down the convertible top, and pulled smoothly from the curb. Chicago late at night is both dark and light, with streetlights burning every few feet. My dad told me that when he was a kid, he remembered old Mayor Daley declaring with certainty that the continuous presence of light would make the city a safer place, and proceeded to plant glowing metal poles everywhere. I cruised through empty streets bathed in fluorescence, the cool, lake-smelling wind against my battered face, and it felt like being alive.

By the time I parked in the alley behind Windy City Gym, reality had returned.

Willy had covertly left open a door anticipating my return.

I entered and locked it behind me, and was alone in the dark again.

There was no light under Willy's apartment door, so I crept quietly across the gym and shimmied with difficulty up to the Crow's Nest, pausing every few feet to shift the heavy briefcase from one hand to another. Finally I hoisted myself inside, shut the trapdoor, pulled the shades, and turned on a lamp. A combination lock held the briefcase together, and I flipped the numbers instinctively to my birthday. Where those significant digits had no effect on the office keypad, now they fell smoothly into place. It was another sign that my dad had anticipated my survival. But at the moment, all that mattered was that the briefcase opened, and I sat back, staring at its contents.

Hundred-dollar bills were stacked in tight green bricks.

The steel skin of a pistol shimmered ominously.

A razor-thin rectangle of plastic bore my name.

The black AmEx credit card imprinted with SARA JANE RISPOLI proved that my dad expected me not only to survive, but to find the briefcase. I set it aside, along with a Sig Sauer .45 conceal-and-carry and ninety-six thousand dollars in cash. I realized that these things were my dad's last, best attempt to protect me, especially since I would now be the protector of the old leather notebook stuffed with secrets.

In the middle of the briefcase sat the ratty, ancient thing, just as I'd suspected.

It was held together with masking tape, rubber bands, and metal clips, and its spine was cracked with age. The leather surface was patchy, dry, and wounded, like mummified skin. Carefully, I lifted and unbound it, opening to the flyleaf.

La proprietà di Nunzio Rispoli, 1922, was written in faded ink.

Below it read, *La proprietà di Enzo Rispoli—Property of Enzo Rispoli, 1963.*

Further down, my dad's handwriting stated, *Property of Anthony Rispoli, 2011.*

The last inscription was the freshest and I touched it lightly, knowing he'd written it in secret, which made me simultaneously sad and mad. If my dad had told me about this—any of this—I could've done more than grope blindly from one life-threatening situation to another. I looked down at the time-worn notebook, at his words written with care, and thought, Maybe this is his way of telling me. I turned the page to a sheaf of paper that had been reattached decades ago, the tape gone yellow, and read the carefully handwritten words, *La Tavola d'Indice*. Below it, someone else had hastily written in English, *Table of Contents*. Underneath were titles of eight chapters, also written in Italian, with the first seven bearing scribbled translations—

1. Nostro—Us

2. Loro—Them

3. *Soldi*—Money

4. *Muscolo*—Muscle

5. *Sfuggire*—Escape

6. *Metodi*—Methods

7. *Procedimenti*—Procedures

8. *Volta*

The last chapter was not translated, but even I knew that *volta* is a common Italian word for "time." As I flipped the pages, I saw some parts of each chapter were written in Italian and others in English. Countless names accompanied by phone numbers and addresses were scribbled, crossed out, and new ones added in their places. Dozens of ancient business cards were held fast by rusty staples. Black-and-white photo booth snapshots of dicey-looking guys were glued to pages. Scraps of paper taped here and there in some sort of order bore phrases (*Toronto, Midnight, February 8, 1973*), names (*Ask for Joe Little*), and figures (*2,000 brl's at 500 per*) that had no significance, since there was no context. It was crammed with handwritten notes, some that appeared as old as Great-Grandpa Nunzio's inscription from 1922 and some as recent as last week. Each section was baffling, and taken as a whole, the scruffy old notebook was simply overwhelming. It was like being the first person to look at the Rosetta Stone or the Bible. I knew the notebook was what Uncle Buddy was after and that it was really important, but I didn't know why. I flipped more pages, hoping for a note from my dad, and that's when the title of a section caught my eye.

Checking quickly, I saw that it was in the chapter titled "*Sfuggire*—Escape."

I flipped back and reread two words written at the top of the page.

Capone Doors.

The section was printed in a neat, blocky script and had a textbook tone to it, with the obvious goal of educating the reader. My skull still ached from the fire truck assault, and my body, shoulders to toes, creaked with the pain of falling into the bakery. I propped up pillows, stretched out on a cot, and read.

"Capone Doors were invented in 1921 by Giuseppe 'Joe Little' Piccolino, the chief officer of weapons and devices, and were installed in and around Chicago between 1922 and 1950. Before Joe Little's untimely disappearance and presumed death in 1951 (see '*Loro,*' section II, pages 3–4) he estimated that upwards of a thousand Capone Doors had been concealed in as many locations, and that despite the ongoing teardown and reconstruction of the city, many remained functional.

"It's important to note that only the Outfit, Chicago's venerable underworld institution, has Capone Doors; no other city than Chicago, and no other criminal organization than the Outfit, had the foresight. Because of technological marvels like these, Outfit members were the actual 'untouchables.'

"Officially, Capone Doors are designated as escape hatches, but during Prohibition (1919–1933) the doors were instrumental in the Outfit's domination of bootlegging and rumrunning, used to import and export alcohol without detection or interference. After Prohibition was repealed, Capone Doors continued their usefulness as conduits to secret casinos and illegal sports books, as white slavery highways and sneak-thievery pathways and as rush-hour avoiders. The ownership of and access to Capone Doors was at the heart of the bloody Battuta-Strozzini Turf War of the 1970s (see '*Nostro,*' section I, pages 9–15) that pitted the North Side of Chicago against the South Side. The dispute was settled when it was decided by ruling panel that Capone Doors were a public utility, with all members of the Outfit allowed free and unfettered access. The panel was chaired by *l'amico di tutti amici*, the honorable Enzo 'the Baker' Rispoli."

I paused, sitting up a little.

I reread the last few lines, picturing my small, gentle, smiling grandpa.

My mind went to the memory of when he shape-shifted into Evil Grandpa, and it clicked. I sat back and continued reading.

"A boon to Capone Doors came in 1938, when the City of Chicago began to dig subway tunnels in order to supplement El trains. A far-ranging and wide-reaching system of secret tunnels already existed beneath the muddy surface of Chicago (see '*Soldi,*' section III, page 109–113) to which Joe Little had long ago connected many Capone Doors, and it was subsequently engineered to access the subway system as well. Since that time, many an Outfit member has participated in the ultimate turnstile jump.

"Generations of Outfit members passed on the locations of Capone Doors to the next generation, but a comprehensive list was never distributed for fear that it could fall into the wrong hands on the right side of the law. As years passed, some were forgotten, others torn down, and still others built over. In Joe Little's original blueprints, he states that 'the key to finding a Capone Door is to imagine them everywhere, in every type of building and location, both public and private. And to train the generally unseeing eye to spot a hidden *C*—the button that activates the door—which will be slightly raised from the surface.' Of course, it should be noted that this wondrous invention was named in honor of our revered founder and inspiring force, Al Capone."

"Al Capone. A.C.," I whispered, remembering the photo in the office of Club Molasses. I turned the page expecting to read more, but instead of the neat, blocky script, the page contained a list written in two different hands which I now recognized as my grandpa's and great-grandpa's. It read:

Monadnock Building, lobby, east wall
City Hall, second floor, men's room
Edgewater Beach Hotel, Yacht Club, behind the potted palms
Green Mill Lounge, beneath the bar
Uptown National Bank, teller cage no. 5
3rd, 11th, 19th, 33rd, and 41st Ward Precinct Houses, lock-up
Henrici's Ristorante, wine cellar
Lincoln Park Boat House, under the dock
Biograph Theater, north balcony
St. Hubert's Grill, in the phone booth
All elevated train stations built before 1935, electrical closets

The list continued on, some locations I recognized, others I'd never heard of, but all of them surely containing (or at least at one time contained) its own personal Capone Door. I dog-eared the page so I could come back and finish, and turned to the next page. It was a new section titled "Safe Houses," and explained how the Outfit owned dozens of hotels, homes, apartments, warehouses, and condominiums under assumed names where any member on the lam could hide out safely. This section contained a list of addresses, and I was skimming it when my eyes drooped and my chin touched my chest. I lifted the notebook and felt something odd, something hard and bumpy. I turned to the last chapter, "*Volta*," flipped the pages aside, and there it was, a tarnished brass key taped to the inside back cover. I didn't remove it, just squinted at it with heavy eyelids.

After that, I don't remember anything until I heard a woman scream.

I jumped awake from the cot like I'd been electrified.

The notebook tumbled to the ground as the woman screamed again.

I rolled to the floor, crawled to the window, carefully pulled back the sun-streaming blinds, and looked down into the boxing ring where Ski Mask Guy was sprawled on his back, plaid rumpled suit still buttoned, tie askew. Across from him, Willy bobbed and weaved with fists cocked, ready to deliver another Sunday punch. Ski Mask Guy got to his feet and shook his head, adjusting his mask and his bulk. The lumbering goon had his back to me and was pointing at Willy while, from somewhere unseen, a woman shrilled, "Lucky punch. Okay, *two* lucky punches, you cockroach! For the last time, give up the girl or get ready to meet Jesus!"

Willy pushed his glasses up on his nose, spit through the ropes, and said, "Bring it, sissy boy."

I craned my neck, looking around the gym for the woman, and then a flash of bodies drew my eyes back to the ring as Ski Mask Guy lunged like a Frankenstein monster. Willy ducked and delivered a one-two kidney punch that doubled him over, followed by a surgically precise left hook to the chin that put the freak on his back again.

Ski Mask Guy cried out in pain.

It was high-pitched and feminine.

It was the same voice I'd heard only a second ago, and it was his.

I watched as the giant lunkhead lay prone on the canvas, seemingly unconscious, and remembered the sugary voice from the mini-camera tape. I'd assumed there was a woman present then, too, but that high-pitched tone belonged to Ski Mask Guy, and it only made him creepier. The fact that he was not Uncle Buddy was no comfort; it only affirmed what I'd been dreading, that there really were three different people out to get me—a turncoat uncle, a faceless freak, and a corrupt cop with a stable of officers at her command. Quietly, then louder, Ski Mask Guy began to giggle girlishly, and then he leaped to his feet with alarming agility. Willy crouched, hands set, but Ski Mask Guy reached out in hyper-speed and grabbed Willy's left arm, yanked and twisted, and I heard old bone crack.

Willy did not scream.

Instead, gritting his teeth in pain, he threw a feeble right.

Ski Mask Guy halted it in midswing and broke that arm too.

Willy, still silent, dropped to his knees, his head on his chest. "You really thought," Ski Mask Guy said, his schoolmarm voice weirdly incongruent with his hulking form, "that a flea like you could compete with a specimen like me? I was play-acting!" He wrapped his hands around Willy's neck and lifted the old man until only his tiptoes touched the canvas. "Okay, this is *really* the last warning," Ski Mask Guy said. "Tell me where the girl is, Uncle Tom, or this face is the last one you'll ever see!"

I was pulling open the trapdoor when I heard the "Uncle Tom" reference.

It was a filthy racial curse, something only a psycho pinhead would use.

It only made the scene in the ring that much more violent and surreal, and my mind went to the .45 in the steel briefcase.

I popped the locks and looked at it lying heavily among the stacks of cash, like some sort of sleek, dangerous reptile at rest. My hand trembled as I reached for it, with everything in me screaming that what I was doing was stupid and wrong. Then Willy screamed, the gun was in my hand, and I held onto the rope and jumped. "Hey, sock puppet," I said as my feet hit the floor. "Let go of my friend before I . . . I put another hole in that mask!" I was so racked by jitters from just holding the gun that I almost dropped it before gripping it tightly in two sweaty hands.

He turned to me while still choking Willy, whose eyes bulged and body squirmed like a fish on a hook. "Well, well. If it isn't little Miss Kick-Me-In-The-Face!" he trilled. "Hey, does that thing squirt water or pop a little flag that says *bang*?"

I climbed into the ring cautiously, raised the .45 directly toward him, and he giggled girlishly. That he was amused by a gun aimed at his face only unnerved me more, and I heard my voice break as I repeated myself. "I . . . I said . . . let him go."

"Hey, didn't anyone ever tell you it's *rude* to point guns at your elders?" he said, tossing Willy aside like a sack of potatoes. The old man hit the canvas hard, groaning and turning onto his side. Ski Mask Guy faced me, cracking his knuckles and rolling his horrible head on a thick neck.

The cold blue flame kindled and flickered in my gut when I saw him move like that, like a career heavyweight preparing for battle. Nervous fear drained from my brain and body, replaced by a jarring it's-him-or-me sense of reality as sharp as the blade of a knife. The .45 suddenly felt weightless in my hands, and I licked at my lips, knowing instinctively that lowering it meant lowering my only defense against the bulky maniac. I didn't want to shoot him, but it was plain that Willy and I were dead unless I kept the gun squarely and confidently between us, which meant that if he took even one step . . .

"Gimme that thing, you silly little . . ." Ski Mask Guy squealed, lunging like a crazed grizzly bear.

And then my finger squeezed metal just once, lightly, as the shot filled the room with an echoing blast and Ski Mask Guy grabbed his shoulder. The bullet had grazed him just enough to cut a line in his filthy suit and the skin beneath it. "You shot me," he said, amazed, touching the surface wound and holding up bloody fingers. "I mean, you barely shot me, but you shot me! I didn't think you had it in you!"

"It was easy," I said, looking at him down the barrel, seeing that my hands had stopped shaking. "Easier than I thought it would be."

"Sara Jane," Willy said weakly from the canvas. "Don't . . ."

"Listen to Uncle Tom!" Ski Mask Guy said, his voice as shrill as fingernails on a blackboard. "Once was funny, a real lark, but remember . . . guns don't kill people! *People* kill people!"

"Where's my family?" I said. "Tell me now, or I guarantee that next time my aim will be much better."

"I'll make you a deal," he said, backing away, holding up his hands like a TV bad guy. "Gimme that old notebook and I'll tell you the whole amazing story, beginning to end, with no commercials! I swear on a stack of Bibles as tall as the Willis Tower!"

I stared at his thick, jumpy body, his facial muscles undulating crazily under the knit mask, and said, "You're lying. You won't tell me shit."

"Quite possibly, but you'll *n-e-e-ver* know if you kill me!"

"True," I said, wanting so badly for this nightmare to end, for the terrible freak not to exist. I stepped forward, close enough to smell rancid meat, and put the barrel of the gun in his face. "Maybe I'll never know," I said. "But maybe I don't care anymore."

"No, Sara Jane!" Willy called. "Please . . ."

The tone of Willy's voice—more desperate than angry— gave me just enough pause for Ski Mask Guy to go up and over the ropes like it was Cirque du Soleil, hit the gym floor like a ton of bricks on two feet, and run for the exit. I watched him go, watched him bow dramatically at the door, and heard his falsetto echo up the stairs as he cried, "Next time, Sara Jane! Oh, how my heart beats for next *ti-i-i-me*!" I looked at the gun in my hand, feeling nothing but bitter regret at my inability to use it, and then dropped it and went to Willy, who was suffering on his back. After I guided him to his apartment, I told him as much as I thought he should know about the notebook—that it, and not me, was what everyone was after, and that it was valuable and I was disposable.

When I was done, Willy said, "Get me a cigarette." I rose, removed one from the battered tin box, put it between his lips, and lit it. He inhaled and exhaled a couple of times, and then said, "That's all I need. Put it out."

I crushed it in a coffee cup, saying, "Those things will kill you."

"At least it would be a slower death than if crazy man did it," he said. "Or you, with that gun."

"He hurt my family."

"You know that for sure?"

"I know for sure he hurt you."

Willy nodded and cleared his throat. "I never told you how my daughter died."

"You just said cars and alcohol."

Willy nodded again, pursing his lips. "What I didn't mention was that I was driving the car she was in when she died. And that the alcohol was in me."

"Oh . . . Willy . . ."

"See, I killed my own daughter, Sara Jane. I was drunk and shouldn't have been behind the wheel of a car, but she trusted me. She died and I lived, and I will never understand how the universe got it so wrong." His eyes were wet behind his glasses but his voice was steady. "Yes, it was an accident. But all those drinks I had weren't. I didn't intend to kill my daughter but I did, and I loved her more than life, and still . . . still the stain won't ever wash out."

"Willy," I said, laying a hand on his shoulder.

"Listen to me and listen good," he said. "You don't want that cancer on your soul. I know your life is upside down and there are some very bad people after you. But the real fight now is your brain versus your heart, doing what you know is right versus what you feel must be done. Killing someone, especially when it's on purpose . . ." His words drifted off. He cleared his throat again and said, "Don't do that to yourself, girl. Promise me you won't."

"Willy, we need to call a doctor . . ."

"Promise," he said, fixing a gaze on me that shone with remorse.

"Okay," I said. "I promise."

Afterward I got him as comfortable as possible and then called an ambulance. When I saw that he had drifted off, I slipped out of the apartment, shimmied up to the Crow's Nest, and grabbed the briefcase. I checked its contents—money, credit card, and of course the notebook—and remembered the gun. On my way across the gym, I climbed inside the ring and retrieved it, and then paused only long enough to scribble some words on a few pieces of paper. I opened the apartment door so the EMT people would see Willy, left behind the bloody, shorn shirt I borrowed from them, and hurried back toward the gym exit. I stopped every so often to post one of the pieces of paper, each of which bore an arrow and read *Guy with broken arms this way.*

I climbed in the Lincoln and started the engine, hearing approaching sirens.

I was leaking tears, wondering if I'd ever see Willy again.

I wondered if I'd be able to look him in the eye if I ever broke my promise.

I'M NOT CERTAIN, but I assume that the life of a fugitive doesn't normally go from sleeping in bloody head bandages on an army cot above a sweat-stinking boxing gym to being saluted by a doorman in epaulets before settling into a four-star hotel suite, gliding from a steam shower Jacuzzi to a warm, enveloping spot between two-thousand-thread-count Egyptian sheets on a bed large enough to host a square dance.

But it did.

I had the notebook to thank.

I couldn't believe it was real until sushi rolled in on a silver cart.

According to the notebook, the hotel I was in—the Commodore, across the street from Lake Michigan—had been secretly owned and operated by the Outfit for seventy years. I'd randomly selected it from the list of safe houses, closing my eyes and pointing at the page. There was a phone number and scribbled instructions next to it—make the call, ask for the manager, and say "Al sent me." Afterward, all I had to do was show up and I would be treated like a VIP, no names taken and no questions asked. When I arrived and repeated the line to the doorman—"Al sent me"—he saluted, said my room was ready, and noted that the Lincoln would be at the curb each morning, ready to go. He looked me over from head to toe and politely enquired whether there was anything else I needed. I said no, but asked his name just in case.

"Al," he said with a wink. "Just like everybody else around here."

And then I was riding a silent, private elevator.

The key was in the door; the room was vast and smelled like roses.

It was after the three-course room service was demolished and my stomach was aching with satisfaction that the extreme quiet and stillness of the place set in. It was a stark contrast to the past three days. I threw the robe on a chair and lay on my back in silk PJs staring at the ceiling as my beaten body took on the composition of a jellyfish, adhering to the wondrous bed beneath it. My mind, which had existed in a constant state of jumpy alertness, downshifted to a low gear, and my hand inched toward a remote control. The enormous flat screen flicked on, and I heard familiar zither music. I turned my head and saw shadows flash against the walls of a black-and-white, bombed-out Vienna, and smiled—it was Lou's favorite movie, *The Third Man*. It felt like an omen—whether a good or sinister one, I can't say—just that it made me feel my little brother was nearby. I closed my eyes and let the music fill my lungs.

Zing-zing-zing.

Tinkle-zing-zing.

Thoughts of Lou moved me closer to my grinning, lanky dad with a permanent five-o'clock shadow and flour on his shoes.

Zing-zing-zing.

Tinkle-zing-zing.

Memories of my dad hugging my mom in the kitchen until she pushes him away, giggling and smoothing her skirt as I enter the room, her face lighting up, so happy to see me, and she opens her arms and I'm right where I want to be, in her embrace. Her arms folded around me, and I smelled her rose-oil perfume and soft dark hair. It was sweet and sorrowful because we were together; I also knew I was asleep and dreaming, but we were together, and asleep, and then I was pitching weightlessly over the edge of a cool blue waterfall, not caring if I ever touched the bottom. Falling, normally terrifying, was a relief. It felt so good that I never wanted to wake up, but I did, because my mom woke me. I felt her delicate hand brush my cheek and opened my eyes without lifting my head from the pillow. She was sitting in the chair across from me, and I said, "Mom. You're alive . . ."

She smiled. "I'm with your dad and Lou, Sara Jane, and we need you."

"I need you, too. All of you. But I can't find you."

"You can't stop now. You've come so far in such a short time."

"I'm tired, Mom." I yawned. "Too tired to go on."

"But darling," she said, her smile fading, "if you don't look for us, who will?"

"So tired . . ." My eyelids fluttered.

"Sara Jane," she said, and the urgency in her normally calm speech forced my attention. "If you don't look for us," she said, folding herself into the chair across from me, "we may never be found."

"Okay, Mom, okay," I said through another yawn. "I'll keep looking. I just need to sleep first, okay?"

Her smile returned. "You're such a strong girl . . ."

Behind her words, another voice warned, "That's a nice girl, that. But she ought to go careful in Vienna . . ."

My mom said, "But you have to be careful in Chicago . . ."

The voice returned. "Everybody ought to go careful in a city like this."

"Everybody," my mom said, brushing my cheek again, "has to be careful in a city like this."

I blinked awake at her gentle touch and looked at the robe folded over the chair. A voice murmured behind me, and I turned to the TV. I'd watched *The Third Man* with Lou so many times that I knew the character's name—Popescu. "Everybody ought to go careful in a city like this," he said gravely. I looked at the robe again and then lay back on the downy pillow. This time I couldn't have stopped crying if I wanted to, the tears fed by the cool blue waterfall over which I'd tumbled. It was late Tuesday afternoon, and small gusts of air-conditioning rippled the curtains, moving golden spots of filtered sunlight around the ceiling. The room was so beautiful and comfortable, so desolate and remote, that it felt like the end of a life. I wanted to get up, pack my few things, and continue on my desperate journey to nowhere, but my body was dead weight.

I tried to lift an arm but it wouldn't move.

I willed my leg to bend but it was paralyzed.

I turned inward to my aloneness and cried until I was unconscious.

When I awoke, the only light in the room was the rectangle of flat-screen TV, glowing on the wall like a secret portal. I looked to it, hoping for an answer, and watched a man bark about politics until his face turned red, and turned it off.

There were so few answers.

So many questions.

There was no one to help me but me.

For the next unknown hours I slept and became conscious and slept again. I remember trying to order room service, slurring my order into the room's phone and then canceling it, trudging across the carpet to pee in the marble bathroom, and then rolling back into bed. It's possible that I would've remained semicomotose forever if my cell phone hadn't rung and led me out of the fog. It buzzed for what seemed like an eternity, but I was so far from wakefulness that I couldn't rouse myself to answer it. After it stopped, I blinked thickly and opened my eyes. Sunlight blared through the curtains. I struggled to sit up, throwing my legs over the side of the bed like they belonged to someone else. I used the heels of my palms to grind sleep from my eyes, not knowing what day it was and not caring. It felt as if my entire being had gone through a gigantic meat grinder and then been slapped and patted back into shape.

It wasn't quite an emotional breakdown that I had.

It was more like a break apart, clean and oil the pieces, and put back together.

I was far from being in a happy place, but at least more prepared for what might lurk outside the door.

That's when I remembered my mom's warning about being careful, since what lurked outside was Chicago. Someone had tried to sneak inside via a phone call, and I looked over at my cell lying silent and inert on the carpet. I bent painfully and picked it up, stared at the display, which indicated the last caller, blinked, and stared again. I'd flexed my emotional abs, prepared for a hard blow to the gut when I saw Uncle Buddy's number, or Detective Smelt's, or worse, unknown digits belonging to a phantom in a ski mask.

I did not expect Max's name and number.

To be honest, I had almost forgotten about him.

Seeing his name now was akin to looking into an alternate universe.

As I inspected the display, the phone buzzed in my hand and I jumped like an electrified rabbit. It was Max again, and I was gripped with the sort of fear that had nothing to do with insane uncles, rogue cops, or masked assassins. Instead, it was old-fashioned crush anxiety—talking to someone you really, really like when you aren't prepared. But the prospect of not talking to him was even worse, so I took a deep breath, told myself, "Casual, casual," and pushed the green button.

"Hello?" I said, as casual as a mental patient.

"Sara Jane?" Max said. "Is that you?"

"Hey, Max. How are you?"

"I'm good," he said. "Are you okay? You sound funny."

"Oh," I said, touching at the bruises on my neck. "Um . . . yeah, my throat feels a little weird."

"So were you sick or something? We were supposed to meet at the Davis Theater on Sunday."

"Max," I said, feeling a blush creep over my face, "I'm so, so sorry I missed the movie. I should have called, but this weekend was just really . . . busy."

"Family stuff?"

"You could say that."

"I know how it is," he said. "When my dad calls from L.A. and my mom answers the phone, the fireworks start immediately. I just want to escape, you know?"

"Absolutely," I said.

"Speaking of family, I met your uncle."

That shut me up. I tried to recover but could only murmur, "Uncle Buddy?"

"Yeah. And your aunt Greta."

"She's not my aunt."

"She called herself your aunt."

"She's *not*," I said, too forcefully, which shut Max up. We were both quiet until I cleared my throat and said, "So where did you meet him?"

"At your house."

"You went to my house?"

"Uh . . . yeah. Your uncle was working on the front door. I held it in place for him while he attached a hinge. Cool old place, by the way."

"Thanks."

"He and your aunt . . . or whoever she is, mentioned that they were staying with you. Your parents and brother are out of town or something, huh?"

"Yeah," I said dully. "Or something."

"Your uncle's a pretty chatty guy. He had a ton of questions about school: what time we go in the morning, what classes we're in, what kind of security . . ."

"I'll bet."

"He told me I could stop by your house anytime."

"What? No, don't do that!"

"Huh?"

"I mean, unless I'm there. Uncle Buddy can really trap you."

"Listen," Max said, "I hope I didn't, like, overstep a boundary, as my mom's therapist would say. It's just, you weren't at the movie and you haven't been in school. I was worried."

"You were?" I said. "About me?"

"Yeah. Well, I mean, me *and* Doug were worried. It's weird when a friend isn't where she's supposed to be, right?"

"Right," I said quietly, that word *friend* from Max's lips feeling like a punch in the heart. "Weird."

"By the way, Doug has this movie, *Goodfellas*, scheduled for . . ."

Max's words faded into the background as my brain kicked into emotional-calculator mode. My home was now off-limits with Uncle Buddy lying in wait plus the fact that I'd brought a curse on Willy and couldn't return to Windy City Gym equaled Fep Prep—the last place where I could be the Sara Jane I was before this nightmare began. No one there knew about my life outside its walls, which provided a comforting suspension of reality. It was like being in bubble—as long as the bubble came with electronic surveillance every five feet and a squad of security guards that wouldn't let a cop inside without frisking him. Plus, it's housed in an old redbrick former shoe factory, with a chiming clock tower that used to call laborers to work (and now warns kids to be in homeroom by eight fifteen), composed of twisting hallways, stairways to nowhere, and out-of-the-way classrooms; only kids who are super-accomplished gamers can easily navigate the place. It's my second year and I still get turned around in that labyrinth.

I looked at myself in the mirror as Max continued to talk.

The high cheekbones and olive skin were aspects of my mom's face that existed in my own.

It occurred to me then that just as important as the strict security of my school was my mom's expectation that I would continue to attend, even in her bitter absence. Like I said before, her philosophy as a teacher—as a person—is that knowledge is power. But more than that, she believes that knowledge is the air we breathe, the food we eat, the rhythm of our hearts. Knowledge is life, and she would expect me to go on living. Just by attending school I would be closer to her, and feel the strength of her confidence flow like lava through my veins. So I vowed not to let her down, then heard a question mark at the end of Max's sentence.

"I'm sorry . . . what did you say?" I said.

"Tomorrow? You know, Wednesday? Will you be back in school?"

"Yeah," I said. "I will."

And then we said good-bye and hung up, and I looked at the phone in my hand. With one call, Max had reminded me how easy it was to track a phone with invasive apps and beeping satellites and meticulous provider records. Now I was sure

I was being listened to and spied on. Just across the street, Lake Michigan winked and sparkled like a blue quilt covered in diamonds. I needed fresh air and my phone needed a permanent, watery resting place. Sometime during my twelve hours of unconsciousness, the old sweats and crusty clothing had been magically replaced with jeans and new underthings, a good pair of shoes and a plain white, super-soft T-shirt, all in my size. Al the doorman, I thought, remembering the skeptical look he'd given me before asking if there was anything else I needed. I dressed quickly, lifted the briefcase, and left the room. He was at his post outside the hotel entrance.

I tapped him on the shoulder and said, "Hi, Al."

He looked at me and the slick little mustache under his nose lifted in a smile. "Hi, Al. What can I do for you?"

"I need a phone," I said quietly.

"Flip-top, candy bar, PDA, or iPhone?"

"Actually," I said, looking around, "something untraceable."

He nodded. "Disposable. How many?"

"I don't know. Three?"

"Let's go three dozen, just to be safe. Nice day, huh? Going for a walk?"

"Just to the lake."

"They'll be in your car trunk when you get back. And listen, don't dillydally. The hotel's throwing a Cinco de Mayo party for guests. Mariachi, mango salsa, and margaritas. You can enjoy the first two, but no booze. Underage drinking is *strictly* prohibited. After all," he said solemnly, "at the Commodore, we respect the law."

"Thanks, Al," I said.

"You're welcome, Al," he replied with a salute, the gold epaulets of his uniform glinting in the sun.

My quick stroll to the water's edge consisted of an extended look over my shoulder and envy. Everywhere I turned, from busy Michigan Avenue to the North Avenue Beach House boardwalk, people were going about their lives. It was at least eighty degrees, a summerlike day making an appearance in May, and everyone seemed to be enjoying the generous sun. They weren't racked with suspicion or desperate to be rid of a phone or carrying steel briefcases full of secrets, guns, and money. The world seemed so ridiculous—some people floated along in peace while others fought to survive, with both groups sharing space and rubbing shoulders. And then sand crunched under my new shoes and I hurried toward the lake, swiveled my body, and extended an arm. The phone skipped across the water like a flat, rectangular stone. It was an early sixteenth birthday gift from my mom and dad, and left a trail of sparkling bubbles as it sank—another small part of them gone with it. And then I turned and looked at North Avenue Beach and realized what a mistake I'd made.

I don't mean throwing away the phone.

I mean walking unprotected in broad daylight.

It seemed like an entire beach full of people stared in my direction.

Some were shirtless on towels, others wore bikinis and held volleyballs, and still others stood with their arms crossed, wearing sunglasses and sport coats. The sunglasses were okay, but my gut quietly informed me that guys in sport coats under a hot sun were not. They had cop written all over them, from the chunky shoes to the blank expressions focused on me and my briefcase. I had no doubt they belonged to Detective Smelt. I felt like a fool, surrounded by acres of hot sand and endless lake. My only option for cover was the old beach house, built to resemble a 1930s cruise liner, complete with smokestacks.

And there it was.

The 1930s.

If it really was that old, maybe it had a Capone Door.

I remembered how Joe Little installed them between 1921 and 1950 in private and public structures, and few things were as public as the beach house. I ran for it, and the cops ran for me. I was panicked in a save-my-butt way but calm, the chilly blue flame flickering in my gut, and was able to file away the fact for further use—*when looking for a Capone Door, look for an old building.* I took steps two at a time and hit the sandy concourse running hard, wondering where it could possibly be, looking past decades of renovation for something that was part of the original structure—*concession stand? No—lifeguard office? Too new-looking—upstairs beer garden? Too exposed*—and hearing them behind me.

"Stop, thief!" one of them barked in a patrolman's voice.

"Stop her!" the other one shouted, trying to get someone to intervene. "She stole a briefcase!"

Well played, I thought, and skidded around a corner, pulling up in front of two entryways, one leading to the men's showers, the other to the women's. They would expect me to go into the women's, so I ducked into the men's, thankful that it was empty. It was a square, tiled room—no doors, no windows, a dead end—until my eyes were drawn to the knobs beneath each of the ancient dripping shower heads, one for hot stamped with little *H*'s, the other for cold stamped with little *C*'s.

Those beautiful little *C*'s.

I pushed them all quickly, one by one, but nothing happened. Looking closely, I saw decades of hard-sealed rust encrusted around the letters.

I pushed each of the *C*'s again, leaning into them with all of my weight, until one moved and a door popped open as silently as if it had been oiled yesterday. I was sealed safely behind the wall before the first cop's shoe squeaked on wet tile, and then it was quiet, neither guy saying a word, just walking slowly around the room. I could feel their frustration vibrating through the wall. Finally one of them said, "Well, shit. Where did she go?"

The other one said, "Smelt's not gonna be happy."

"Smelt was born unhappy," the first one said. "That's why she's always at Twin Anchors. Sweet liquor eases the pain."

"That's funny. You're a funny guy. You should tell her that."

"I'm dumb," the first one said, their footsteps receding, "not stupid."

It was the second time I'd heard of Detective Smelt's hangout—Twin Anchors—and filed away that nugget too. And then I turned to a painted hand on the wall pointing down a flight of stairs that ended at a hallway, which branched in opposite directions. One wall bore the words "Lincoln Park Boathouse" with a hand indicating right; the other read "Commodore Hotel" with its hand pointing left. I turned down the dim hallway listening to something thump and echo above me, and realized I was passing beneath Lake Shore Drive. A few minutes later my foot kicked a bottom step. I climbed a short flight to another door. It unlatched quietly and I lowered myself into a toilet stall. I shut the Capone Door, eased from the stall, and turned to a dozing men's room attendant. The old guy was propped precariously in a chair next to a display of mints, aftershave, and crumpled dollar bills. I tiptoed past but my shoes were wet, the rubber soles complained, and he sat up and stared at me.

"I went through the wrong door," I said with a shrug.

He smacked his gums, mumbled, "It happens," and closed his eyes.

I turned the corner and heard a cheerful "Ay-yi-yi-yi!"

"Cinco de Mayo," I murmured, the date reminding me that school would be out soon. That meant I'd lose the security of Fep Prep for the entire summer, which added even more urgency to what felt like an increasingly hopeless quest. The music grew louder and I heard people milling about, margarita glasses tinkling, voices raised in celebration. The lobby was crowded with partiers as the mariachi strummed and tweedled in the corner. I pushed through the throng, headed for the elevator, anxious to reach my suite in the sky, when something odd caught my eye.

There were five musicians in the mariachi band.

Four wore sombreros and played guitar, violin, horn, and accordion.

The fifth, in a rumpled plaid suit and plastic devil mask, plunked a ukulele.

Even without the Satan-head mask, I realized Hawaii was

a hell of a long way from Mexico, and I didn't freeze, didn't pause, just made a U-turn and cut back through the crowd. The last thing I saw was Ski Mask Guy's neck twisting in my direction. I flew down the hall and then remembered that I was in the Commodore, and that the name of the Outfit-run hotel probably began with the third letter in the alphabet for a reason. I stepped around a corner and stared at a wall covered in flocked wallpaper. The pattern was end-to-end diamond shapes with small raised *C*'s in the middle. I pushed one, and then another, and another—I realized Ski Mask Guy would be rounding the corner any second—and pushed another, and one more, and then I thought screw it and took a fire extinguisher from the wall, listened for galumphing footsteps, and stepped out swinging.

I nailed him at solar plexus level.

He staggered backward groping at air, caught himself, and charged.

I went low on the next shot, kneecapping him, and he squealed like a debutante.

And then I was gone, down the hallway, pushing through the revolving door briefcase-first and sprinting for the Lincoln, yelling, "Al! Throw me the keys!"

"Head's up, Al!" he said, flipping them through the air.

I snagged them, leaped in, and called out, "Thanks, Al!"

"My pleasure! Watch your back, Al!"

I roared from the curb, waved from the window, and hoped for more Als just like him.

WHEN YOU TELL A LIE but you don't mean to tell a lie, it's not really a lie. It's an alternate version of reality, or sincere disinformation, or in my case, the truth deferred.

I told Max I would be at school the next day and meant it.

Because I meant it, it wasn't a lie, although I didn't actually return to Fep Prep for a week.

First I had to hide inside a brick wall.

It all began with a hundred-dollar bill. I needed food and gasoline, except, as I learned, a sixteen-year-old kid peeling off Franklins tends to raise eyebrows among the average mini-mart merchant and fast-food vendor. The last thing I needed was unwanted attention, or the police called based solely on suspicion. So, after I fled the Commodore Hotel, I stopped off at a currency exchange on North Avenue, told the teller that my dad needed change for a hundred, and walked away with a pocketful of fives and tens.

That's when Ski Mask Guy materialized out of thin air,

catching me with a huge open hand across the mouth that drew blood. I ducked under his fist, which swung like a wrecking ball, and answered with a perfectly aimed right that sounded like it broke his nose. He reeled and stumbled, and I took off down the sidewalk like my hair was on fire.

I was fast, but he was pissed.

He was on his feet in a flash.

I ran through the nearest open door, into the North Avenue train station, and was charging toward the platform stairs with him galloping behind me. And then, in the long second when there were only inches between my swinging ponytail and his grasping fingers, the air grates popped open and began raining rats.

Ski Mask Guy gasped and began swatting at the writhing gray bodies, while I took the opportunity to run for my life. I remembered what the notebook said' about Capone Doors being located in every El station electrical closet built before 1935 and hoped this one was at least that old. I rounded a corner and spotted a door bearing the words DANGER: ELECTRIC— NO ADMITTANCE, which cracked and yielded to my very determined shoulder. I ducked inside, located a tiny *C* covered in grime, and leaped into the wall, followed by a gang of rodents. It wasn't the steamy heat or pitch blackness or cobwebs adhering to my face like a second skin that sucked so badly, or even my bleeding mouth dripping over my lips that I couldn't wipe away because the space was too tight to lift an arm.

What sucked were the rats.

Wedged between brick and mortar, I was unable to bend down.

It sucked that I couldn't caress their hot spiky hair and wormy tails, and scratch lovingly between their triangle ears, since they had saved my butt.

For an hour I stood between two walls—in the intervening years since the Capone Door was installed, another building had been built against the station, cutting off the escape tunnel—while dozens of rats skittered and clicked over my feet. Now and then I felt a cold nose inch its way up my ankle. There was tentative nibbling at the end of my little toe and one of them squeaked, then stopped, and then started again: squeak, stop, start, repeat, for what seemed like a hundred years.

It was so narrow I could smell my own bloody breath.

Through layers of old brick, I heard the El train pass overhead.

For thirty of those minutes I listened to him out there in his creepy ski mask shuffling around, trying to figure out how I (and a crowd of rats) had disappeared in a train station closet with no windows and only one door, the same one he'd run through a few steps behind me while peeling off rats. He pushed over boxes and punched at the ceiling, got on his knees and felt along the dirty tile floor, exhaling the F-word with every girlish breath. When he was done, he sat down and crossed his arms, waiting for me to reappear. Even with a wall between us, his nauseating fuzzy pork chop odor was inescapable.

Through a pinhole, I watched him bob his foot impatiently.

Rats swirled around my feet excitedly.

They were jumpy, like my heart.

I remained motionless for another half hour, unwilling to take the chance of exposure, not after what I'd seen in Ski Mask Guy's eyes after I broke his nose. Finally, he kicked over his chair and left the closet. When he was gone, the rats scattered too.

They departed like a herd of silent little ghosts.

They never even gave me a chance to thank them.

I emerged from the wall, bloody and dusty, but with a revelation—I would continue running blindly until I understood *why* I was running. Of course it was to find my family, but whatever happened to them had occurred because of the notebook. It was time to unearth the secrets that lie between those old pages and use them to my advantage. After all, as my mom drilled into my head, knowledge is power.

To do that, I had to get off the street.

I had to hide out and start reading.

I chose a ninety-first-floor apartment in the Hancock Building from the list of safe houses. It was a glass box in the sky where Lake Michigan spread out as if the whole world was submerged beneath cold blue water. I locked myself inside and began studying the notebook, but my paranoia alarm went off Thursday morning and I moved to another location, an ancient brick warehouse overgrown with ivy and weeds, surrounded by gutted cars and encircled by a rusty barbed wire fence. The windows were covered with cages and the door was a giant rolling wedge of iron that locked by dropping a metal bar into the cement floor. I appreciated the airiness of the Hancock but needed the reliability of thick brick and heavy metal—it reminded me of Windy City Gym, and Willy. When

I opened the notebook in that old place, the past came roaring back to the present; alive, jumpy, and dangerous. I continued my crash course, and by the time I closed the notebook and pushed it aside, the rest of the week had passed.

What I learned came off the pages like a sick whisper.

Most of it was shocking, some painful, the rest shameful.

All of it involved my family.

A realization sunk agonizingly into my consciousness like a dull needle inserted by a sadistic nurse. Something made the notebook shake—I saw that it was my own hands—as the need to scream crept up my throat and into my mouth. It gurgled like sour nausea, but when I parted my lips, all that dribbled out was a faint "Oh . . . my . . . God," that didn't sound like my voice. It was as if someone else were in the room, because there was—another me, the one I didn't know existed until I read it in the notebook.

It told how the Rispoli clan was so deeply embedded in the Outfit that the bloody organization couldn't operate without us.

It wasn't an implication or a rumor. Worse, it was a secret, which is just another term for a concealed fact. It stated in black and white how three generations of men in my family aided and abetted Chicago's (and the world's) most psychopathic and murderous organized criminals, which made them criminals, too. If it was true, and the zillions of microscopic icicles knifing every inch of my skin said it was, then the life my parents had carefully constructed around me was a lie.

I licked my dry lips, staring at words on the page, while that other girl said it again. "Oh my God."

．．．

There are things I wish I did not know about my long-gone great-grandfather, my dear dead little grandpa, and my own dad, whose fate is questionable.

There are facts about molasses that make me hate the sugary, syrupy substance in a completely unrealistic way.

Over and over again those wishes and that hatred interrupted my reading as I delved deeper into the notebook's first chapter, *"Nostro*—Us," which refers to the entire Chicago Outfit. Within that chapter was a section titled, *"La storia della famiglia Rispoli e' la storia del Outfit a Chicago,"* meaning, "The story of the Rispoli family is the story of the Outfit in Chicago." It was there that I learned of not only my family's unique place in the criminal organization, but also how it all began with molasses.

Molasses, which can be easily fermented to produce alcohol.

Rum in particular, but other types of cheap booze too.

My family was the source of that sugary syrup for Chicago and beyond.

When I say source, I don't mean plain old sales and distribution. I mean the entire supply of molasses into Chicago was controlled by Nunzio "Blue Eyes" Rispoli, my great-grandfather (who knew he had a nickname?). He opened Rispoli & Sons Fancy Pastries in the twenties as a front business, since bakeries required large amounts of sweet raw products like molasses and wouldn't draw the attention of federal agents. Nunzio's operation grew and grew until he was covertly importing thousands of gallons of the stuff from Canada as the main supplier to dozens of secret distilleries.

He was tight with the Outfit's boss of bosses, Al Capone.

Their relationship was not founded on admiration or respect.

It was cash, tons of it, paid by Nunzio for the right to operate.

Capone ordered every illegal booze maker in town to buy precious molasses exclusively from Nunzio, and in exchange Nunzio gave Capone's organization fifty percent of his profits. Capone took half of the booze makers' profits too—not to mention what he shook out of the thugs who delivered the liquor, the rumrunners and bootleggers. The Chicago Mafia made so much money from illegal liquor that it was able to expand its criminal operations across the country and the world. And unlike the Mafia in other large cities, the Chicago organization was multi-ethnic. There were lots of Italians at the top, but everyone—Greek, Jewish, Irish, African American, and at least one very bad English guy—was welcome, as long as they earned money. Eventually, it even rebranded itself with a business term rather than an ethnic one—the Outfit. All of this sounds innocent by today's standards, even a little romantic, like some of the stuff I've watched in the Classic Movie Club. Except that if any of those booze makers disobeyed Capone and bought molasses from another source, his guys would beat, maim, blind, disfigure, or murder the offenders and their families. They pummeled people with bats and pipes and tire irons, drove them around in car trunks filled with bricks, pounded nails into their heads and feet, set fire to them, drowned, choked, stabbed, smothered, and hung them, and sometimes even mercifully shot them.

It was brutal and done with intent, the opposite of romantic or innocent.

The Outfit called it doing business.

Nunzio did business with them from the beginning of Prohibition to the end.

In fact, the speakeasy he built far beneath the bakery was the Outfit's gathering place of choice. Long after the bakery closed each day, a procession of criminals and their significant others rode the oven-elevator down to Club Molasses to drink their own illegal product and gamble away the profits they made selling it. Meanwhile, through his molasses business, my great-grandfather provided a foundation for modern organized crime in Chicago. Illegal booze financed the Outfit's investments in prostitution (everyone is a victim), gambling (shreds souls and lives), extortion, loan-sharking, labor racketeering, and on and on, including the precursor of illegal drugs. The system of distribution, laid like railroad tracks during Prohibition—who imports, who brokers, who sells—is the same one the illegal-drug train runs on today. In the margin of the notebook, Grandpa Enzo scribbled a reflection: "The money that began with molasses was a puddle seeping toward a rivulet, the rivulet trickled toward a stream, the stream bubbled into a river, the river rushed toward the sea. And now, we are the sea . . . the bottomless, churning sea." The tone seems self-satisfied, almost proud, but at the same time overwhelmed, like it's all too much to deal with.

Eventually it became *way* too much.

The Outfit extended its reach to Cuba, Hollywood, Washington D.C., and beyond.

Meanwhile, the organization in Chicago was in chaos.

Al Capone was sentenced for tax evasion in 1931 and locked away in Alcatraz penitentiary in the middle of San Francisco Bay. Among his many evil attributes, he had been a master of crime management, keeping competing interests and rogue personalities in line by sheer force of will. Among his many failings was a weakness for the spotlight. Big Al was a publicity hound, constantly showing off his expensive cars and shiny diamond stickpins, and even shinier women.

He opened soup kitchens for the poor and spent lavishly on orphans in an attempt to change his public reputation from crime lord to benefactor. In the end, all that it did was attract attention to his lifestyle. The FBI wondered how it was that a guy with so much disposable income never paid taxes, and he was quickly convicted and sent away. Upon release from prison eight years later, he retired quietly to Miami. Capone never returned to Chicago, and it was said that he'd died in Florida, but no one ever saw his dead body. Crooks around the world speculated about what had happened to his vast personal fortune, estimated at a hundred million dollars in cash. It was rumored that he hadn't died, but instead snuck off to Italy with his money. Another rumor, scribbled in a margin, was that Capone was spotted in Chicago as late as 1951, holding secret meetings with none other than Giuseppe "Joe Little" Piccolino, the inventor of the Capone Doors.

The Outfit didn't care what happened to him.

They were just glad he was gone.

They vowed never again to seek the spotlight and to go as far underground as possible, since publicity served only to weaken the organization.

As soon as Capone was gone, a thug with a low profile and big brain named Frank Nitti stepped into the void.

Nitti, it turned out, needed Nunzio.

During Prohibition, Nitti's job was to distribute Nunzio's molasses among the illegal distilleries. He was impressed—dumbfounded, really—at my tiny, gentle great-grandfather's ability to control the smugglers, liars, and thugs who worked for him. These were bad men with small brains and short tempers, yet each one was intimidated by Nunzio, and Nitti never forgot it. By the time he took over, Prohibition had ended, liquor was legal, and the ocean of cash that flowed from illicit booze dried up. Still, the Outfit had plenty of income from all of its other businesses, both legitimate and nefarious. By 1940, Nitti realized that the time had come to restructure, and after studying several corporate models, concluded that consolidation was in order. He split the Outfit in half, with the moneymakers (sales, loan-sharking, bribery, investments, and banking) on one side, and the muscle (intimidation, beatings for hire, enforcement, collections, and executions) on the other. He knew the entire organization could be boiled down to those two divisions, since each one depended on the other—without money, they couldn't protect their business, and without protection, they couldn't make money. Because he was a modern man, he named himself chief executive, and appointed a vice president to each division.

Genarro "The Gent" Strozzini was the very first VP of

Money, a position and title that were handed to his son, his son's son, and on down the line.

Agosto "Gus Batters" Battuta was the first VP of Muscle, and a Battuta had been the Outfit's chief knee-cracker ever since.

Strozzini and Battuta were oil and water and hated each other from the beginning.

If Battuta's guys were slow to collect a debt, then Strozzini was slow to pay Battuta's guys, and then Battuta's guys exercised their knuckles on Strozzini's guys, and so on. Nitti was tempted to erase them both and start over, but he had selected them because they were so good at what they did—Strozzini could pinch a penny until it squealed, while Battuta was a born killer with no conscience—and because they commanded the loyalty of large gangs of their own. He needed to get them under control, but if he focused on one versus the other, he would lose the edge of impartiality so critical to his stature— and that's when he thought of Nunzio. He remembered the little man's outsized ability to control sour personalities, and while he held no real hope that Nunzio could tame Strozzini and Battuta, he thought it was at least worth a try.

The end of Prohibition ended Nunzio's molasses business but he had made enough money to retire from the Outfit and become an actual baker, which he found that he loved. My great-grandmother, Ottorina, ran the front of the store, and with a wink and a nod, they offered a specialty: molasses cookies. Grandpa Enzo was a little kid, already working in the kitchen, and here I learned something strange. Apparently, Nunzio named it Rispoli & Sons, plural, because there had been another son—Grandpa Enzo had a younger brother whose name and fate are not recorded, only the fact that he existed. In any event, Nitti asked Nunzio to intercede between Strozzini and Battuta, and Nunzio agreed. Only he, Nitti, and the two men were present at the meeting. The notebook is vague on details, stating only that Strozzini and Battuta left arm in arm, professing undying loyalty to each other. Whatever Nitti witnessed was enough—from that day on, Nunzio was the Outfit's official feud breaker and peacemaker. He took the title counselor-at-large and settled disputes at Club Molasses, which evolved from a speakeasy to a quasi courtroom.

There's nothing written in the notebook that explains Nunzio's methods for making hardened criminals make peace and get along. There is, however, a scrap torn from some sort of history book stapled to a page. It's old and yellow, taped together from many pieces as if someone shredded it, thought about it, and reconstructed it. I could hear my heart pounding in my ears as I read it, because I was reading about me.

"After a grueling trip, the team of researchers reached the remote Sicilian village of Buondiavolo in 1906, set among arid hills at the southernmost tip of the island, which consisted of the ancestors of an obscure tribe captured in Egypt after Alexander the Great's troops engaged it in a skirmish. Alexander was amazed to watch the fierce, outnumbered clan fight completely without emotion. There were no battle cries or shouts of anger. Meanwhile, his troops were intimidated to the point of inaction; had Alexander not ordered reinforcements, they would have fallen one by one from sheer fright. Seeing an opportunity, he made peace with the tribal leader, the most vicious yet serene warrior among that people. Alexander was intrigued by the chief's eyes, which were described as 'small circles of ice lit by chips of burning gold.' The chief spoke of how it had passed down from the Pharaoh—that the rare salts found in the precious metal were not only life-sustaining, but bestowed otherworldly powers. Producing a satchel of shining sand, he declared that only the tribal leader had the privilege to eat gold. Alexander made a show of respect for this custom, as he did toward all savages whom he conquered, and absorbed the tribe into his army, making it an elite unit, first to engage difficult enemies. The last place he sent it was Sicily to destroy rebellious Greeks, but then he died prematurely. His empire crumbled, history stumbled forward, and the tribe remained in the place that became Buondiavolo.

"Researchers found modern residents of the village to be mild and pleasant, even when aroused to anger. One team member, Dr. J. Reginald Huff, inadvertently offended a young man when he failed to remove his hat in the presence of the man's mother. As Dr. Huff reported, 'Smiling brightly, the lad explained precisely what he would do to my intestines with a dull fish knife if I did not right the situation. The chill blue of his eyes and serenity of his demeanor terrified me to the point where I would have doffed not only my hat, but any other article of clothing, had he so ordered.' The team experienced it again and again—calm rage that froze a person in terror, making him utterly complacent. As Dr. Huff noted, 'I've always been terribly frightened of knives. When the young man invoked a fish knife to my belly, it was as if he were reading my fear.'

"What's more, there was a rumor of an even more mysterious property to the phenomenon. Supposedly, there was a family known for its blue eyes flecked with the same gold as their Egyptian ancestor. These people, it was said, were capable in times of extreme pain or passion of emitting a charge or spark from that fearful gaze. While this attribute was not witnessed by the research team, it did note several volatile electrical storms happening in and around Buondiavolo. It was also noted that every home, without exception, bore a lightning-scarred weather vane.

"Over the centuries, residents mixed with a host of conquerors—Romans, Byzantines, Normans—until at last they were Sicilian. This 'thinning of the blood' is the basis of the research team's theory of why not everyone displays the unusual trait; in fact, it is not even consistent in families. One man may possess it while his brother does not. Inhabitants recognize it as something to be feared and respected, and many who have it hold positions of authority. The local term is 'il ghiaccio furioso'—pronounced phonetically as 'il gee-ah-cho fury-oh-so.' In English, it loosely translates to 'the cold fury.'"

Which Uncle Buddy does not possess, and neither does Lou.

Great-Grandpa Nunzio, *yes*; Grandpa Enzo, *check*; my dad, *for sure*.

And me—*oh, hell yeah*.

It's like I knew what it was before I knew what it was called or where it came from. The first time I experienced it was at age thirteen when Mandi Fishbaum called me a slut. I've never forgotten how I radiated that cold fury through my eyes and Mandi winced as if something had bitten her brain. I could feel her terror—I was channeling it—which was horrible for her, but only made me stronger. In fact, the more I thought about it, a strange recollection bubbled to the surface. As I stared at Mandi, a vivid image had appeared between us of her mother connected to a chemotherapy machine—it was as if we were sharing the picture in our minds. In the years since the incident, Mandi's mom did indeed die from cancer, and it devastated her. I hadn't seen the future—worse, I had peered into the buried part of Mandi's soul where terror lived.

Looking at the notebook, I knew that there was something inside of me that absorbed a person's deepest fears—the ones kept carefully locked away at the bottom of a soul—and projected them back in psychic HD. The creepy-crawlies normally left free to roam a subconscious were dredged to the top of a person's brain and projected back from my gaze. Lou once told me that all real fighters have something burning at their essential core, and that it was inside of me too. Remembering it made me realize that, like boxing, I was born with an innate ability that meant little unless I could learn to control it.

I pronounced the words silently, feeling the truth of them.

Ghiacco furioso—"gee-ah-cho fury-oh-so."

Grandpa Enzo and my dad felt it too.

According to the notebook, each in turn served as counselor-at-large to broker internal peace for the Outfit. Grandpa Enzo took over after Nunzio died in 1963, just as organized crime was rocked to its roots. A New York gangster named Joe Valachi tried to avoid the death penalty by testifying before Congress about the secret inner workings of the Mafia. He discussed extortion, heroin trafficking, and murder after murder after murder. Before his testimony, the public doubted that organized crime existed; when he was done talking, its rotten underbelly was fully exposed. Valachi committed the cardinal sin of Mafiosi—he ratted—and mobsters across the country came under intense scrutiny. The Outfit receded further into the shadows, growing greedier and more violent among its own as it became harder to earn a dishonest living. Grandpa Enzo had his work cut out for him, and it affected him in an unusual way.

He began to have doubts.

Some of them are scribbled in the margins.

He wonders about morality, and "truth vs. loyalty," and "the future of my family."

My grandpa realized that his role in the Outfit would affect the children he would have someday, and it gave him pause. He was still a young man and considered quitting, except there was no quitting—once you were in, you were in. The only ways out were death or talking to the Feds and begging for protection. The Outfit's attitude toward rats is captured in a newspaper item taped to a page, dated 1969. It details the impending execution of convicted hit man Eddie "The Exterminator" O'Hara, who brutally beheaded an Outfit associate as well as his wife and children. Unrepentant, O'Hara is quoted as saying, "The bum was a rat, and rats breed. You can't kill just one. You gotta kill the whole damn family." In other words, turning informant wasn't a healthy option, and so my grandpa continued on. The notebook makes it clear that my dad and uncle knew about his role in the Outfit, that my dad's inheritance was evident from childhood, and that he was destined for that role too. The inverse was true of Uncle Buddy. He obviously didn't possess ghiaccio furioso—in fact, he didn't possess much more than a loyal nature and the ability to take a punch, and the loyal part was BS.

Early on, my grandpa and dad began to keep secrets from Uncle Buddy, with the notebook being a prime example.

My uncle thought they were excluding him and grew to hate them for it.

They did it to protect him from the Outfit because they loved him.

My dad's concern for his brother is contained in a letter to me, folded into the notebook. It's dated a year before the disappearance, which means he'd been considering telling me about our family for a long time. Its tone is apologetic and vague—he regrets what I've probably learned from the notebook but can't state anything explicitly for fear of the letter falling into the wrong hands. He says that he began as counselor-at-large before my grandpa died (I wondered why he often worked late—who has to work late baking cookies?) and mentions that he and my mom have a plan to "free the family," which must be a reference to their whispered conversations. He tells me to watch out for Uncle Buddy (good advice) but also to watch over him (not going to happen) and then relates an odd anecdote that I think was an attempt to tell me something without saying it. Apparently, Nunzio had a special way with animals (like Lou with Harry) and kept two unusual pets.

A pair of rats.

The big gray type with worm tails that dine and swim in the sewers of Chicago.

Nunzio called them Antonio and Cleopatra.

He knew that if he fed them and provided a warm place to live—Club Molasses—they would guard their territory, family, and all things Rispoli with ferocity. Antonio and Cleopatra bred and bred, and soon they and their offspring were patrolling the speakeasy like stealthy packs of tiny Dobermans. I have no doubt it was Antonio and Cleopatra's great-grandchildren who sensed a Rispoli in trouble and saved me at the train station.

Antonio—Anthony—is my dad's name.

Was he named after a rat?

Is that what he was trying to tell me—that he had become one?

So far, it's a question that even the notebook can't answer. What endless hours of reading has made clear, however, is that the Outfit has no code of honor, no ethnic allegiance, and no loyalty. There is only the accumulation of power and its twin purposes of making money and destroying people who try to take that money away. I'm sure that's why Great-Grandpa Nunzio began writing things down—he did it to protect himself, by recording secrets about and evidence against other Outfit members in case he ever needed leverage.

But then he went further.

In great detail, he documented the locations of secret escape routes all over Chicago, while also providing the confidential contact numbers for nameless, dangerous allies and the passwords needed to access them, putting a shadow army of homicidal thugs at his fingertips. It was a practice carried on by Grandpa Enzo and my dad; they each updated those invaluable Outfit secrets to their respective generations. And then there's the last chapter, "*Volta*," written in some form of incomprehensible Italian, and the mystery key taped to the inside back cover—I'm sure the power contained in those words and that jagged hunk of brass is considerable. Why else would they be disguised and unexplained? It was that very realization—the cumulative power of its pages—that turned on a lightbulb for me. The notebook isn't a family history, and it isn't an archive of criminal evidence.

It's an instruction manual for operating the Outfit, from its secretive, singular boss at the very top of the organization, down to its soldiers on the street.

There is a kind of danger on those pages that can strike and kill quickly, quietly, and efficiently.

It's a leather-bound nuclear weapon, and I won't hesitate to use it.

AFTER WHAT SEEMED like an eternity of running and fighting for my life, making it back to school was a relief, but also surreal, as if I'd stepped into the calm, orderly existence of that previous Sara Jane. I was standing outside of homeroom, my face knit with hatred as I thought about how I planned to deploy the notebook's power on that masked, lurching freak, when someone said hi.

"Hey," I growled without looking up.

That was how I said hello to Max when I finally saw him.

After a whirlwind of fleeing, punching, and reading, I'd cocooned into something slightly less than human—a defensive, monosyllabic armadillo girl, ready to fight or flee at a moment's notice. But when I looked up at Max's grin and warm brown eyes, my heart began to beat again. I was so happy to see him that it was almost impossible to stifle a hug. He was too, but not romantic happy; his expression was mainly friendly, and it hurt as much as getting punched by Ski Mask Guy.

"Jeez," he said, inspecting my face. "You got hit hard, huh? Is that why you were out for so long?"

I had already told Max that I was a boxer. He knew I sparred regularly, and I went with it. I told him about a tough opponent I faced at Windy City, how the freak dodged and weaved, but that I intended to take him down in the future.

"A rematch, huh?" he said.

"Definitely," I said. "It's inevitable."

One of the best things about Fep Prep is that it allows my mind to take a much-needed rest from my troubles, and being with Max only made it better. We ate lunch together and talked about nothing in particular—his week, what I missed at school, what we each had planned for summer break. It felt so good, like my brain was purging itself of urgency and fear, and I said, "Hey, what about *Ten Seconds to Zero*? Did you see it?"

Max's face changed. It went from relaxed to concerned, and he said, "Movies . . . that reminds me. Have you talked to Doug?"

I shook my head. "I haven't seen him yet. Why, what happened?"

"Something bad," Max said solemnly. "Something very bad."

He explained how Doug had brought his precious *About Face* screenplay to a discussion in social sciences class, since, in Doug's words, the film "offers a succinct analysis of non-violence that is still applicable to our geopolitical world," or something. He was crossing campus when Bully the Kid spotted him, and at first it seemed like the same old thing, with Billy calling him idiotic names while Doug went into emotional lockdown and Billy's entourage of morons stood around yukking it up. But this time was different. This time, for whatever reason—maybe it was confidence from having just discussed *About Face* or maybe he'd finally had enough—Doug had the nerve to say something. When there was a lull in the taunting, he cleared his throat and said, "Your eyes are really close together."

Billy paused, scrunched up his monkey forehead, and said, "Huh?"

"Close-set eyes," Doug said. "They're a genetic indicator of mental disabilities."

Someone snickered and Billy's neck turned red. He moved closer to Doug and said, "Mental dis— Wait, are you calling me a retard?"

"From a cognitive function standpoint, 'retard' is an unacceptable term," Doug said. "But using it as slang certainly applies."

Billy's eyes got smaller as he said, "Is that a yes?"

Doug said, "Possibly."

Billy smiled in a slow, toothy curl and said, "It's on!" and shoved Doug to the ground. Doug rolled like a human burrito and struggled to his feet. Billy pushed him again, and the screenplay skittered across the grass. "I won't fight back!" Doug huffed. "Push me all you want! I won't fight!" But Billy wasn't listening. Instead he was holding the screenplay, staring at the title page.

"*About Face*," he said, with that same evil lip curl. "A . . . butt . . . face. A butt-face. Hey, is this your life story?"

"Give it back," Doug said, lunging at it, with Billy acting

like a toreador, stepping aside and shoving the fat, clumsy bull to his hands and knees.

"A butt . . . ," Billy said, putting his foot on Doug's big rear end. "Face!" he squealed, pushing Doug flat to the ground like a puffy starfish. Billy sat on him and turned to the first page. "Chapter one . . . I am born!" he said, mock reading. "The doctor slaps my face, thinking it's my ass!" While the pinheads laughed, Billy ceremoniously ripped off the first page and threw it over his shoulder.

"Don't!" Doug said, struggling to get up. "Please!"

"Chapter two," Billy said. "Mom tells me I have shit for brains and I say, well duh! What do you expect? I have a butt for a head!" He dug a handful of pages out of the screenplay and threw them into the air.

"No!" Doug screamed, writhing helplessly beneath Billy's bulked-up body. And then there was more laughter, more pages torn out and thrown away, and by the time Billy got to chapter ten, the screenplay had scattered like dry leaves in the Chicago wind. No one could have caught the pages and no one tried, because only Doug loved them. When Billy was done, Doug was done too, unable to hold back tears. It was what Billy had been working and waiting for all year. When Doug began to sob, Billy leaped to his feet, threw his arms in the air, and exploded into a victorious hyena laugh. Doug was an inert, weeping pile, his eyes squeezed tight, and was still lying there when the last gaper finally drifted away.

"I didn't hear about it until the next day," Max said. "I walked into the theater room and there's Doug, working on his laptop like his fingers are on fire. I tried to talk to him about what had happened but he wouldn't even look at me. He just kept saying it was urgent that he finish the screenplay."

"Poor Doug," I murmured.

"I warned Billy that if he goes near Doug again I'd kick his ass in a way he'd never forget," Max said. "It was him and those morons he hangs with, all of them flexing and giving me the dead-eye. He said, 'Oh yeah? Well you better start doing push-ups because I can't get enough of that fat sack of shit.'" Max shook his head, and said, "Seriously, the first time I catch him alone, he's dead."

"Doug wouldn't want that," I said.

"It doesn't matter. If someone doesn't do something, Billy's just going to keep abusing him. Sometimes violence is justified."

And there I was, straddling the line between Willy's philosophy, that fighting outside the ring only led to more violence, and my own reality, of having spent days on the street fighting to survive. Doug would contend that any type of physical confrontation, inside a ring or out, was wrong, but Max had a point—*something* had to be done to help Doug, and the first thing was to get him to talk.

"Where is he?" I said.

"Theater room," Max said. He's been there every day between classes, working like crazy on his screenplay."

"I need to see him."

"Sara Jane," Max said, taking my hand and giving it a quick squeeze. "I'm glad you're back."

It was so much better than a hug.

Hugs are commonplace and benign; everyone hugs, from NFL players to enemies.

Hand-squeezes are one short rung below a kiss.

I turned away feeling strong and headed for the theater room. It was empty and dark, the light from Doug's laptop piercing the gloom. I expected to see dead bags of junk food and killed soda cans, but the only sign that he'd been there recently was the glowing computer screen. I looked at the page and saw that the first half was dialogue between two characters.

GOOD KING DOUG

But you are too softheaded and without moral compass to lead a kingdom.

VILE LORD BILLY

And you, sire, are as disgusting and bloated as a stuffed toad!

GOOD KING DOUG

I would never raise a hand in violence. In this, I am true.

VILE LORD BILLY

You never raise a hand to anything! You sit all the day long watching while other men do! You are weighted to the throne by inaction and flab!

GOOD KING DOUG

But at least I wish no man any harm.

VILE LORD BILLY

A wish, too, is unmoving and unreal. It is fluff and cotton candy, of which you look as if you've eaten a metric freaking ton.

GOOD KING DOUG

But . . . but . . .

VILE LORD BILLY

Butt-face, you fat load! You fat effing loser! Why don't you go watch another movie and eat another bag of Munchitos and then eat a bag of rat poison, you fat prick!

GOOD KING DOUG

You . . . you . . . are right, my lord. I'm . . . I'm . . .

I watched the words drift off and then resume not as dialogue but as disjointed thoughts that bumped into one another, crowding for space.

". . . I'm better off dead, I'm better off dead, because Billy is right, I've always known he was right, I'm a fat piece of shit, I'm a fat effing loser, I can't and won't do anything, not even defend myself, not even stand up for myself, all I do is watch, I sit on my fat butt-face and watch life go by, I deserve to die, I stare at movie after movie because I'm useless and unequipped and scared of real life, so I'd rather not live, I'd rather die, and that's what I'm going to do, I'm going to do it, I'm going to eat a bag of rat poison, and at least I will have done that . . ."

"What are you doing?"

I looked at Doug standing in the doorway. This was no time to act as if I hadn't seen what I'd seen, and said, "Don't do it, Doug."

He walked quickly to the table and slammed down the laptop, mumbling, "That screenplay is private property."

"It's not a screenplay," I said. "It's a suicide note."

"No, it isn't," he said bitterly. "The word *note* implies that someone will actually read it. I don't have anyone who would care enough to do that."

"You have me," I said, feeling my throat tighten. There were gray rings beneath his eyes and he seemed looser and a size smaller, as if part of him had deflated.

He avoided my gaze, saying, "Who the hell are you? My little movie friend?"

"Not movie friend," I said. "Friend, with nothing attached."

"Except sympathy for the fat kid with a brain crammed full of stories about other people's lives," Doug said. "Well, save it for some other loser. I won't need it anymore, and you and everyone else will be better off without me."

"You're wrong," I said, shaking my head.

"No, *you're* wrong!" he screamed, and it was the most life I'd ever heard come roaring out of him. "My parents are divorced, my pothead dad's long gone, and my mom, who lowers a vodka bottle only long enough to tell me what a disappointment I am, is married to some asshole lawyer who hates my fat guts! I have no siblings or friends—nothing except movies, don't you see? I have nothing, and I have everything!"

"No," I said.

"You have great parents!"

"No."

"A brother, a whole family!"

"No!"

"A home where everyone loves you!"

"No, damn it! I don't!" I shouted, and broke into a crying jag that was like a tsunami in its force. It drew Doug back to the surface and he was silent. I wiped my face in my hands, pushed my hair behind my ears, and repeated myself. "Don't do it, Doug."

Quietly, with what sounded like real curiosity, he said, "Why not?"

"Because," I said. "I can't lose another person I care about."

"Who else have you lost?"

"That's my business, Doug," I said, pushing away a stray tear. "That's my life, not yours."

He nodded slowly, studying the floor, and then looked me in the eyes. "You know why I loved that screenplay? The sincerity of the language. It might not be the greatest movie ever made, but Charlie Huckleman believed every word he wrote about nonviolence. There's power in sincerity, Sara Jane. There's real power in words."

He was right—the words I'd read about my family had changed me forever. I said, "What do you want, Doug? If you could have anything, what would it be?"

"I want a life. I want a . . . purpose. Fep Prep used to be my refuge . . ."

"I understand. Really, I do."

"And I want to be left alone so I can figure out what that

purpose is. I just want Billy to stop harassing me forever."

Staring at Doug's sallow face, the edges of his mouth drawn down, I realized that I could help him—I could confront Bully the Kid, let my cold fury flicker and burn, and do what I was born to do. The problem was that I still didn't know if I could summon it, or if cold fury just sort of happened. There was also the issue of Fep Prep—did I want to bring that part of my life here, inside *my* refuge?

And then a familiar lightbulb flickered and buzzed.

I remembered the notebook, my own personal Outfit instruction manual.

It was a loaded weapon, custom made for a situation just like this one.

All I had to do was make a phone call—I remembered one unlisted number in particular—but paused, wondering exactly what kind of force I'd be unleashing. The notebook made it crystal clear that there were no good guys in the Outfit, no thugs with hearts of gold. There were only enforcers who used car batteries and pliers on mopes, and killers who used knives, guns, and Lake Michigan on victims. On the other hand, the notebook's instructions were precise, obviously designed to control its own power and reduce collateral damage. I'd made the decision to use it if necessary, and I couldn't think a situation as dire as this one.

"Will you do me a favor?" I said. "Will you do nothing? For twenty-four hours, don't do a thing."

"What difference will a day make?" Doug said without a trace of hope.

"Exactly," I said. "It's just one more day. Promise me? As a friend?"

He was looking at the ground, pursing his lips, and when his head began to nod, I stepped forward and wrapped my arms around him. He didn't cry, just put his head on my shoulder, and I felt his magnetic, overdue need to be embraced.

I was wrong about a hug.

It's not commonplace or benign.

It sounds like a silly bumper sticker, but a hug can keep a person alive.

THE PHONE CALL was awkward, phlegmy, and weird, but at least it was short.

After school I headed south on Lake Shore Drive, past the museums, past Soldier Field, doubling back in case I was being followed, and I left sunshine behind as I slid down the ramp to Lower Wacker Drive. It's a subterranean boulevard following the same route as Upper Wacker Drive—in effect, a double-decker street designed decades ago to help regulate traffic. There's a third level that goes even deeper underground (my dad refers to it as "*Lowest* Wacker Drive") but today I stayed on the second level. Lower Wacker is punctuated with nooks and crannies, abandoned loading docks and forgotten turnarounds, while the Chicago River meanders past only a dozen feet away. A car can pull into one of those shadowy spots and disappear not only from traffic but daylight itself. I found a dark little corner, eased the Lincoln to a stop, and got out. The river inched by on the other side of a low chain-link fence—the perfect place to make a call without a chance of being seen or overheard—and I dialed the number from the notebook. It started with someone hacking on the other end, really working something out from the back of his throat, and then a voice like wet gravel said, "BabyLand."

I rechecked the number—it was correct—and then read the password. "Uh . . . Saint Valentine is a friend of mine?"

There was a pause and the voice said, "Be at the Green Mill in an hour."

"Where's the Green Mill?"

The answer was a wet cough with a slurp at the end, then he barked, "What, you ain't got a map?" and hung up. I stared at the phone, which felt infected in my hand, silently thanked Al for dozens more, and whipped it into the river.

An hour later, after consulting an actual phone book, I stood in front an old-time cocktail lounge where green neon announced THE GREEN MILL. I pushed through the door and the bright afternoon was swallowed up in barroom gloom. The bar stretched from the front door all the way back and then made a sharp left and kept going. Tiny booths lined the wall, ancient sconces oozed pink light, and a bandstand stood empty at the back of the room. The bartender, bent over a newspaper, looked up at me disinterestedly and went back to the page. There were only two other people, a large broken-nose-looking guy on a stool staring hard into a glass of something brown and an old man parked at the bar in one of those golf cart–wheelchair things called a Scamp. My bet was on the broken nose, so I approached and said quietly, "Are you him?"

"No," he said, picking up his glass. "I'm drunk."

"Hey, Einstein," the wet gravelly voice said. It was the old man in the Scamp, and he dipped his head at me. I walked down the bar and he said, "Take a load off."

I climbed a barstool and looked around. "Can I be in here?"

He took a greasy fedora from his head, removed a previously lit, disgustingly chewed cigar from its band, and said, "How old are you?"

"Sixteen."

He snapped a match and lit the turd, blowing smoke through ancient yellow teeth. "Jesus. You're younger than the other one."

"Which other one?"

"Don't worry about it," he said, breaking into a coughing fit that shook his bulky frame like he was enjoying his own personal earthquake. I noticed then that he was even older than I thought, and a lot bigger. The hands he used to cover his mouth were as large as catcher's mitts, the knuckles like red, broken walnuts. His face was mapped with a scar that began above his left eyebrow, traveled across the bridge of his nose, and ended just past his bottom lip. All in all, from the sickly pale skin to the pinkie ring the size of a meatball to the Sansabelt slacks and Velcro sneakers, he was pretty creepy to look at, much less talk to. When he'd cleared his lungs, he took another deep drag and said, "So who the hell are you and how'd you get that number?"

"It doesn't matter where I got it," I said, knowing I'd arrived at a make-or-break moment. Contacting the Outfit via the notebook had been a risk; if the criminal organization had suspected my dad was a rat, they might have been the cause of my family's disappearance. I was aware that as soon I revealed my identity, I'd know what the Outfit knew, and I should be prepared to run for my life. Inhaling a deep breath, exhaling through my nose, I said, "My name is Sara Jane Rispoli and . . ."

"Whoa-whoa," he said, lifting a massive palm and squinting angrily. "Rispoli? *Anthony's* kid?"

I ran my tongue over my braces, working up the nerve, and swallowed once. "I . . . yeah, I am. Is . . . is there a problem?"

"I'll say there's a *problem*!" he barked. "Where the hell's your old man? I been calling and calling, and nothing! He's supposed to broker a thing between me and Strozzini and what, he takes off on a *goddamn* pleasure cruise or something? Who the hell does he think he is, *Mussolini*? And lemme tell you something else about your dad . . ."

He was leaning forward in the cart with his eyes bulging and the scar a deep red. I guess I should've been intimidated, but instead I was relieved—the Outfit was obviously unaware that my family was gone, which meant that it wasn't responsible for their disappearance. On the other hand, it also meant I couldn't ask Knuckles if he knew anything about Ski Mask Guy—there was no credible way to bring up a mysterious freak assassin without raising suspicion. And then I was hit by a speck of Knuckles's stinking hissy-fit cigar-spit, and a cool, clear anger rose up inside. It had been three years since I'd experienced the cold blue flame, but when it began dancing in my gut, it felt as if it had been burning there my whole life. It rose and rose, and I seemed to inhale it into my eyes as I locked onto his and said quietly, "Stop yelling at me, old man."

Something changed in his face; it went pale and slack as he and I shared a stark, vivid scene of the fear that was attacking him.

I saw a metal casket without flowers in a small, cold room. I saw his funeral with no one in attendance but his own empty corpse.

He sat back slowly and whispered, "Yeah," with an involuntary shudder, "you're a Rispoli." He coughed into his fist, displaying a big, creepy hand again, and said, "Dominic Battuta. Call me Knuckles."

The blue flame huffed out and died as fast as it had appeared, and I had no idea what made it jump or where it had gone. All I knew was that it had gotten the old man in line, and that he was looking at me now like a rabbit in the carrot patch, staring at the farmer. "I know who you are. I know you're the VP of Muscle for the Outfit, just like your dad and grandfather before you," I said, repeating my lesson from the notebook.

"Some things are best left in the family. You should appreciate that," he said. "What do you need?"

I was conflicted about what I was about to do, but certain that Doug would hurt himself, or be hurt further by Billy, if I didn't. "Intimidation," I said quietly.

"What kind of intimidation are you looking for?"

"What kind do you offer?"

Knuckles spread his arms wide and said, "On this end, we have mild harassment. On this end, beaten senseless."

"What's in the middle?" I said.

"Crapping his pants."

"Yeah, that one. And I need it done tomorrow. But look . . ."

"Hang on a sec," he said, producing a scrap of paper. He slid on a pair of half-glasses, licked a pencil tip, and scribbled, murmuring, "To . . . morrow. Crapping . . . pants."

"But I don't want you to hurt the guy. Just scare him really badly. The person I'm doing this for is an advocate of nonviolence."

Knuckles looked over the top of his glasses. "Talking to me about nonviolence is like recommending the veggie plate to a lion."

"You have to promise," I said. "Just scare him."

"Okay, fine. No kneecapping. I'll put my scariest man on the job," he said. "But in return, you gotta do something for me."

"What's that?" I said.

Knuckles sighed like a dragon, blowing cigar smoke from his nostrils. He explained how his division was engaged in a bitter dispute with the other major division, Money, about getting paid. It had grown worse in the past several months since the FBI began investigating front businesses, trying to figure out what the Outfit was doing behind all those supposedly legitimate operations. "Like this place. The Green Mill was a front for decades. Supposedly belonged to a hood called 'Machine Gun' Jack McGurn, but Big Al was the real owner."

"Is that right?" I said, looking around for the Capone Door.

"Tell you one thing. Ain't no Feds snooping around BabyLand."

"What's BabyLand?"

"My store. It offers everything for new parents, from clothes to furniture to them weird bags they stuff the kid into and strap to their chest." Knuckles shook his head and said, "What kind of a man would wear that thing?"

"Kid stuff doesn't really match your personality," I said.

"That's the beauty of it. The Feds look at traditional businesses . . . limos, concrete, strip joints . . . but who ever thinks to look behind a baby?" He sucked on the cigar like a pacifier, hacked up smoke, and said, "The problem is StroBisCo. You think it was too damn *huge* to be suspect, but the G-men are even peeking behind Wonder-Fluff Carmel Bars. 'Course, they ain't gonna find nothing. The books have been cooked on Stro-BisCo since day one, you know what I'm saying?"

"Uh, yeah . . . for sure," I said as casually as possible, as if I knew what he was talking about. Fortunately for me, he kept talking, and what I heard was amazing. Everyone on the planet had heard of StroBisCo, since it churned out a majority of the population's junk food. What no one on the planet knew, except for a select few criminal Chicagoans, was that the gigantic corporation was also the Outfit's most important front business. Its complex of factories on the West Side went on for miles, the smokestacks belching out the afterburn of thousands of conveyor-belt crackers, cookies, doughnuts, and anything else that can be packed with sodium or injected with sugar. Its most famous snack is the Wonder-Fluff Carmel Bar, which my dad says contains so many additives that it causes teeth to fall out. According to Knuckles, besides promoting world obesity, StroBisCo was also a massive money-laundering operation for the Outfit—dirty dollars went in one door, were shaked and baked, and came out another door perfectly clean and untraceable. The VP of Money was also the CEO of StroBisCo. In order to avoid suspicion, he was withholding all payments to Outfit members until the Feds quit poring over false payroll ledgers and doctored expenditure sheets.

"VP of Money," I said, remembering what I'd learned from the notebook. "Last name Strozzini?"

Knuckles nodded. "My grandfather hated his great-grandfather, and my father hated his grandfather, and I hate him. I haven't been able to pay my guys in a month, and they're the ones out there doing the heavy lifting and leg breaking."

"But doesn't it make sense? I mean, if the FBI is paying that much attention . . ."

"Ah, it's all BS. Strozzini is holding on to that money just to screw with me. The mutual animosity between the Battuta and Strozzini clans is legendary," Knuckles said, with something like pride. He went on to say how my dad was scheduled to sit down with both men to resolve the situation, and asked me to urge my dad to fulfill his duty as counselor-at-large and do the deal.

"I can't. He's . . . not well."

"He's on a cruise, ain't he, kid?"

"He's not well," I said quietly, locking onto his rheumy eyes while narrowing mine threateningly, as if I could call up the blue flame at will. "In fact, he's so ill we had to close the bakery temporarily."

Knuckles blinked heavily, whispering, "Sorry to hear it. Give him my best." A moment later and a shade paler, he said, "How about you?"

"Me what?"

"Do what your dad does, what Enzo the Baker used to do," he said. "Sit down with me and Strozzini, use your gift or whatever it is, and get my guys paid."

"No, I couldn't. What if he doesn't listen to me?"

"He might not. Doing business with broads isn't exactly an Outfit tradition. On the other hand, you got the Rispoli thing in spades with the eyes." He shivered.

"I don't know . . ."

"Okeydoke," he said, revving the Scamp. "Well, good luck to that nonviolent pal of yours. He'll be fine. Maybe." He touched his hat and rolled toward the door.

"Wait," I sighed. "Okay, I'll do it. But I can't guarantee anything."

Knuckles buzzed in reverse and greeted me with a nauseating display of cigar-stained teeth that was, in theory, a smile. "Club Molasses, right? When?"

"Uh . . . no, not there. My uncle Buddy is doing some odds and ends at the bakery while it's closed. You know, painting and, uh . . . mopping."

"Buddy Rispoli," Knuckles said with a chuckle. "What a schlub."

After all that had happened, the dismissive way he said it affected me strangely—it actually made me a little sad for my uncle. "Why do you say that?" I asked.

"Listen, kid, no offense, okay? Buddy's not a bad guy, he's

just not your dad. Frankly, I never seen such a wannabe in all my life. The guy should stick to mixing batter or rolling dough or whatever it is he does. His own pop, Enzo the Baker, didn't even trust him enough to tell him that Club Molasses existed under his *own fat feet!*" Knuckles guffawed, and then wiped his eyes. "Naw, the Outfit ain't for him."

"Who's it for?"

"A Rispoli like you. Hell, you'd be perfect if you weren't a girl," he said with a wink. "Now then, how about the Bird Cage Club?"

I remembered it from the notebook; it was the other place guarded by Nunzio's rats. "Fine. Where is it?"

"Come on, kid, I ain't got time for this. You know where it is."

"Right. Of course," I said, making a mental note to read up on it.

We talked details a while longer—what I wanted him to do tomorrow, and whom to do it to, when the meeting with Strozzini would occur—and then Knuckles held out a catcher's mitt and showed me those teeth again. "So we got a deal?" he said.

"Deal," I said.

I shook a hand that had busted many bones over the decades.

Those bones were smaller pieces of shattered lives.

I had just agreed to be a part of that sick process, and it broke my heart.

EVERYONE HAS A TALENT, even the most seemingly untalented person, even if it's something that other people wouldn't consider particularly entertaining or useful, like performing an entire opera on a kazoo or flipping an omelet blindfolded.

My sometimes-friend Gina's talent is gossip.

The time had come to deploy the full power of her awesome gift.

I'd asked Doug to wait twenty-four hours until he did anything crazy like hurting himself, and the time was almost up. When the bell rang at the end of first period, I was out the classroom door and down the hallway before it filled with slow-moving loud-talkers, waiting at Gina's locker. I'd made sure to conceal my bruises beneath makeup so her full attention was on what I was about to tell her. Gina's place in the Fep Prep firmament—Gossip Queen—makes her the be-all, end-all of the buzz, dish, and dirt, and I had a juicy morsel now that was (literally) custom made for her.

When she saw me, her incredible gossip ESP kicked in and she said, "Let me guess. Max is going to fight Billy Shniper."

I looked around carefully and then stared at her. "No," I said. "Doug is."

There are few things as sweet as seeing surprise register on Gina's face. Watching her process unexpected information is like watching a great chef experience a new flavor. "When? Where?" she said hungrily. "More importantly . . . how?"

"Don't fool yourself," I said. "Doug has moves."

"Yeah, one toward a bag of Munchitos, the other toward a remote control. Seriously, Sara Jane, is this really going to happen?"

I looked around again, and said, "I swear. Today, right after school. Under the El tracks, behind Bump 'N' Grind. And Gina?"

"Yeah?"

"Doug's a friend of mine, so don't tell anyone, okay? He said that after he breaks Billy's nose . . ."

"He said that?"

"And after he makes Billy get down on his knees and apologize like the little bitch that he is . . ."

"Doug said *that*?"

"Then he just wants to put this whole silly thing behind him and get back to concentrating on his girlfriend. The model. Who lives in Canada." There, I thought, looking at Gina's *O*-mouth, that should do it.

It did it all right.

By last period, the tidbit had spread from kid to kid like flu in a preschool.

Everyone seemed to know about it except Doug, who never talked to anyone.

When the last bell rang, the entire student body flooded out the doors and headed for the grassy patch beneath the El. I'd made a plan with Doug to get an espresso at Bump 'N' Grind after school, and he was waiting for me on the sidewalk, confused at the back pats and "good lucks" being showered on him by kids he didn't know and had never spoken to. "What's that all about?" he said.

"Maybe they just like you," I said as we started walking.

"No one likes me."

"Doug . . ."

"I know, I know," he said, shifting his laptop from one arm to the other. "You do. But I've been thinking about it—I can't stop thinking about it—and it's not enough to . . ."

"Hey! Doug!"

I looked up at Max waiting across the street, hands on hips, angry and concerned, and I realized I'd forgotten to factor him into the plan. "Crap," I mumbled.

"Crap what?" Doug said as we crossed the street. The mosh pit of kids crowding behind Bump 'N' Grind was impossible to miss. "What's going on here?" he said.

"What the hell are you doing?" Max said, stepping in front of Doug.

"Just getting an espresso," he said, taken aback. "Maybe a scone."

"You're going to *fight* Billy Shniper?" Max said.

"What?" Doug said, turning bright pink.

"You are?" I said innocently.

"No. No . . . I would never . . ."

"Hey, chunky!" Billy shouted. Apparently he'd been waiting behind Bump 'N' Grind doing calisthenics or something, warming up for the takedown, and now he came around the corner with his idiot crew in tow. A throng of kids followed, and then it was Billy and his friends on one side and Doug, me, and Max on the other. Billy strutted like a muscle-bound peacock, saying, "Bad-ass versus fat-ass! This is gonna be *awesome*!"

Doug said, "I don't understand what's happening, but I won't fight you."

Billy shrugged. "You don't have to. Just stand there and I'll beat your ass."

Doug looked around at the crowd, processing it, and then back at Billy. "Aim for the head. It'll save me from buying rat poison."

"Huh?" Billy said.

"You're gonna kill me, kill me. Get it over with," Doug said calmly. "What are you, scared? I'm not."

Billy's smile drooped, he looked around at his guys, who were as confused as he was, and turned back to Doug. "What is this, like, some kind of mind game?"

"Hit me!" Doug roared, making Billy and his guys step back. "You effing loser! You effing freak!"

"Doug," I hissed, grabbing his arm, "stop talking. Just . . . wait."

"Wait for what?" he bellowed, and turned on Billy. "Hit me! Kill me! Do it now, you . . . you effing *retard*!"

Billy's face fell when he heard that word. He made a hard red fist and said, "My pleasure," through clenched teeth, but was interrupted by the gentle toot of a car horn. The crowd turned to the curb, where a Fiat older and smaller than my mom's creaked to a halt. It was a tiny Italian car with a tiny Italianate man emerging from it. He was in black from head to toe—black suit, black shoes and shirt—except for his tie, which was white. His black-rimmed glasses magnified his eyes like two dark marbles and were worn beneath an impressive head of white hair. The tune he whistled was carefree and so was he, strolling toward the mosh pit with his tiny hands in his tiny pockets. Watching him approach, I thought, If this is Knuckles's scariest guy, Doug is dead. He stopped a few feet away, took his time surveying the crowd, then raised his black eyebrows and grinned with a mouthful of white Chiclet teeth.

"Yo, Dougy," he said with a dip of his head.

The crowd was silent, a train rumbled overhead, and Doug said, "Me?"

"How's it hanging, buddy boy?"

"Uh . . . fine, I suppose," Doug said, confused. "Listen, I'm not . . ."

The tiny man moved closer and looked up at Billy, inspecting him like he were in a petri dish. "Who's this jag?" he said. "President of the Hitler Youth Club?"

"Something like that. Pardon me, but who are . . . ?"

He shook a box, popped a Tic-Tac, and said, "Listen up, everybody, and get the wax outta your ears. Dougy here is my man, my very best chum, *amico mio numero uno*, you get me? Anyone"—he paused, smiling at Billy—"and by anyone I mean you, Adolf Junior, bullies, teases, touches, taunts, screws with, or looks askance at him, you're gonna have to deal with me."

An empty plastic bag scratched past like a tumbleweed.

Someone coughed quietly.

Far away a siren moaned.

The tiny man raised his arms like a preacher. "Are we square?"

Billy snuffled stupidly and said, "I don't know what that means, but I know it's gonna take a lot more than some old midget to back me off of fatty-pants here. Hell, I'm just getting started!"

"Old midget," the tiny man said, smiling. "Why are guys like you always so dumb? Can't you see I'm a harbinger?"

"A what?" Billy said.

"Harbinger . . . of doom," Doug mumbled as a *shreep* of brakes sounded at the curb. It was an anonymous car, dark and unidentifiable, just like the three guys who slinked out of it. Billy and his well-muscled crew were twice the size of the small, wiry trio, who wore jeans and heavy boots and plain T-shirts, and had biceps like small round rocks under their yellowish skin. They said not a word, just fanned out behind the tiny man. One of them had a tattoo but I can't remember what it was, and I think another wore a ball cap but I can't be sure if it was Cubs or Sox. I would be hard-pressed to pick any of them out of a lineup except to say that they were not big and looked sort of bored, but they smelled dangerous.

Violence crackled in the air, and the tiny man pointed at Billy and said, "Jigsaw puzzle. Small pieces."

"Them"—Billy snorted and then gestured at his 'roid-rage crew—"versus us? Are you serious, midget man?"

I hated to agree with Billy but he seemed to have a point. The three guys looked like second-string ballet dancers, not even mean-looking, just standing there.

"So dumb," the tiny man said, shaking his head. "Boys? You're on the clock."

The first guy moved slowly, like a thin, bored cat, but somehow Billy was on the ground holding his face and screaming while the other two were kicking him all over. There was movement, someone huffed, and one of Billy's friends was in a pile weeping while another held a bloody nose and screamed for help until he got punched in the mouth. It was like a three-man tornado of ass kicking that whipped around Billy and his buddies with no sign of stopping, hypnotizing the crowd with its pure, poetic violence. I sidled up to the tiny man and whispered, "You were only supposed to scare him!"

He nodded politely. "You're the Rispoli, huh?"

"Knuckles promised!"

"One thing you should know about Knuckles: he's a liar," he said, showing me white Chiclet teeth. "We all are. That's why we're in this business, right?"

I looked back at the whirlwind of violence I was responsible for—fists, blood, and teeth—and it made me want to puke. The spectators emitted a collective *huh-huh-huh!* howl, like a capacity crowd at a cow-butchering contest. I walked away quickly, hustling toward the Lincoln, and heard my name called as I rounded a corner.

"What did you do?" Doug said in a tone that was pure accusation.

"I don't know what you're talking about," I said, and kept walking.

"Who are those guys? You were talking to the little one, I saw you!"

"Go away, Doug," I said, anxious to be alone, away from the scene. "Go home and don't kill yourself, okay?"

"Back there, before he showed up, you told me to wait!" Doug said, grabbing my arm and spinning me around. "You knew he was coming!"

I shot a finger in his face as fast as I throw a left and said, "At least you could say thank you!" The car keys were in my hand, and then I was in the car gunning the engine, and Doug threw himself in the passenger seat as I squealed away from the curb.

"It wasn't your place!" he shouted. "I'm against violence!"

"Oh, shut the hell up, Doug, you big girl!" I screamed, roaring onto Ashland Avenue. "I am too, but it happened! It's not like they're going to kill him . . ."

"Kill him?!"

"And now Billy will never bother you again! No one will! You'll have all the space you need to figure out the mysterious destiny of Doug Stuffins!"

"It wasn't your place! You have no right!" he said, but his voice faded and my view through the windshield narrowed as my windpipe quit working. I was choking, something biting into the skin at my neck, and I smelled putrid meat before looking into the rearview mirror at the same plastic devil mask from Cinco de Mayo leaning over the backseat. The wire Ski Mask Guy was killing me with was digging into my throat. I couldn't make a sound while Doug gazed out the window, sighed, and said, "Life is so unfair," as I cranked the wheel. I smashed into a parked van on the left, sending pedestrians scattering like cockroaches hiding under a refrigerator. Doug screamed, and I did it again, this time crushing the side of a sluggish bus on the right, its passengers pressing their shocked faces against windows. Ski Mask Guy slid from side to side but his grip only tightened. Doug saw him and went mute, squeezing himself into the corner.

"You're next, chub-bub!" Ski Mask Guy squealed in his schoolmarm voice.

I pressed the gas pedal to the floor, speed and motion my only defense. It was the second time the maniac had tried to choke me to death and this time it was working—this time I had no Harry, only Doug, and he was a gaping frozen meatball. I whipped the car back and forth, sideswiping a Toyota and crushing the mirror of a minivan. Ski Mask Guy's grip slipped and I gasped, "Doug! Do something!"

"Fatso ain't gonna do *nothing*!" Ski Mask Guy cackled. "He's just watching!"

"Watching," Doug muttered. "Not doing." And he lifted the laptop and swung it hard against Ski Mask Guy's head. When the freak sprang back, Doug hit him again, shouting, "Let her go, you son of a bitch!" And he did, slamming a shoulder against the back door and tumbling from the car.

Doug's laptop flew out too, shattering into a million pieces against the pavement. I could breathe, but barely, and looked into the empty backseat, where the devil mask grinned slyly up at me.

I gaped into the rearview mirror as Ski Mask Guy rolled to his belly and his head popped up.

I caught a glimpse of a face that was melted.

It was branded with a reverse R, just like the cake pans from Rispoli & Sons.

And then I told Doug everything.

I told him about the scene at my house, and my family that had now been missing for more than two whole weeks.

I talked about Uncle Buddy, Ski Mask Guy, Detective Smelt, and Club Molasses.

I explained the Outfit, ghiaccio furioso, and especially the notebook.

At the end, I sat back against the driver's seat and closed my eyes, waiting for the disbelief, the questions about my sanity, maybe a polite query about possible drug use.

Except Doug believed me.

He believed every word I said.

In fact, out of the six and a half billion people who populate the earth, Doug Stuffins was precisely the right person to believe me. He had spent his life memorizing, internalizing, and vicariously living through stories on film that were as unbelievable as mine, and even more so, and they were alive to him just as mine was now. If I had told him Ski Mask Guy was a carjacker, Doug would have scoffed, but explaining that he was an insane masked assassin trying to kill me for an Outfit instruction manual that I found in a steel briefcase hidden inside a buried speakeasy was completely believable.

We were parked at the Superdawg Drive-In, and Doug stared at the demonic mask in his hands, saying quietly, "It all makes sense now."

"What does?" I croaked, holding ice against my neck.

"Like you said, my destiny . . . what I was born to do and meant to become."

"Who?"

Doug turned to me with a look of certainty. "The sidekick."

"The what?"

"The sidekick. Robin to Batman. Doctor Watson to Sherlock Holmes. Tom Hagen to Michael Corleone . . ."

"Whoa, wait a minute," I said, sitting up.

"Don't you see?" Doug said. "I've been writing my life all wrong. I cast myself as the hero when I'm actually the loyal and able wingman with a quick mind and the intellectual resources, i.e., a brain brimming with movies, to help solve any problem."

"Doug, this isn't a movie . . ."

"I know it's not. It's real life, finally."

"It's too dangerous."

"I can help you. I *need* to help you," he said, his words both a promise and a plea.

The idea of help was so foreign to me, so utterly unavailable, that I had forgotten how badly I yearned for it. There was nothing adventurous about the bloody web I was caught in, nothing exciting about the black void my family had disappeared into. I was trapped all alone inside my reality and had ceased hoping that it would ever be any different. But now Doug was offering to pierce that sick bubble and join me. I doubted that he could help—I doubted that anyone could help me besides myself—but I didn't want to be alone anymore. "You can't tell Max anything."

"I won't, I swear."

"As long as I'm confessing, I . . . I think I might love him. Maybe."

"Yeah," Doug sighed. "Me too."

There was a pause between us, and I glanced at Doug inspecting the devil mask. "Doug . . . are you gay?"

"I don't know yet. I might be," he said. "Age sixteen totally sucks when it comes to absolutes."

"But you just said you love Max. That sounded pretty absolute."

"No I didn't. I said 'me too,' in agreement with your 'maybe.' What I meant is that I have a somewhat murky and as yet undefined feeling for him."

"But you also like him as a friend, right?"

"Of course! You and Max are my . . . ," and he stopped before saying "only friends," and stared at the floor. When he looked up, there was certainty in his eyes, and he said, "If I were the sidekick, do you know what my advice would be?"

"What?"

"That it's time to confront your enemies. You've been chased enough," he said. "Remember when we watched *Shane*? How Alan Ladd finally straps on his six-shooter and faces down the bad guys who have been giving the innocent farm family shit for two hours? Remember *The Pope of Greenwich Village* with Mickey Rourke?"

"And Eric Roberts," I said, seeing what he was leading to.

"At the end, Mickey Rourke walks into the mob boss's private club and tells him to go bite himself because there's nothing else he can do. But at least it's something."

I thought of Uncle Buddy at my house and Detective Smelt at Twin Anchors.

They didn't know where I was but I knew where they were.

Just like that, Doug had given me an idea.

Maybe Batman was onto something with the whole sidekick thing.

THE MORNING OFFICIALLY BEGAN with sunlight tiptoeing through the caged windows of the warehouse, throwing crisscross shadows on the cement floor, but by then I'd been up for hours. Waking early is what I do and who I've become out of fear and necessity. My brain, which clicks off at night like a low battery and pops back on when it's recharged, is especially active at the very start of a day. Conscious while the rest of the world sleeps, I make decisions, filter facts, and steel my gut for what lies ahead.

Today I began at four a.m.

I did a hundred push-ups on the cold floor and a hundred sit-ups.

Afterward I cracked the notebook, searching for guidance.

First I learned that the Bird Cage Club, where I was scheduled to meet Knuckles and his counterpart, Strozzini, was located at the very top of an old skyscraper in the Loop, on the thirty-third floor. It provided a general location (but oddly, no address) and a warning—never enter through the main entrance, only through a Capone Door hidden in the adjoining barbershop. Next, I studied the chapter titled "*Loro*—Them," which explained in detail the many different groups regarded as a threat to the Outfit and how to avoid or neutralize them. It includes sections on the police ("Bribing a Cop"), the FBI ("Planting a Mole"), methods to avoid prison sentences ("Feigning Insanity and Faking Cancer"), dealing with rats ("Dead"), and on and on. Each section echoed Doug's advice—when all else fails, take the fight to *loro*—them.

At seven a.m. I was parked down the street from my house.

Balmoral Avenue was deserted and the streetlights buzzed off.

The .45 was freshly loaded and I flicked the safety on.

The homes on my street are too tall and far apart to travel from roof to roof, like at the bakery. Cutting through the backyard meant an exposed patch of grass, and besides, there was no way I was going through those dark cellar doors again. In the end, there were no safe options to approaching the house—it was all risky—so I lifted the gun, crossed the street, and walked up to the front door. I was prepared to kick it off its hinges and enter swinging, but there was no need—it pushed open easily. I hadn't been inside my home since I'd fled from Ski Mask Guy in the pouring rain. Now I had a gun, and more than that, a dangerously low tolerance for bullshit. Uncle Buddy and Greta had taken over our house—*our damn house!*—and they were now going to tell me everything they knew about my family, or else. Any anxiety I'd felt about shooting that freak had vanished like smoke up a chimney.

I entered imitating a cop flick, looking left to right with the .45 raised in both hands, and froze.

What I saw was a funhouse déjà vu of the last time I walked through the door—complete disarray—except that there were no longer any signs of violence. The shades were drawn, curtains pulled, and the odor of old socks and dead cigarettes was pervasive. Yawning pizza boxes and greasy carryout cartons competed with crushed beer cans and empty liquor bottles, with ashtrays overflowing on every surface.

Just like last time, noise cut through the gloom.

It was clearly a voice; talking, stopping, repeating itself.

There was desperation in it, and it was on TV.

I walked over to the big flat screen where I'd watched so many movies with my family and recognized the scene immediately—one man, lanky and drawn, spread out on a chaise lounge, raging helplessly at a smaller, darker man who stood by watching coolly. The DVD was stuck, playing over and over again, with the man on the chaise saying, "I'm your older brother, I was stepped over! . . . I'm your older brother, I was stepped over! . . . I'm your older brother, I was stepped over! . . ."

I lifted the remote control and pushed a button, the scene went forward, and the smaller man said quietly, "It's the way Pop wanted it."

The lanky man clawed at the air around him, jittery and pissed, saying, "It wasn't the way I wanted it! I can handle things! I'm not dumb, Christ, like everyone says! I'm smart . . . and I want respect!"

That scene in *The Godfather, Part II,* is the reckoning

between the younger brother, who has taken control of the Mafia, and his older brother, who was passed by—the exact opposite of my dad's and Uncle Buddy's relationship. There was a stink of fantasy to it, as if my uncle had been obsessively staring at what he hoped for. I turned it off and the screen went black, further darkening the room. In the sudden quiet I heard the *tink* of cutlery. I checked the gun and moved toward the kitchen door, which I opened silently to Uncle Buddy sitting alone at the table, shoveling cereal into his unshaven face. A box of Froot Loops sat to his right, a half-drunk bottle of vodka to his left, and a burning cigarette in an ash-packed coffee cup before him. I pointed the gun at him and the motion drew his attention. He looked up, bleary-eyed, and said, "Greta left me."

I held the kill-shot position just like I'd seen in movies, uttering the only thing that occurred to me. "Greta's smarter than I thought."

Uncle Buddy nodded slowly. "I deserve that," he muttered, in a voice that was sincere and bitter and completely wasted. "I ruined it. I ruin everything."

"Where are my parents and Lou?"

"You know what Greta told me before she took off? She said, 'Even if you *had* gotten your hands on that notebook, you would have *screwed it up!*' She spit at me and said, 'Your old man and your brother were *right*, Benito . . . you were born to mix dough!'" He took a swig of vodka and said, "So, anyway. At least she gave me the ring back. I wonder where I put it . . ."

"Uncle Buddy," I said, feeling the blue flame flicker and

ignite, filling me from the pit of my stomach to the tip of my brain with a cold fury that strongly advised a bullet to his booze-blasted skull. The ghiaccio furioso was so powerful and alive that it threatened to take me over completely, sending sharp little electrical volts to urge on my trigger finger. Maybe it was because I'd once loved Uncle Buddy and now hated him, or because the terror he'd caused me now seemed so small and cowardly, but this time I held on to the cold fury and focused it behind my eyes, controlling it rather than being controlled by it. I said it again, "Uncle Buddy," and when he looked up at me, what he saw looking back registered on his puffy face in an awful way.

"No, please," he said, shaking his head. "Not you too."

"Where are they?" I said, moving toward him. He shrunk back into the chair, cowering, until I was standing over him. "Look at me," I said. "Look at me right now and tell the truth. You don't have a choice."

"I don't know," he mumbled at the table. "That dog, what's-his-name . . ."

"Harry?"

"He was here, hanging around, like he was waiting for Lou."

Or me, I thought, and I'd suddenly had enough of this mumblefest. I grabbed a handful of greasy hair and yanked it back until his unwilling eyes, wide and wet, locked on mine. "Where are they?" I said, so calmly that it sounded dead to my own ears.

He stared at me, and I saw what he feared most.

It was himself, not old and alone, but worse—young and alone.

It was Uncle Buddy, not hated, but forgotten.

He paused, jaw trembling, and said, "I swear I don't know where they are! I swear to God!"

"What about the government? Did my dad make some kind of deal?" I said, remembering Uncle Buddy's confrontation with him, how he'd implied that he had spied on my father's voice- and e-mail.

Uncle Buddy was crumbling under my gaze, looking paler and more translucent by the second. His mouth was wet and sloppy when he said, "I picked up the other line at the bakery. There was a woman on the phone, real official sounding, saying something to your dad about 'coming in safely' and 'guaranteed anonymity.' And the letter . . . the letter was just a list of towns and cities . . ."

"Where we could relocate," I said to myself.

"But the government?" Uncle Buddy stammered. "The government doesn't take in witnesses by tearing apart a house like I found this place." He was shaking now, sucking air like a beached whale, and said, "Please . . . I don't know anything."

"You know about the notebook," I said, feeling frost on my tongue.

"My pop and Anthony, they used to have this weird language, like a pig Latin that wasn't English and only sort of Italian," he said, swallowing thickly. "They'd use it when they didn't want me to know what they were talking about. Except one time, right before my pop died, I was hiding in the broom closet. And I overheard him and Anthony talking about it in plain old Italian, explaining that it contains *potenza ultima* . . . ultimate power."

"What does that mean? Ultimate power?"

"I don't know!" he cried. "Anthony was telling my pop he wanted nothing to do with it! But whatever it was, *I wanted it!* Oh God, I wanted it so badly!"

"So badly that you turned on us, even though we loved you," I said. "You took over our home. You tried to take over our lives."

Uncle Buddy stared with his mouth open and then said softly, "I wanted what Anthony has. Not just a family and a home, but power . . . what you have . . . the ghiaccio furioso. I thought the notebook would . . . that maybe it could . . ." And he paused, licking at his dry lips. I let him go and he slumped back, whispering, "I still want it."

"What about Detective Smelt?" I said. "What about the freak in the ski mask?"

"I don't know about any cop or freak. I'm the only freak I know." Something clicked in his muddled mind, and he said, "Sara Jane . . . are you in danger?"

It was the first time I laughed in weeks.

The sound of it rolling from my mouth was strange to me.

There was no joy in it, only tired irony.

I wiped at my eyes and looked around the kitchen at filthy dishes, scummy counters, and molding food. The line of blood where Harry dragged himself into the basement was still there, dried brown on the tile floor. My uncle, who had once been my buddy but was now my personal Judas, took a swig of vodka and said, "Whoever they are, it must have been my pop's death that brought them out of the woodwork."

It was the first relevant insight he had. "Go on," I said.

"That means they must have Outfit connections. My pop was 'Enzo the Baker,' 'Boss,' and 'Biscotto' to the mob, but to the rest of the world he was just a little Italian pastry maker down the block."

Following his line of thought, I said, "Only someone who knew Grandpa was counselor-at-large would have known my dad was next in line, and that he would inherit the notebook."

"Next in line, yeah. Notebook, I'm not so sure," he said. "I didn't even know it existed until I overheard Pop talking about it. I finally confronted your dad . . ."

"At Grandpa's funeral," I said, remembering my dad dropping Uncle Buddy with a lightning left hook.

He rubbed his jaw absently. "Your dad admitted it existed. He told me Nunzio started it, Pop continued it, Anthony added to it, and that it was a Rispoli family secret, full of secrets. He was clear that no one else in the Outfit knows about it."

"Unless someone does," I said. "Who would it be, if someone did?"

"I don't know," he said. "Like I said before, I don't know anything."

"Uncle Buddy, look at me," I said, and when he did, he winced in pain but was unable to turn away. "Who would it be?"

"I . . . I don't know," he said. "Please believe me!"

Actually, I did. As he gaped up at me, I saw Uncle Buddy for what he was—a two-bit schemer who, through bitter jealousy, had helped tear my family apart. I was gripped by a pity that was equal to my anger, and I pushed him away, taking a final look around. "I'm leaving now. Either clean this place up or burn it down."

"No, wait!" he said, lunging for me, grabbing at my arm. "I can help you, Sara Jane! Give me the notebook! If that's what they're after, I'll be the target! Please!"

"Let go, Uncle Buddy," I said, trying to pull away.

"Give it to me, goddamn it!" he shouted, tightening his grip and rising from the chair. "I want it! I *need* it! It's my goddamn turn! It's my—" And before he could tell me what else was his, I spun and cracked the gun against the side of his skull.

Uncle Buddy sat heavily in the chair and went face-first into his Froot Loops.

I lifted his head out of the bowl so he wouldn't drown in sticky milk.

I hate him and hope I never see him again, but after all, he is my uncle.

SO NOW I KNEW that Detective Smelt and Ski Mask Guy were somehow Outfit connected. But I also knew (with Uncle Buddy as a prime example) that a connection doesn't make a person *part* of the Outfit.

As counselor-at-large, I was learning that, besides being a violent criminal organization, the Outfit was also a gossip factory that put Gina Pettagola to shame. The most hardened thugs whispered cattily about one another and to one another like a bunch of gun-toting grandmothers. If the people that mattered within the Outfit knew what Detective Smelt and Ski Mask Guy knew—that my family was gone—there's no way the word wouldn't have gotten around and that I, a Rispoli, would have been allowed to serve as counselor-at-large, much less exist with legs unbroken, or worse. By now, I was chillingly aware of what happened to suspected rats and their suspected rat children. Whatever knowledge or inside information that Smelt and Ski Mask Guy had gained, whatever their ultimate goal, they were not operating inside the organization. What I didn't know was how that connection had been made; how did they learn about the existence of the notebook?

And then I faced another equally puzzling question.

What exactly does one wear to a Mafia sit-down?

I went conservative in all black—skirt, blouse, boots—and at ten until noon on an overcast Saturday stood outside an ancient skyscraper.

CURRENCY EXCHANGE BUILDING was etched in stone over the entrance, with the year it was built, 1926.

It was tall, thin, sooty, and smudged, its general neglect indicating that no currency had been exchanged there in a very long time.

For fine arts class at Fep Prep, we took a tour of architecturally significant buildings in the Loop and learned that Chicago was the birthplace of the skyscraper. Structural steel allowed buildings to climb high into the sky, just as the Currency Exchange Building did, far beyond the El tracks that nearly touched the old building's filthy façade. Many old Chicago structures had been renovated to perfection, but the one I stared at now seemed to have been forgotten. Maybe it was the building's location—jammed into a crowded and not beautiful stretch of Wells Street between Washington and Madison with the train rumbling past, fat purple pigeons pecking at litter, and people rushing by without even seeing it. And then I realized that was the point—it was right there, hiding in plain sight—and I noticed something odd. The address of the building on one side was Forty-Three North Wells and the address on the other side was Forty-Five North Wells, but the Currency Exchange Building, squeezed between them, had no address at all.

Yep, I thought, this has got to be the place.

I remembered the instruction to avoid the main entrance and enter through an adjoining barbershop. It must have been an out-of-date entry in the notebook; the business next door was a shabby carryout with a pigeon-crapped awning that read PHUN HO—TO GO! I entered a cramped space with a bored-looking guy in a greasy apron staring at something Asian on TV. I tried the women's room door but it was locked, so I approached the counter.

"Excuse me," I said. "May I use the restroom?"

Without looking away from the TV, the guy threw a thumb over his shoulder.

A sign tacked to the wall read NO PAY. NO PEE.

A few minutes later I was in possession of a bag of egg rolls and a key. I paused, remembering being chased by cops at the North Avenue Beach House, and how I would've been screwed if I had chosen the women's shower. It didn't seem to have occurred to Joe Little, the inventor of the Capone Doors, that a woman would ever need to use one. The counter guy wasn't watching, so I slipped into the men's, which contained a sink and an old-time porcelain urinal. I looked closely at its faded logo—Chicago Hygienic Inc.—with the *C* in "Chicago" slightly raised. I wasn't thrilled about touching it, so I used a paper towel, gave it a push, and the porcelain *pissoire* slid smoothly sideways, revealing a dimly lit alcove. I stepped inside, hearing the urinal *thunk* back into place. Before me hung a steel elevator cage that looked as if it had been hewn from black lace. It had three buttons—Up, Down, and Garage. Figuring a place called the "Bird Cage Club" had to be up, I pushed that button. Something clanked and whirred, and I rose skyward. I was almost there when I heard a thick wet cough above me, the elevator stopped, and through the cage I saw Knuckles in his Scamp.

"Welcome to the Bird Cage Club," he hacked. "Best views in the city."

I stepped into a circular room, which must have been the dome of the building. The beams were constructed of the same black, spidery steel as the elevator. The round walls, which were all glass, displayed incredible views of the Loop and far beyond, all the way to the lake. A bar clad in black leather stood against a wall, but there was no other furniture. The floor was made of white octagon tiles, and besides a large, round, raised platform in the center of the room, it contained nothing but Knuckles and me.

Or so I thought.

I heard someone else clear his throat politely.

I looked over at a man with his back to me, and my heart punched my chest when he turned and smiled.

He had thick black hair and deep green eyes, skin the color of smooth copper, and thick black eyebrows that arced when he saw me. He was as tall as Max, with broad shoulders that fit perfectly into a tailored suit, and his smile was warm and confident. More surprisingly, he was barely older than me. There was something familiar about him and I couldn't help myself, I said, "You . . . look like that actor, from that movie . . . he was a pirate, I think."

"You too," he said, inspecting me with the same intensity. "Not a pirate, I mean. No, you look just like . . ."

"A young Sophia Loren," Knuckles said, lighting a cigar. "I noticed it right off. Except maybe around the nose area. You got a little extra real estate there, kid."

"Actually, you're better looking than her," he said with a smile, and my heart punched me again. "So you're her? The Rispoli?"

"Sara Jane," I said, my tongue feeling thick and dopey.

"Tyler," he said, taking my hand. "Tyler Strozzini. Sorry to hear your dad is sick, but it's cool to meet you."

"What kind of an Italian kid is called Tyler?" Knuckles mumbled.

"This from a guy who derives his nickname from finger parts," Tyler said, grinning. "The answer is, a kid who's half Italian and half African American." He turned to Knuckles and said, "That probably didn't fly in your day, huh, old man?"

"The Outfit has always been an equal opportunity organization," Knuckles said primly. "Except for broads, of course."

"Sorry if I'm being rude," I said. "But aren't you a little young to be VP of Money for the Outfit *and* the CEO of StroBisCo?"

"I'm seventeen. How old are you?"

"Sixteen."

"And yet here you are." He smiled. "How did that happen?"

"Just . . . odd circumstances," I said.

"Same with me," Tyler said. "My dad held both positions before me, and my grandfather before him. I knew I was next in line, I just didn't think it would happen so soon. But then my parents were killed in a plane piloted by my dad. He was a really skilled flier, had logged thousands of hours. But, to use your term," he said, shooting Knuckles a look that was unfiltered hatred, "they crashed under odd circumstances."

"Real tragedy," Knuckles murmured. "Then again, your old man was even slower paying my guys than you are." He looked at his hands, whistling and inspecting his crusty old nails.

The bad blood between them was so thick that it smothered the conversation.

Tyler turned to the window to cool off, and Knuckles continued his cuticle exam.

I realized then that Tyler and I were members of an unusual and exclusive club—we were Outfit kids. Although I'd only recently learned of the organization, it was undeniable that the Outfit was woven into my personal history and DNA. Doug accepted the existence of the Outfit, and the reality of my surreal life, from a dramatic and historical perspective. But Tyler lived it. Yeah, he was cute—my heart did mini backflips when he looked at me with those green eyes—and if anyone could offer me guidance on how to live two separate lives, it was him. I would never tell anyone that my family was missing, the danger was simply too great, but if circumstances were different, Tyler was the one person who would understand what I was going through.

He broke the silence, saying, "So, your dad ever bring you up here?"

"Uh . . . the Bird Cage Club, you mean? No . . . he didn't."

"Kept it a secret, huh? Just like my old man used to do . . .

always held something back, just in case." He grinned slyly, showing perfect teeth, and said, "Did you even know about it? Your great-grandfather Nunzio took a hundred-year lease on it from my great-grandfather. It's not up for another ten years or so."

I wondered then if my dad had even been aware of the lease; it was completely possible that Grandpa Enzo kept it from him, just like my dad had kept secrets from me. Or even that Nunzio had kept it from Enzo for some reason. I cleared my throat and said, "Not until he got sick and I stepped in as counselor-at-large. Then he told me everything about . . . everything."

Tyler grinned again, sadly instead of sly. "My dad never had a chance to tell me anything but the basics about the Outfit and our place in it. I didn't even know we owned this building until after my parents died."

"You own the entire building?"

Tyler nodded. "It was the original front for Money. My great-grandfather had the brilliant idea of letting the working people of Chicago launder the Outfit's profits, so he opened currency exchanges all over the city. Filthy dollars were traded for sparkling new greenbacks, one utility bill, money order, and city sticker at a time."

"There's a currency exchange on every block," I said.

"The money laundry was consolidated under StroBisCo in the seventies," he said. "Currency exchanges are a still a rip-off, though."

"Remember me, kids?" Knuckles said through a haze of smoke. "We gonna deal or not?"

"So where do you go to school?" Tyler asked.

"Fepinsky Prep. How about you?"

"Newton Minow Academy. I graduate next month."

"Cool, you must be excited. Where are you going to college?"

"Hello? Anyone?" Knuckles said.

"Local . . . University of Chicago. Majoring in economics," Tyler said. "Gotta mind the family business."

"Makes sense," I said. "I haven't even started thinking about college yet."

"Do you want to go away?"

"Yeah, I think so."

"Won't your boyfriend be upset?" he asked, smiling again.

"What the hell's going on here?" Knuckles demanded.

"Boyfriend?" I said, thinking of the dance where Max and I didn't dance, of the movie we didn't see together, and worst of all, how he called me his (ugh) friend on the phone at the Commodore Hotel. "I guess . . . I'm not really seeing anyone. Officially," I said.

"Me neither," he said with a grin. "Not officially."

"Enough!" Knuckles thundered, bringing down a catcher's mitt on the edge of the Scamp hard enough to split metal. "Are we gonna resolve this thing or not?"

"What?" Tyler said, still looking at me. "Oh, you mean the payroll thing? Uh, what do you think, Sara Jane?"

I shrugged and said, "I think Knuckles is right. You should pay his guys."

"Okay," Tyler said. "I will."

"Huh?" Knuckles said. "You will?"

Tyler turned to Knuckles and said, "The counselor-at-large says yes, so yes."

And then we talked for a little while longer, Tyler explaining how the big round empty thing in the floor used to hold an enormous lightbulb that could be seen for miles from the top of the building, how the Bird Cage Club had been one of Chicago's most popular speakeasies during Prohibition—and then he asked if he could call me sometime.

I was unable to explain that not much was happening between Max and me, but that I hoped it would. My heart definitely belonged to Max—still, I'd be lying to say that Tyler's attention hadn't gotten to me a little. It felt strangely good to be known as Sara Jane Rispoli, Outfit Somebody, rather than Fep Prep Nobody, and to be attractive to a guy who looked like Tyler Strozzini. I guess that's why I hesitated; instead of telling him that calling me probably wasn't a good idea, I explained that I was between phones, which was true. Tyler winked and said no problem, that getting in touch with untouchables was his specialty.

Something occurred to me, hearing that word—untouchables.

I couldn't remain in the warehouse safe house forever; metal cages on the windows aside, if someone really wanted to get his hands on me, it wouldn't be impossible. I thought then of how tough it had been to reach the Bird Cage Club—without knowledge of Capone Doors, it would've been impossible—and that twenty-seven floors in the air with only one way in and out made it the perfect hideout. I tried on my own smile and said, "By the way, my dad . . . he wondered if you had an extra set of keys by any chance? He misplaced his."

"For you," Tyler said, rummaging his pocket, coming up with a key chain, and removing one key, "anything." As I took it from him, he held my hand and gave it the same kind of squeeze Max had. "By the way," he said, nodding toward Knuckles but holding my gaze, "ignore what the senior citizen said about your nose. It's perfect." And then he turned and climbed on the elevator, waved as the doors closed, and my heart ached a little.

"Beware," Knuckles said, relighting the cigar. "He's a sneaky little bastard. He'll use anyone and anything to get a leg up."

"In what way?"

"In every way. That's why he's so good at his job." He exhaled smoke through his nostrils, smiled like a corpse, and said, "You're about to become a very busy girl. When this gets around the Outfit, how you convinced Money to come across with my payroll? Thugs will be lining up for you to settle their disputes with that gift of yours."

That was the thing. I hadn't used the ghiaccio furioso. I used another power I didn't even know I had, and it made me blush thinking about it. I said, "No way. It's not my responsibility."

"Whose is it? Your dad's, who's inconveniently under the weather? Or on a cruise? Or perhaps," he said, squinting suspiciously, "somewhere else?"

"I told you, he's ill."

"I know, I know . . . so ill you had to close the bakery," he said in the same mocking tone he'd used to call Tyler's parents' death a "real tragedy." Knuckles leaned over the handlebars of the Scamp and said, "I just want to remind you that we all have a boss . . . me, Strozzini, and your dad. And not just any boss . . . the boss of bosses. If your dad's duties go unful-filled, you can bet Lucky will start asking questions."

I don't know why it hadn't occurred to me—of course there had to be someone in charge of the Outfit, its CEO, just like Frank Nitti had been so long ago. I swallowed thickly and said, "Remind me again why he's called Lucky?"

"You'll know if you meet him. Thing is, you don't want to meet him. The rare instances when Lucky himself whistles someone in is when the old man has serious questions," Knuckles said, leaning forward in his Scamp. "And woe be it to the poor S.O.B. who doesn't have the right answers."

Maybe Knuckles knew something and maybe he didn't, but I understood his meaning clearly—if business did not proceed as usual, the Outfit would make it its business to find out why. And if it turned out that my dad really had gone to the Feds, I wouldn't be able to run fast enough or far enough to save my own life. I stared at the old man who had been around for-ever, who went back so far in the Outfit that he had known Nunzio. I was sure he was full of answers to the questions I was dying to ask—like, for example, why had Nunzio taken out a hundred-year lease on the Bird Cage Club? But I couldn't—I had to pretend I knew everything.

"Yeah, okay, I can handle it," I said, remembering my dad's words from long ago. "I can handle anything."

"I have no doubt," Knuckles said. "That's why I need an-other favor. A couple animals that work for me, both first-rate knee-crackers, are about to kill each other over a broad. I can't afford to lose either, so you gotta talk to them, set them straight."

"Okay," I said, thinking of Detective Smelt. "Then I need a favor from you."

"*Una mano lava l'altra.* One hand washes the other," Knuckles said with a grin and extended a catcher's mitt. "You know, kid, we work well together."

"I guess we do," I said.

We shook on it and, to misquote one of Doug's favorite movies, *Casablanca*, it looked like the beginning of an ugly friendship.

THERE ARE TWO TYPES of people in the world: those who enjoy eating barbecued ribs and those who are turned off by gnawing on pig bones covered in goop.

The Twin Anchors Restaurant & Tavern has a long, storied history of serving the former. Pork ribs have been its bread and butter for eighty years, including the period during Prohibition when it was a speakeasy, providing patrons with Chicago-made moonshine in soda pop bottles. Decades ago, Frank Sinatra loved the joint, as did every notable Outfit member, and sometimes they found themselves at the same table with him, and sometimes Grandpa Enzo was at that table too. Remembering that it was Detective Smelt's hangout of choice, plus her possible Outfit connections, led me back to the notebook, where I learned all of this and more. Apparently, Grandpa Enzo even bought a piece of the business from its owner, someone named Roberto, whose last name isn't supplied. It doesn't tell what happened next, only that my grandpa eventually sold his piece, and that was that.

The notebook mentions that the Twin Anchors has a Capone Door.

Hopefully I wouldn't need it.

Hopefully Detective Smelt wouldn't be the she-devil I suspected she was.

I pushed through the entrance without the gun, armed only with ghiaccio furioso and a determination to use it on her just as I had Uncle Buddy. It was a cozy place with a cheery bar and Sinatra murmuring from the jukebox, and although I'd never met the detective, I spotted her immediately at a round leather booth in the corner. She wasn't a she-devil, but she was a ghost, or a zombie, and she looked up at me and smiled.

"Sara Jane," she said in that unmistakable voice, a piercing combination of West Side Chicago and a phlegmatic lion.

"Elzy?" I said to my dead nanny, because, despite the black beehive that had been replaced by a henna buzz cut, and despite the retro-mod wardrobe that had been replaced by no-nonsense detective wear, she still wore the cat's-eye glasses, and it was still her. I approached slowly, sensing movement bristling around me, her people ready to pounce if I did. "It's not possible. I went to your funeral."

"You went to the funeral of an empty casket," she said. "Have a seat. You want a Coke or something?"

I sat heavily, staring, until I managed to say, "Do my parents know?"

"That I didn't die? Of course not, that would have ruined it."

"Ruined what?" I said.

"Me taking over the Outfit. That's why I need the note-book," Elzy said, sipping something brown with cherries in it.

I paused, watching her lick her lips with a pointed little tongue. "You know about the notebook?" I asked.

"I know about a lot of things I'm not supposed to know. But for heaven's sake, be patient, we've got some catching up to do," she said with a wink. "Personally, I'm an expert at being patient. I waited years for the opportunity to take over the Outfit, and then your grandpa Enzo provided it by dying. Or, I should say, your dad provided it, by being himself. Brains, tenacity, DNA—Anthony Rispoli had everything it took to eventually become boss of the whole Outfit. The problem is that he had too much." She pointed a finger, saying, "He had you and your little brother. Oh, many were the conversations I eavesdropped upon, hearing him tell your mom how he didn't want you and Lou to ever have anything to do with the Outfit, how he loved you far too much to allow it to poison your pristine little souls. Over time, I realized that when Enzo died someday, your dad would be caught in a moral quandary—do I continue on in the Outfit tradition, or do I take my family and disappear?—and that pause for reflection, that dropping of the guard, so to speak, would be my chance to pounce for the notebook."

"In other words, you were waiting not only to exploit my dad's conscience, but also his grief," I said, hearing the acid in my voice.

Elzy nodded, smiling proudly. "In the old days, Outfit thieves pulled a nifty move called a 'Rest in Peace.' They'd scan obituaries for funeral times of the wealthy dead, and while the family wept at the graveside, they'd ransack their homes. So yeah, it's something like that." She sipped at her drink and then waved her hand, saying, "You like this place? Snug, isn't it? Personally, I love it—I grew up here, did you know that?" I shook my head like a mummy, and she said, "My father owned it."

"Roberto . . . ?" I said, recalling what I'd read in the notebook.

"His nickname was Bobo . . ."

"Zanzara," I said. "Your last name. Bobo Zanzara . . . didn't he work for my grandpa at the bakery?"

"Very good," she said. "Yes indeed, in the kitchen, just like an indentured servant. It was quite a comedown from having been the owner of such a glorious front business like this one, but he had no choice. You see, Daddy had a dice problem, as in they refused to roll his way. He ran a successful gambling operation for the Outfit but was a terrible gambler himself, and he lost his piece of Twin Anchors back to the Outfit."

"His piece," I said. "My grandpa owned the other piece."

"That's where the story gets bitter," she said with a mirthless smile, crinkling her nose. "Of course you know that your grandfather was counselor-at-large for the Outfit. He had power and he had money . . . it would've been so easy for him to simply give his piece of Twin Anchors to Daddy. Your grandfather didn't need it and wouldn't have missed it, while Daddy needed it desperately."

"But wouldn't your father have just gambled it away, too?"

"That's not the point!" she hissed. "Enzo Rispoli sold his piece to the Outfit and made a tidy profit, and then took my father into the bakery like . . . like an employee!"

"Maybe my grandpa was just trying to help him," I said.

"My father didn't *need* help," she said. "He was a proud son of Buondiavolo, born in the hills of Sicily, just like your people . . . well maybe not *just* like your people. But he deserved power! He deserved respect! And what did he get? An apron and a cookie sheet."

"It's better than nothing, isn't it?" I said. "At least it was an honest living."

Elzy snorted, emptied her glass, and said, "Let's cut the bullshit, sweetie. There was *nothing* honest going on behind closed kitchen doors at Rispoli & Sons Fancy Pastries. From Nunzio's molasses business to Enzo holding court at Club Molasses to your dad being crowned counselor-at-large, your family was just one big multigenerational lie. And what do you have to show for it? Ninety years of a Rispoli family tradition of crime and that precious little notebook packed full of black secrets."

Elzy's speech was poisonous and targeted, but it didn't hurt—by then I had already been wounded by the truth of my family. Instead, it gave me an insight, and I said, "It was Bobo, wasn't it? He found out about the notebook."

"Indeed he did," Elzy said, grinning broadly.

"Your dad wasn't just a lousy gambler. He was a disloyal sneak who spied on my grandpa at the bakery."

Her eyes flashed, as if she hadn't expected me to hit back so accurately. "Daddy suspected the notebook was hidden in

270

Club Molasses and was caught trying to climb into the oven one night after hours by Enzo the Baker. And your sweet little grandfather, always the soul of charity, called on the Outfit to dole out punishment. Of course he couldn't admit that the notebook existed, so he told them that Daddy had stolen a large sum of money from the bakery. The Outfit framed Daddy on a trumped-up charge of something or other, and in the blink of an eye, he was sent to prison for life. Except . . ."

"My grandpa wouldn't do that," I said, not sure of my assertion in the least.

"His sentence lasted only a few weeks before he was stabbed by an inmate. Typical prison death, they said. Murder for hire, I said. Of course, in order to survive, I had to pretend to believe that the absurd frame-up that sent Daddy away was real, pretend to be ashamed of him, and pretend to know nothing about the notebook. Except that I did." A fresh drink was delivered. Elzy sipped and said, "Daddy told me he'd overheard your grandpa telling your father when he was just a young man that the notebook contained a secret so powerful, whoever possessed it could control the Outfit."

"What secret?" I said, remembering what Uncle Buddy had told me about *potenza ultima*—ultimate power.

Elzy shrugged her birdlike shoulders. "He never found out. Your grandpa seized the notebook, Daddy went to prison and then to heaven, and the notebook has been in Rispoli hands ever since. But no matter, my little brother and I decided that we would get the notebook ourselves and tear it apart until we found the answer to that untold secret. So, feigning ignorance and loyalty, I went to work in your parents' home and my brother went to work at the bakery. While I monitored your family, he would succeed where Daddy had failed by infiltrating Club Molasses and stealing the notebook."

"I remember you talking about him," I said, trying to recall his name.

"He was such a handsome youth, a mere twenty-year-old sprig of a man when he began rolling dough in that stinking kitchen," she said. "He despised your grandfather of course, and your father, but he saved his purest hatred for your uncle." She paused and her face changed from frosty self-assurance to twitching rage as she spit, "Buddy Rispoli . . . Buddy-god-damn-Rispoli! He just desperately needed to boss someone around, and the fat schlub rode my brother day and night. More flour, less salt, roll the dough lengthwise not vertically, until my brother wanted to twist his neck."

"Twist his neck," I repeated, feeling my bruises.

Elzy slammed the drink, a fresh one replaced it immediately, and she told me how her brother was working alone in the kitchen one morning. He'd just removed trays of cakes from the oven and was sampling one when Uncle Buddy showed up. My uncle berated Elzy's brother for using his bare hands, delivering a blistering speech on kitchen hygiene, and her brother flipped off Uncle Buddy and told him to go to hell. That's when Uncle Buddy made the mistake of shoving him. Elzy's brother beat him to his knees but my uncle wouldn't stay down, and Elzy's face changed to something that was not self-assurance or rage, but horror.

"Buddy was on the ground, struggling to get up, and my brother charged him," she said slowly, her words tinged with revulsion. "At the last minute, Buddy grabbed his ankle. My brother tripped, lost his balance, and fell face-first onto a white-hot, overturned cake pan stamped with the Rispoli *R* . . ."

Oh my God, I thought, feeling my spine freeze, that means Ski Mask Guy is . . .

"Poor Kevin," Elzy said mournfully. "Half of his beautiful face, his neck, and his vocal cords. It drove him to the brink of insanity and he had to go . . . away. Years later, when he escaped from the . . . hospital . . . I broke out too, from my existence, and we reunited," she said, blowing her nose into a cocktail napkin. She put on a smile that would've startled a snake and said, "And here we are."

"Here we are," I said, seizing control of the rapidly rising ghiaccio furioso just as I'd done with Uncle Buddy, trying with all of my strength to focus it across the table. Elzy blinked rapidly behind the cat's-eye glasses as I said, "But where's my family? What have you done with them?"

To my great surprise, she ceased blinking and chuckled. "Who knows? Maybe dead in the ground somewhere. Worm food first and then gone forever."

As she spoke, I felt a little electrical storm break across my head and shoulders.

The cold fury popped and faded, and I was flooded with exhaustion.

I sat back heavily, struggling even to hold up my head.

"I'll be damned. So you're the one who got the gift," Elzy said, staring at me with curiosity. "Even though you and your brother both have blue eyes, I never would've guessed it would be you. Amazing how sexist we're all trained to be. Even I naturally assumed that a man would get the power." She sighed and said, "By the way, it doesn't affect me."

I shook my head, confused, and she sat forward smiling.

"You have a weakness, you know that?" She sipped, swished, and swallowed, and explained that no, she didn't possess ghiaccio furioso, nor did anyone in her family. But she reminded me that her father was from Buondiavolo and had shared an ancient secret with her and Poor Kevin that only people from the village knew—how to avoid the immobilizing grip of cold fury. "Don't ask," she said. "What kind of nemesis would I be if I told you? But I will tell you that I have no idea where your family is. Yes, Poor Kevin tried to get his hands on them . . ."

"I saw it," I said, finding my voice. "Frank Sinatra's head."

"Ah yes, my darling Frank. I gave him to your parents on the pretext that poor me, the trusted nanny who cared *so* deeply for their precious children, would soon be dead, and that a nanny cam was an absolute necessity in my absence. I even showed them how to use it and placed it in that central location myself. Of course, my real hope was that they'd discuss the notebook and it would be caught on tape. My intention was to sneak into your house and steal it, but someone was *always* home—you Rispolis just never went out, did you?" She shrugged and said, "After a couple of years, I gave up on ever getting my hands on it. Who knew your mom and dad would continue to use it? Anyway, Poor Kevin would've succeeded if he hadn't been interrupted. He was this close when—don't laugh—when a whole caravan of black ice cream trucks surrounded your house, tinkling their merry tune. My nimble brother hid in the basement, and your people have been gone ever since."

"Ice cream trucks?" I said. "That's ridiculous. You're lying."

"Oh yeah? If I had your family, do you think I would've gone to all the trouble with my cops and Poor Kevin trying to hunt you down? I would've just sent you body parts a piece at a time until you gave me the notebook." She paused, smiling serenely, and said, "Whoever has your family or wherever they've gone, none of that matters now. What matters is that you have the notebook, and you're here."

"Who says I have the notebook?" I said.

She looked at me over the top of her cocktail and said, "Well . . . do you?"

I said nothing, trying to assume a poker face.

Elzy grinned and said, "Yeah, you have it, just as I suspected. You know something, you might not believe this, but I always liked you. You were a sweet kid and a straight arrow . . . just as bad a liar then as you are now. But you were also a tough little kid, and now you're a tough young woman, and I say let's let bygones be bygones. I say let's do this thing together."

"What thing?" I said calmly, stifling an urge to punch her teeth down her throat.

"Take over Chicago. It's our time. Have you read the notebook?"

She knew I had it; it was too late to act as if I didn't. "Parts of it."

"I'm curious," she said. "How much of it explains women's roles in the Outfit? How much of it talks about your great-grandmother, grandmother, or mother? Where does it discuss the wives, sisters, and daughters of all of those Outfit bosses and thugs?"

"Nowhere," I said.

"Exactly. Organized crime is a boys' club, with no position of power or responsibility for a female." She narrowed her eyes and said, "We're all God's children, except a woman connected to the Outfit. Then she's less than a second-class citizen. She can be a faithful wife who won't testify, or a *goomah* on the side, or an Italian mama who cooks meatballs for her sonny boy as he shines his pistol, but nothing else. That's precisely why I faked my own death. With Poor Kevin back at my side, I was done being little miss Elzy-Do-This-Do-That. With my organizational skills, nerves of steel, and almost complete lack of moral conscience, it was time to be the Elzy I was born to be . . . the head of the Outfit." She sipped her drink and said, "Unfortunately, I was born a female. If I'd openly infringed on Outfit business, the boys' club would've crushed me. My head would be fish food in Lake Michigan and the rest of me scattered in the Sanitary Canal. If I was going to take over, I needed to disappear . . . to remove the thought of Elzy Zanzara from anyone even remotely connected to the Outfit, so that I could take it by complete and utter surprise. My work would have to be done covertly and unseen, working in the shadows until I made my move. And for that, I needed an edge."

"You mean the notebook," I said.

She stared at the ice in her glass and nodded. "With the information contained between those covers, plus my vision and your gift, we can rule this dirty town. It's high time that someone who thinks with her brain first is in charge."

"No," I said, shaking my head slowly. "Never. It doesn't matter if it's a man or a woman. The whole thing has been rotten from the beginning and it will never change."

"I don't want to change it, you little fool," she said. "I want to control it. But okay, fine and dandy, I'll do it alone . . . well, not quite alone. I have Poor Kevin. He's my ultimate weapon because he loves me and only me, and would happily travel to hell and back at my command. He almost got you the first time, in the basement of your house, if it hadn't been for that filthy little dog."

"The basement," I said, feeling again at my neck. "He almost killed me."

"He was just trying to squeeze the notebook out of you," she said, sipping. "I suppose it was a bit painful, but Poor Kevin despises you Rispolis. But then, don't we all?" And then she lowered her voice and glanced around at her people. "Of course, I never told my officers about Poor Kevin. Better to have them all working independently. That's good leadership, Outfit style. Never let your employees know exactly what you're doing, or whom you're doing it with. Secrecy is the key to success."

"You mean secrecy plus a masked lunatic, don't you?"

"Tsk-tsk, sticks and stones," she said, crinkling her nose. "Poor Kevin is my avenging angel. Nothing short of a Mack truck can stop him."

"I guess I'll have to get a Mack truck."

Elzy finished her drink, patted her lips, and said, "This has been fun, but I want that notebook and I want it now."

"I'll never give it to you. Why should I? You don't have my family."

"Oh, but I have something," she said, tossing a pair of books on the table. I glanced at the titles, Roger Ebert's *The Great Movies*, volumes one and two, and recognized Doug's well-worn copies. "Your chunky friend traced Poor Kevin's devil mask to a novelty store, asked a few questions, and actually tried to catch him," she said with a small smile. "It didn't work out too well."

"Where is he?" I said quietly, using every ounce of restraint not to flip the table and stomp the answer out of her. "I swear to God, if you've hurt him . . ."

"Don't swear, and yes, of course we've hurt him. All you have to do is trade the notebook for your bloated buddy and Poor Kevin will let him go," she said, narrowing her eyes behind the cat's-eye glasses. "Of course, now that you're here, I could just keep you, couldn't I? Let Poor Kevin convince you to give up the notebook in his own special way. I have more than enough people here to . . ." But she spread her arms at an empty bar. Her officers were all gone, with cigarettes still smoldering and drinks unfinished, as if ripped from their posts by silent, unseen hands.

That's when one of those hands lit on my shoulder.

Elzy looked behind me and her jaw muscles rippled.

One of Knuckles's dark and anonymous guys said, "Time to go, girly."

I rose and saw his two companions, one near the bar, one at the door, and wanted to ask what they had done with Elzy's people, but it wasn't a Q&A moment. Elzy crossed her arms and said, "I see you've learned a couple of things from the notebook."

"More than a couple."

"Two hours. Come alone, unarmed, or you'll have a fat corpse on your hands."

"Where?"

"Rispoli & Sons Fancy Pastries." She smiled coyly.

The bakery, where her brother lost his face.

Club Molasses, where my family buried its secrets.

Where everything began and where, I realized, she intended everything to end.

An hour and fifty-eight minutes is not much time to speed-read part of a chapter, scribble a list, grab cash from a steel briefcase, drive like a maniac to one store and then another store, and then build a bomb.

Actually, the notebook calls it an "incendiary device."

Chapter six (*Metodi*–Methods) describes it as ideal for "scare tactics, arson, and safe-cracking."

It also cautions that it could kill someone, which might be a good thing.

After I aged the brand-new leather notebook I'd purchased by backing over it with the Lincoln and beating it with a hammer, I very carefully wired it with the device. Everything I needed to assemble the little bomb was available at the corner hardware store, which in my former life would've been extremely disturbing. My present life was a different story—one that could end prematurely at any time—and I had no moral issue whatsoever about blowing off the rest of that evil sock puppet's face.

At the hour-fifty-nine mark I pulled up in front of the bakery.

The time for parking down the block had passed.

Leaping roof to roof seemed suddenly ridiculous.

I lifted the notebook, climbed out of the car, and walked through the front door of the bakery, the bell jingling behind me. I'd thought about bringing the .45, but it was bulky and hard to hide, and besides, if my scheme went off as planned I wouldn't need it. The front of the store was dark and so was the kitchen, but it didn't matter, I knew where they were, and went straight to the Vulcan. I folded myself inside, whooshed quickly below the earth, and pulled open the heavy steel door of Club Molasses.

It was dark inside except for a single spotlight.

It shone on Doug in the middle of the dance floor.

He was slumped in a chair, chin on his chest, shirt soaked with blood.

I ran to him, set the notebook on the floor, and gently lifted his head. It was impossible not to grimace at his beaten, swollen face. I whispered, "Doug. It's me, Sara Jane," and he blinked heavily, trying to focus. Quietly, I said, "Where is he?"

Doug worked his jaws, spit out a tooth, and said, "Right behind you."

There was no panic, only action, and I spun with my right fist curled at my chin and my left fist in front of my right. Poor Kevin bowed like a huge, rumpled maître d', emitting a gust of rotten-meat cologne from his melted head. "Welcome to Club Molasses! Table for two?"

"I have the notebook," I said, vibrating with ghiaccio furioso, feeling it quiver and fade as it had with Elzy. It was plain me versus maniac him, and I said, "Take it and let us go. That was the deal."

"Let you go? Oh no-no-no!" he trilled, pumping his arms in time to his words like a crazed sports fan. "Not until I inspect the no-no-notebook!"

"You want it?" I said, kicking it across the parquet dance floor. "Go get it."

Poor Kevin watched it slide like a hockey puck and then looked at me. The pupils of his eyes through the ski mask holes grew larger and smaller, like two crazy cameras trying to find focus, and then he shrugged and shambled after it. And then everything sped up—me lugging Doug toward the door, Poor Kevin picking up the notebook, me bracing for an explosion and then hearing a soft, gentle *pop*. I turned to him staring at the blank, smoking pages that did not blow up, and then he lifted his horrific head and said as coldly as a frozen knife, "You think I'm stupid?"

"It's a misunderstanding," I said, backing toward the door with Doug attached to me like a three-hundred-pound anchor.

"It's a death sentence!" he squealed, galloping across the floor. I dropped Doug, ducked and moved, and Poor Kevin's massive fist missed my head by inches. When he turned, I was waiting with a hard left-right combo that stopped him. He shook his head and then went into a fighter's crouch too, and we squared off on the dance floor. "Hey, this is gonna be fun!" he said as we circled. "Just like the old days when I used to beat the dirt out of that schlub uncle of yours! You Rispolis are all the same, blah-blah-blah, all talk and no . . ." and then he had to stop talking because my fist was in his mouth—once, twice, three times—and he skidded backward. Then he charged forward, and I dropped a shoulder and threw my Willy Williams left hook.

The sound of fist on jawbone cracked across Club Molasses. Poor Kevin stumbled and reeled to the floor like a train off its tracks.

He slid face-first and hit the bandstand, and I ran for Doug.

"Come on!" I grunted, sitting him up like an enormous toddler, and he was almost to his feet when we both went down. Doug rolled but I was trapped under Poor Kevin, his knee on my back and his big leathery hands finding my neck again, for what I knew would be the last time. His thumbs went to my windpipe and the edges of the world were trimmed in black. Doug lifted up on a shoulder and fell, then tried again, but he was like a newborn turtle with his bruised, closed eyelids.

Dying was not okay, I told myself. There was no resolution or freedom in it. I struggled against it with every muscle and tendon in my body, and when I felt my brain emptying itself of oxygen, I thought of Lou.

No, wait—not Lou—I meant Lou's dog, Harry.

He blasted out of the darkness like a tiny Italian ball of cold fury and chomped his needle-sharp jaws onto Poor Kevin's butt cheek, with the freak shrieking and flailing his arms. I had no idea how the crafty little canine got inside Club Molasses—I thought the only way in and out was through the oven elevator or the Capone Door in the office—but realized then that there had to be other doors, yet to be discovered. I rolled onto my back, sucking air, and watched Poor Kevin rip

Harry free and throw him softball-style into the backseat of the convertible Ferrari.

Ferrari, I thought, hacking spittle and grabbing Doug by the ankles.

I knew the keys were in the ignition.

I prayed to God there was gasoline in the tank.

I dragged Doug across the parquet floor, my feet stuttering a mile a minute as Poor Kevin sprinted toward us, and then it was all over, done, we were dead, except that a gray hairy sausage dropped from the ceiling. The rat landed on Poor Kevin's shoulder, snarling and ripping, and he grabbed it and squeezed its guts out. As I shoved Doug into the passenger seat, the masked psycho spun the bloody rat pelt by its worm tail and screeched, "That's it? That's all you got? One little mouse!" right before a dozen pissed-off rodents fell on his head. Nunzio's rats, bred to protect all things Rispoli, were fulfilling their DNA with gusto. Poor Kevin made a noise that was half six-year-old girl, half fingernails on a blackboard. I cranked the engine, and the incredible machine roared to life. Since there was nowhere to go, no way to escape the subterranean space, my simple intention had been to back over the homicidal creep until he stopped moving. But then the headlights popped on and I looked at the wall in front of the Ferrari.

A pattern of bricks formed a large but subtle *C*.

I suddenly realized how someone got the car down here in the first place.

There were Capone Doors, I thought. Why not Capone Garage Doors?

I leaped from the Ferrari and touched the wall—nothing—and then leaned against it—nothing—then threw a desperate shoulder and heard a creak and a rumble, and the wall lifted slowly, revealing a wide, dark tunnel. I was back in the car with inert Doug and shivering Harry, and I paused only for a glance back. Poor Kevin squeezed rats, bit rats, swatted and stomped rats, and then a dozen more of Antonio and Cleopatra's offspring dove from the ceiling, hissing and clawing at his masked head, his raw fingers, and then another dark mass, and another, until the freak looked like a rat Christmas tree, all of it squirming and ripping, and I couldn't tell his squealing from theirs.

I had tried to blow him up and then used his head like a speed bag, he had been attacked by a dog, and he was now being nibbled and sliced by a hundred rats, and still he fought on ferociously. I remembered Elzy's description of her brother—nothing short of a Mack truck would stop him—and leaned heavily on the gas, fishtailing into the tunnel. It twisted and climbed with the cold smell of earth all around me until I heard wheels on concrete, and then the blast of a truck horn as I screeched onto Lower Wacker Drive. My dad's Lincoln is a fast car but the Ferrari is a fast something else, somewhere between automobile and airplane, and I flew above the pavement. I spun onto Congress and then onto the Eisenhower, and I was gone, going nowhere in particular, just as far away from Poor Kevin as possible. I wept violently on that dark, empty stretch of expressway, expelling leftover fear and fury. I stopped and began again, and then it passed away.

That's when my disposable phone with the unlisted number rang.

I answered, and a voice said, "Hey, it's Tyler. Did I catch you at a bad time?"

"Where . . . how did you get this number?" I said.

"I'm me, remember . . . the guy who gets in touch with untouchables? Listen, what are you doing for dinner later? Have you ever been to Rome?"

"Is that a restaurant?"

"It's a city in Italy. I'm leaving on the company jet in an hour for business and I want you to come along."

"Italy," I murmured, that golden place where I'd dreamed of going, so far away from all of this, except that all of this was my life. "I'd love to," I said, "but I can't. Tonight just . . . doesn't work. But . . ."

"But what?" he said hopefully.

"But . . . have a good trip."

"I always do."

"Tyler?" I said. "Rome . . . is it beautiful? I mean, this might sound weird, but . . . is it golden?"

He chuckled and said, "The food's good," and hung up.

I felt my heart twist into a knot, looked at the dark phone, and threw it out the window. Until I'd heard his voice, I'd been speeding on a path to no place in particular, with no plan, and no options.

Then I remembered the key he'd given me to the Bird Cage Club.

I'd almost lost my life deep below the earth.

Tonight I would sleep in the clouds, high above Chicago.

WATCHING THE MORNING SUN illuminate the Loop is to see miles of shadows change from gray to red to bright shining boxes, rectangles, and obelisks. Pulled puffs of cottony clouds meander past, change shape, and dissipate, and far beyond it all, Lake Michigan stretches to the horizon, first pale green, then blue black.

I stood at the window of the Bird Cage Club thirty-three stories in the air, watching the world come alive again, feeling dead inside.

I'd confronted Uncle Buddy, Detective Smelt, and even Poor Kevin, and all I had to show for it was a beaten, kicked-in friend and a small dog sleeping beside him.

I'd parked the Ferrari in the underground garage and decided to inspect it closely before hefting Doug up to the Bird Cage Club. To my surprise, someone (my dad?) had packed it with getaway provisions, as if the need to speed from middle earth at the drop of a hat was a definite possibility. There was bottled water, a first-aid kit, canned Italian delicacies, even a couple of thick Ferrari traveling blankets. I'd patched up Doug as well as I could the night before, and tried to make him comfortable. Harry walked in a small circle and then lay at his side, the first real sign of affection he'd shown anyone besides Lou. Doug rubbed the dog's back and said, "You saved my life."

"Barely."

"I'm sorry, Sara Jane. I was trying to help."

"You can't do things like that, Doug," I told him. "You could've gotten killed."

"As beatings go, it was worse than I imagined," he said. "But not half as bad as what I probably deserved."

"What movie is that from?" I said.

"The movie of my life. By the way, the sidekick approves," he said, gesturing around the room.

"Of what?"

"Our hideout," he said, yawning hugely. "It's perfect."

Afterward he rolled over painfully, Harry snuggled closer, and the two of them were still asleep when I woke at dawn. I walked the perimeter of the Bird Cage Club, looking out every window, and discovered that a sturdy stone terrace surrounded the dome. One of the windows was a door. I wrapped myself in a blanket and stepped outside, and then I was inhaling the chill morning air. Thirty-three stories is a long way down, and I was stricken by a sense of despair that made existence seem pointless and hollow. All of the running, all of the fighting and surviving, and I still didn't know where my family was—it occurred to me again that I might never know. Slowly, I peered over the edge of the terrace, feeling the terrifying-exciting pull to jump, to abandon earth and its disappointments, when I heard Doug mumbling, "I think Harry is sick."

I turned to his hefty, ass-kicked form in the doorway.

He was bruised and puffy, looking very much like an enormous crushed grape.

"He's trying to throw up but seems stuck."

We walked inside and Doug was right, Harry was hacking and retching, his jaws working and his ribs drawn tightly to his chest. "Harry," I said, stroking his back, and he coughed once, twice, and puked out a tiny, clear plastic tube.

"What the hell is that?" Doug said, embracing poor, panting Harry.

I picked up the slimy thing—it was the length and size of a cigarette butt—and looked at it closely. "There's something inside," I said, twisting it until a tiny top popped off and a tightly rolled length of paper fell into my hand. I opened it carefully and read a quickly scrawled paragraph.

In Italy, for thirty years under the Borgias, they had warfare, terror, murder, bloodshed, but they produced Michelangelo, Leonardo da Vinci, and the Renaissance. In Switzerland, they had brotherly love. They had five hundred years of democracy and peace, and what did that produce? The cuckoo clock.

Beneath it, in the same handwriting, read—

Once around at noon, only on Sundays.

A wave of dizziness washed over me, my hands went numb, and the paper fluttered to the floor. I walked outside to inhale fresh air, my mind spinning but also clicking at warp speed. Doug appeared beside me, read the note, and said, "I don't get it."

"I think I do," I answered, staring across the vista at Navy Pier jutting into the lake, its convention buildings, tourist boats, and Ferris wheel like a collection of children's toys. "Is today Sunday?" I said. Doug nodded, and I thought of what Uncle Buddy said, how Harry had been hanging around my house. When I didn't show up, the cagey little animal must've made his way back to the bakery, and Club Molasses, to wait for me—but how, and for how long? "I hope it's the right Sunday," I said.

"For what?" Doug asked anxiously.

I looked at the concern etched on his face and knew that he would do anything I asked. But just by proximity I'd drawn him nearly to the point of death, and I would not allow it to happen again. "I have to do something, and I have to do it alone. You can't follow me or try to help me," I said.

"Please," he said, "I owe you."

"I told you about the notebook . . ."

"Yeah, but I want to be part of this, whatever it is."

"Doug," I said, summoning the ghiaccio furioso, locking eyes until his chin began to quiver. "You will *not* be a part of this. Do you understand me?"

"Yes, yes," he said in a voice that was small and alone, and I saw his fear—a snippet of a movie in which Poor Kevin finished what he started with Doug in a bloody and violent way.

"The notebook," I said, "is here, in the steel briefcase. If I don't come back, I want you to burn it. Burn it, Doug . . . every damn page, handwritten note, old photo, and unlisted phone number. It's *mine*, it's *my* life, and you will do as I ask."

"Yes," he whispered, and I looked away. Doug sighed with

relief, and when he found his voice he said, "Of course I'll do whatever you say. You're the hero."

"I'm no hero," I said. "How can a victim like me be a hero?"

"According to some of the greatest movies ever made, by not becoming like the assholes who victimized you," Doug said. "Hitting that masked creep with my computer was the right thing to do, the *only* thing to do, because he was trying to kill you. On the other hand, I still don't know if what happened to Billy was justified. All I know for sure is that being smarter than an enemy is better than resorting to violence. The great hero is always more patient and much more observant. And then he . . . she . . . wins." He wiped at his nose and handed me the note, saying, "Did you notice the upper-right-hand corner?" I hadn't, and I now looked at part of a business letterhead, which read MISTER KREAMY KO— with the rest torn away. "It has to be Mister Kreamy Kone. You know, the chocolate-dipped frozen concoctions sold from the black ice cream trucks."

"I guess I never noticed them . . . I don't eat that stuff," I murmured, remembering what Elzy said about black ice cream trucks surrounding my house before my family disappeared.

"It's so awesome. The truck stops, you insert money into the side like an ATM, and out pops the deliciousness. You never even see a driver. All the windows are tinted black too. Kind of weird, isn't it?"

"Weird," I said, thinking how the CEO of StroBisCo might have useful information about another Chicago junk-food company. Or, if it was unionized, Knuckles would have to know something—deploying strikebreakers fell under his job description. And then, of course, there was my own personal Talmud-Bible-Koran, the notebook. If Mister Kreamy Kone had even the slightest thread of a connection to the Outfit, it would be in there. Right now, however, was not the time to study; now was the time to get my mind and gut ready for what I had to do at noon.

"Is there anything else?" Doug asked.

"Yeah," I said. "If I don't come back, take care of Harry."

"You have to come back," Doug said. "We have final exams next week."

I realized then that I hadn't studied Italian in almost three long weeks.

I grabbed my Italian-English dictionary and looked up three words.

destino—fate

resa dei conti—reckoning

vendetta—revenge

BY TEN UNTIL NOON, the cool morning sky had been replaced by a sun that shone so brightly it felt like nails being driven into my head.

There was no wind, no clouds, only light and heat.

The Technicolor blue sky looked cheap and fake, and I was tense being out in broad daylight.

I paused at the entrance to Navy Pier, watching tourists come and go carrying plastic bags full of expensive junk and eating large, sweet, colorful garbage, and then moved cautiously up the boardwalk. Twice in that short walk I was overcome by paranoia so strong that I spun in a half crouch, only to see slow-moving people with cameras and fanny packs and cotton candy. I yawned with jittery nerves, my heart beat irregularly—both signs of OD'ing on adrenaline—and I paused.

I stood inside an enormous round shadow.

I shielded my eyes and looked up.

One hundred and fifty feet in the air, the Ferris wheel crept in a slow circle.

My brother Lou is twelve, and in that time he's probably seen his favorite movie, *The Third Man*, a hundred times. He has the entire film memorized, but his favorite part of all is when Holly Martins encounters his friend Harry Lime, whom he believed to be dead. Instead, it turns out that Harry faked his death and has been in hiding to escape punishment for a heinous deed. Harry doesn't feel bad or guilty about his crime; he merely considers himself an opportunist, someone who's made the best from a bad situation (not to mention a profit). To make the point, Harry delivers a short speech contrasting the amorality of a ruling family in Italy with that of placid Swiss democracy.

Every time the scene played, Lou would recite the monologue with him.

It began "In Italy, for thirty years under the Borgias, they had warfare, terror, murder, bloodshed . . ."

Harry delivers this lesson on criminal creativity on a Ferris wheel.

Lou regards it as a genius meeting place since it's on earth but above it, and public but also stratospherically private. He knows that I'm all too aware of his love for that seminal scene. I climbed the steps to the platform with my heart hammering my chest and saw strolling tourists, lingering tourists, tourists gaping into the sky, but no one else. And then—

"Sara Jane."

He was behind me, and I turned to a kid who was my brother, but not.

He was snowy pale with deep circles under his eyes, his thick black hair shaved away.

He wore clothes that were not his own, jeans too big, a pale green hospital shirt beneath a coat too heavy for such a hot day.

Without another word, he turned to enter the Ferris wheel. I followed as he handed an attendant two tickets, we boarded the gondola with its open-air windows, and the great disc made its slow turn toward the sun. By that time we were holding each other tightly and I wept into his shoulder while Lou burrowed against me making low murmuring noises that were not words, but feelings. There was a faint metallic smell to him, like old batteries, and when we parted, sitting opposite of each other, we simply stared while the wheel climbed. Finally I said, "You're alive," and he nodded, and I asked, "Are they?"

Lou paused, then said, "Barely."

"Lou . . . where did you all go?"

"I don't know. We were taken."

"By who? The government?"

"I don't think so. I don't know for sure. But I have to go back."

"No," I said, shaking my head. "I won't lose you again."

"I don't have a choice. Right now, they don't know I'm gone. But if I'm not where I'm supposed to be in an hour, they'll probably kill Mom," he said absently, looking down at the ground, and I saw deep red burn marks on the side of his skull.

"Lou," I whispered, leaning forward and gently inspecting his head.

"They attach wires. I know they do it to Dad, too, or did, every day. I heard him screaming when they turned on the computer." He turned to me, and in a quiet, blank tone he said, "They want something."

"The notebook. Do you know about it, Lou?"

He nodded. "Our family, the Outfit, the notebook. It's very valuable, you know. There's something incredibly powerful in its pages, or so I've been told . . ."

"They can have it," I said. "I'll give it to them now, today, if they'll let you all go."

He gazed down at the ground again. "They don't want it."

That stopped me. The notebook was a deadly burden but also my single strongest edge—my sole bargaining chip in a twisted reality where all lives had prices on them—and now it was worthless. "What do they want?" I asked.

Lou touched my forehead lightly. "What you have. What dad has."

"Ghiaccio furioso," I said slowly. "What you don't have."

"They don't know that yet. That's why I've been here, waiting for you every Sunday for a month. It became too dangerous. This was my last try."

"I don't understand."

"I don't either, exactly. I think they think ghiaccio furioso can control other things besides people. I saw the screen of the computer I was attached to . . . it looked like something medical, like a diagram of a brain or something. I don't know what they've gotten from Dad, but they've gotten nothing from me, and pretty soon they're going to realize that they never will. And then they'll want you." My brother looked at me impassively and said, "Run, Sara Jane. Run far away from Chicago. Leave, and don't look back."

"Never."

"They know you exist, of course, but it's as if it hasn't occurred to them that a girl can possess ghiaccio furioso," he said, looking absently down at the ground far below. "They assumed it was me because I'm a boy and I have blue eyes. But they'll figure it out soon enough and by then you have to be gone."

"No," I said. "I've still got the notebook. Whatever's in there, I'll find it and I'll use it. I swear to God, Lou, I won't stop until you're free."

"It's not . . . possible," he said, his gaze widening.

"It is. It is possible," I said. "You have to trust me."

Lou pointed past me and shuddered. "Down there. Tell me it's not real."

A Ferris wheel is like a wagon wheel, its center held in place by spokes, and I turned and looked down at Poor Kevin inching up the one beneath our gondola. He climbed quickly, like a plaid, mad Spider-Man, and although his face was masked, I could tell he was grinning. There was no time to do anything but shove my little brother behind me as Poor Kevin pulled himself toward the gondola—we were halfway to the top and it swung wildly under his weight until he was inside. The metal car was built to hold six people, and he filled the entire space with the smell of rancid meat while wagging his finger at me. "You, you, *you!*" he squealed, and I felt Lou cower against me as Poor Kevin said, "Rodents and Ferraris and Ferris wheels . . . you're just all over the map, aren't you? And lookie here, if it isn't little brother! Aren't you gonna say hello? What's the matter . . . rat got your tongue?"

I stared with ghiaccio furioso frigid and bubbling in my gut. "Stay back," I hissed, but he repelled it, blinking it away while cracking his big knuckles.

"'Cause I'll tell you something, a rat got part of mine!" he shrieked, and before he could touch us, I dropped to the floor and swept his ankles. He went down heavily on his back, the gondola careened wildly, and I knew it was all useless. The masked demon was my fate—he always had been, right from the beginning. Even as I fought on, I was having the type of sensory revelation that a person on her deathbed must experience seconds before she exits her body, knowing suddenly that it's going to happen—I knew, too, even as he staggered to his feet and I peppered the evil sock puppet's face with a flurry of rights and lefts and he took them like a giggling speed bag. I could hammer away all day, I could bite, kick, and run, but in the end he would grab my neck and squeeze me to death. And then something landed on top of us like a load of bricks. We all froze—Poor Kevin staring at the roof, me in a crouch, Lou against the wall. Poor Kevin stuck his ski mask over the edge, craning his neck this way and that, only for a pair of boots to kick him in the jaw so hard he flew across the gondola. The boots were followed by thick legs as another bulky man swung inside. "Uncle Buddy?"

"Geez, I *really* hate heights," he said, his whole body shaking.

"You . . . you jumped?"

"From the gondola above," he said, with another violent shudder. "Don't ever do something like that."

Poor Kevin stood shaking his head like a wet dog, and

when he looked up, his crazy eyes popped crazier through the ski mask holes. "You schlub!" he cried. "It's really you, isn't it? Buddy Roly-Poly Rispoli! Buddy More-Cannoli Rispoli!"

"Poor Kevin," Uncle Buddy said with a sigh.

"Oh, how I've longed for the day when I could tear your arms from your body and beat you retarded with them!" Poor Kevin bleated. "I mean, *more* retarded! I dreamed about it when I was in the hospital!"

"You mean the nuthouse," Uncle Buddy said.

"Nuthouse, loony bin, cracker shack, you name it, I escaped it, and now here we are, just me and the Rispoli three! It's gonna be fun, like killing rats!" Poor Kevin squealed, breaking into a sick little jig.

"I don't understand," I whispered to Uncle Buddy.

"After you left the house, I picked up your trail and followed you," he said grimly, staring at Poor Kevin. "I wanted that damn notebook so badly. It's all I wanted. And then I saw him."

"Buddy-Buddy, two-by-four, can't fit through the bakery door!" Poor Kevin sang in his schoolmarm falsetto.

"My brother would never forgive me if I let him hurt you," Uncle Buddy said. "And I could use some forgiveness."

"Buddy-Buddy, two-by-four, I'll use your ass to mop the floor!"

"Yeah, you mopped the floor, all right, you mutant!" Uncle Buddy barked. "And if it wasn't done the way I wanted it done, I made you mop it again!"

Poor Kevin stopped dancing. In fact, it was first time that I ever saw him stand completely still. "Oh yeah, well . . . you're fat," he said.

"What's he doing?" Lou said. "He's only making him madder."

"Uncle Buddy," I hissed, but he ignored me, moving carefully toward the door of the gondola.

"You rolled dough for shit, too, you know that?" Uncle Buddy said. "You screwed it up every time, and every time I had to go back and make it right."

"Not . . . every time," Poor Kevin said.

"Absolutely the worst baker I ever met . . . even worse than your old man! All the *paisani* on the block knew it, and they all laughed at you behind your back."

"Not . . . everyone," Poor Kevin said, and he was moving again, his big body twitching under the plaid suit like it was crammed full of small, angry animals.

"Hey, kids, you know the only thing this freak ever baked that was worth a damn?" Uncle Buddy pointed at him and guffawed. "His face!"

Poor Kevin stood bristling, the ski mask moving on his neck like a bobble-head, and he shrieked like a pig in heat and charged. My uncle went into a crouch, and then at the last minute dropped to the floor and snagged Poor Kevin's ankle. The freak stumbled to the door of the gondola and it popped open. He was half in, half out, making circles with his arms and squealing, and I couldn't help myself—it was instinct—I grabbed him by the greasy suit coat and pulled him back inside.

"Sara Jane, no," Uncle Buddy said slowly. "You shouldn't have . . ." But he didn't finish his sentence because Poor Kevin kicked him in the mouth. Uncle Buddy rolled, spitting blood as the maniac tried to stomp his head, but Lou leaped from the wall, pushing him off balance. Poor Kevin backhanded my little brother, and he spun like a bleeding top into my arms. I set him gently on the bench and turned to my uncle, who was displaying his primary talent as a boxer, taking blow after blow from Poor Kevin that would have dropped a lesser man.

"Hey!" I screamed. Poor Kevin twisted his neck, and I broke the cardinal rule of boxing, sucker-punching him with everything I had.

The maniac's neck twisted back and Uncle Buddy pounded him with a right.

When Poor Kevin's head came back into view, I threw my left hook so hard that it knocked the ski mask from his head. In that long moment, I gasped at the flaming red *R* pressed into the gooey meat-lump that was his face. He made a slow pirouette—revealing scars like old bacon across his throat, skin holes where there should have been ears, and two lidless eyes as black as burned tar—just before he went down. I saw the terrible disfigurement that had driven him insane, and for a split second, I felt more than a twinge of sympathy for Poor Kevin.

My uncle stood back as if it were all over, but I'd been in similar situations with the masked freak before. Our gondola was almost at the top of the arc, and I was warning him to be careful when Poor Kevin jumped to his feet, grabbed Uncle Buddy in a headlock, kicked open the door, and flipped him out. Uncle Buddy grabbed the edge of the gondola and held on with both hands, his feet bicycling air. Poor Kevin leaned on his knees looking down at him and shrieked, "Spring's almost over and summer's too damn hot . . . but at least you'll have a nice fall!"

"Sara . . . Jane . . . ," Uncle Buddy gasped.

"And don't forget to look back! These two will be right behind you!"

"Sara Jane," Uncle Buddy said, "now!"

I was about to break my promise to Willy.

There would be a stain on my soul, and I suddenly did not care in the least.

I got a running start and pushed Poor Kevin out the door.

There was the *whoosh* of his body as it was sucked into the sky, it was silent, and then the gondola creaked and tipped precariously. Someone screamed somewhere far below. We'd reached the very top of the Ferris wheel's arc as I looked out at Poor Kevin holding on to Uncle Buddy's ankles, both of them swaying like an enormous pendulum. I scrambled for my uncle, screaming, "Hold on! I'll pull you up!"

"Oh yes, please do, hero girl!" Poor Kevin shrieked. "Because when he comes up, I come up! Pull me in, kick me out again, and I'll just keep coming back! I'll never stop and . . . I . . . mean . . . *never!*"

Uncle Buddy looked at me with a decision already made, his eyes crystal clear as he said, "Tell your dad for me . . . your mom . . . tell them . . ."

"Uncle Buddy! No!"

He didn't make a sound as he let go.

Poor Kevin screamed like a girl all the way to the concrete.

It wasn't a Mack truck, but it would do.

I pulled Lou to me, holding him tightly, feeling the Ferris wheel beginning its descent. He moved away slowly and looked over the edge, and I did too, at the crowd of ant people forming around the two twisted, leaking bodies. I saw Lou's head move and I followed his gaze past the scene to the curb. Even from a hundred feet in the air I could hear the haunting jingle of the little black ice cream truck. Without looking at me, he said, "We have a friend inside, Sara Jane. One friend. She brought me here, and now she has to take me back."

"No," I said, feeling my chest cloud with tears. "Please."

"Do you want me to tell Mom and Dad anything?" he said.

The relief that my family was alive was smothered by a deathly feeling of isolation—that I was not yet among them and no one was safe. "Tell them . . . tell them that they shouldn't have done this to us, goddamn it," I said, with water springing from my eyes. "It's their fault, all of it, because they didn't tell us anything . . . they didn't warn us, or tell us who we really are. And please, Lou . . . please . . . tell them that I love them." My brother nodded, and maybe it was what had been done to him with the wires, or maybe because he was only twelve years old and it was all too much for him, but besides a bleeding nose, his face remained as pale and impassive as it had been since we met. Sirens cut the air and I saw how near to the ground we were. "Don't give up on me," I said. "Whatever happens, I'm going to save you. Remember . . . I have the notebook."

The Ferris wheel was twenty feet from the ground, then five feet, and then Lou blinked as if seeing me for the first time. The corner of his mouth rose in a small smile and he extended a pinkie. "All or nothing," he said quietly. "Right?"

I hooked mine with his and said, "All or nothing," and felt him slip something into my hand. It was cold and hard, and I stared down at my mom's gold signet ring with the Rispoli *R* winking up from sharp little diamonds. When I looked up, Lou was gone. The door swung lazily and I leaped free of the gondola, cutting quickly through the crowd before any badges or uniforms reached me. When I was far enough away, I stopped and looked for my brother, but it was as if he never existed.

Except that he did.

My mom, my dad—they all existed in this time, somewhere in this town full of secrets and lies.

To be alive is sometimes to kill and I knew now that I was capable of it, and so much more.

I AM CONVINCED that there are other types of Capone Doors all over the world—secret black holes where people exit one life and enter another and, when the time's right, reappear somewhere else. Some of these doors possess an actual physical form, like the ones I travel throughout Chicago, while others may be legal loopholes, or cracks in the system, or unenforced laws. For example, the notebook outlines several simple methods for obtaining false ID documents—birth certificates, social security cards, driver's licenses, passports, even library cards—and in effect, these are Capone Doors too, since they allow a person to travel through the world undercover.

The notebook contains a phone number that was answered at police headquarters.

I said, "J. Edgar Hoover wore women's underwear."

There was a pause, then a voice asked what I needed.

I told him, computer keys clicked, and he muttered a meeting place.

I knew him by his lunch—he told me to look for a guy in Daley Plaza near the Picasso eating peanut butter from a jar. He was a classic mole, a bland-looking Outfit lifer who had burrowed into the police department as a records clerk with access to the department's vast computer network full of information about everything. No, he explained, there was no record whatsoever of a Chicago police detective named Dorothy Smelt. I told him other cops had worked for her, someone must know something, and he paused, working peanut butter from the roof of his mouth, and lowered a hand slowly in front of his face from his forehead to his chin, as if lowering a curtain. I have since come to understand that in the secret sign language of police, it means no one knows anything, no one saw anything, and no one will say anything, ever.

So Elzy was gone.

She'd exited her life as Detective Smelt through her own Capone Door.

My gut told me that eventually she would reenter through another door, as another person, but with the same twisted ambition to control the Outfit.

She was correct about one thing—I believe that in the twenty-first century, it would be impossible to do that without the notebook.

The official story is that the Outfit is weak, broken, and on its last legs after a long series of trials and convictions. The fact that most people believe this fantasy goes to show how well the Outfit has learned, in a hundred years of existence, to protect itself in a chameleonlike fashion by becoming invisible. The open displays of its existence—think Al Capone driving a Rolls-Royce convertible down State Street smoking hundred-dollar cigars and giving nickels to orphans—are so long gone, it's like they never happened. The organization has wormed its way so deep into legitimate businesses that every time someone orders a latte with extra foam or downloads a movie or upgrades a phone, the Outfit gets its cut. Yes, there are still plenty of limo companies and cement companies and "gentlemen's clubs" where the management uses "dem" and "dose" in daily conversation, but in general, the public accepts the bullshit that the Outfit has shrunk so small as to be almost nonexistent.

And then, out of nowhere, a headless, handless body stabbed sixty-six times will bob to the top of the Sanitary Canal.

A judge will commit suicide, and six hundred thousand dollars in cash will be found hidden in a shoe box under his bed.

There will be a long weekend of South Side shootings, which Chicagoans will dismiss as "drug-related gang activity" without realizing who's actually selling the drugs, and how they use modern street gangs as their sales force.

Only the notebook explains how to access and utilize all of the forces of the Outfit. It contains the past and present of the snaking, unseen organization, and in doing so, lays out a blueprint for its future. Most important, it makes crystal clear that the Outfit is a heartless, soulless business—not a family or a club but pure, grinding commerce—and that the Boss of Bosses, the old man referred to only as Lucky, demands that every single day is business as usual. As Knuckles recently told me, my real job as counselor-at-large is not peacemaker but profit maker, since conflict, infighting, and turf wars serve only to shut down the cash-making machine. He told me that I'm at the center of everything in the Outfit because its center is the almighty dollar.

Knuckles doesn't know that my family has been taken away.

What I've seen and heard as counselor-at-large, and the fact that I've been left alone to do the job, leads me to believe that no one else in the Outfit does either.

They don't know that behind the papered windows of the bakery and the sign that announces a renovation in progress, the place is still and empty.

They also don't know that the notebook exists, or that I'll use it to tear the whole rotten Outfit apart to get my family back.

In the meantime, I had to push myself forward to Fep Prep for final exams before school let out for the summer.

The first thing Max and I talked about on Monday was Bully the Kid, how bizarre the whole butt-kicking thing had been, and when he would be out of the hospital. We were in the theater room, waiting for Doug to show up with the movie, and Max took a long look at me and said, "You sparred recently, huh?"

I thought about Poor Kevin, about the melee in the gondola and about Uncle Buddy, and turned away, stifling a crying jag. When I was sure that it had passed, I said, "Yeah. A couple of times."

"You didn't answer your phone all weekend."

"Oh, yeah. It got . . . wet. I'll get a new one soon."

Max stared at me, looking past the bruises. "You seem different. Like something happened to you. Like . . ."

"It did, for sure."

". . . you met someone else?"

It was my turn to stare, and after a long pause I said, "What do you mean, else?"

Max blushed from the neckline of his shirt, up past his warm brown eyes, right to the tip of his curly hair. He swallowed thickly and said, "This has been a tough couple of months for me, Sara Jane. My parents' divorce, my dad moving to California . . . I feel like I lost my family, you know?"

"Yeah," I said. "I know."

"I mean, I totally understand if you met someone you like, and you want to . . ."

"I did meet someone, but—"

". . . see him, or whatever. I understand, because I don't have much to give right now. Sometimes I don't even feel like myself. Does that make sense?" he said, searching my eyes.

It made so much sense I had nothing to say except, "Max. Have you . . . ever been to Rome?"

"Italy?"

"Yeah."

He nodded, smiling. "Once, when I was little kid. We went as a family, traveled all over Europe. Funny you asked that, because Rome was my favorite place."

"What's it like?"

"It's beautiful. You'd fit right in," he said, and smiled a little. "My mom woke me up early one morning, before dawn. She wanted to walk the streets while they were empty, and we were crossing a piazza on the Capitoline Hill when the sun began to rise. We sat on the edge of a fountain to watch, right by an old church. I'll never forget how sunlight touched the dome and the whole city seemed . . ."

"Golden," I whispered.

". . . golden, like it was lit from above and below, and on all sides." He was quiet for a second, and then said, "We should go there sometime."

"Okay," I said, knowing I would go with him anywhere on earth.

"By the way," he said, pointing at my neck, "I like that a lot."

"Thanks," I said, touching the signet ring, which hung from a chain. "My mom gave it to me."

"It's showtime!" Doug said, bustling into the room, opening his new laptop.

Max stared at the bruises covering Doug's face. "Let me guess. You sparred this weekend too."

"What?" Doug said. "Oh, that. I got a ski mask stuck on my head."

"Huh?" Max said.

"Long story. Okay, today we're watching a classic film noir called *White Heat*, starring our favorite little gangster, James Cagney," Doug said, reaching into a paper bag. Instead of a ginormous root beer and a king-sized bag of Munchitos, he took out a bottle of water and a healthy apple. "His character, Cody Jarrett, is a ruthless criminal who's obsessed with his mother, and . . ."

"Whoa, whoa, whoa," Max said with a grin. "What's with the apple?"

"Pardon me?" Doug said.

"The apple. Where's the salty, crunchy junk and carbonated sugar water?"

Doug cleared his throat. "I'm trying to lose weight. There are things I need to be prepared for. If I'm going to live a long, healthy life, I mean."

Max nodded and lightly punched his shoulder. "Good for you, Doug. I'm proud of you."

Then it was Doug's turn to blush, and he looked at Max's hand and sighed as he turned on the movie. Toward the end, Cody Jarrett made his last stand against the police high above the ground, pacing the top of a building that looked suspiciously like the Bird Cage Club. I glanced at Doug, who winked, as Cody Jarrett screamed, "Made it, Ma! Top of the world!" right before dying in a huge, fiery explosion.

I gave Doug a WTF stare.

He mouthed back, "Ignore . . . that . . . part," and winked again.

I looked back at Cody Jarrett as he was eaten alive by white, crackling flames. Doug's little joke was hard to ignore, since I live at the Bird Cage Club now.

Its isolation in the clouds made it a logical and necessary decision.

Plus, I have a smart, loyal, and (somewhat) humorous sidekick and a small dog with the confidence of an angry buffalo to help guard the door.

I tried one more safe house the day after the Ferris wheel incident, an empty apartment in a three-flat on a desolate street in Lawndale, but as soon as I was locked inside, the phone rang. It was old-fashioned with a rotary dial, mounted on the wall. I lifted it and listened without saying anything. I heard movement and muffled voices but whoever held the phone was simply breathing. I hung up, paced the room, peeked out the window, and it rang again. There are few things as creepy as an old phone *brrr-ring*ing in a hollow apartment, insisting that it be answered as if it knows you're there. I tried to ignore it but it wouldn't stop, so I picked it up again. There was silence, and then very quietly I heard the haunting jingle-tune of an ice cream truck.

"Lou?" I said desperately. "Mom? Dad?"

The line went dead.

I hung up, stared at it for a beat, then lifted the briefcase and fled the apartment.

Maybe it had been a wrong number dialed twice or maybe it was just an eerie coincidence, but both my gut and my paranoia politely disagreed. I rode the steel elevator up to the Bird Cage Club, and I'll stay here until the day my family is reunited at our house on Balmoral Avenue. It's times like these, late at night when I'm studying, that I think about home most often. I can picture us there, my mother making petite, delicious ravioli, my dad trying once again to reattach the old lightning-struck weather vane to the slate roof, and Lou and Harry absorbing something obscure and intelligent on TV. I can't see Uncle Buddy there anymore but at least I love him again, and forgive him.

This is the last entry I'll make in my journal tonight but will continue writing in it tomorrow, and the day after that, and every day until I find my family.

I realize now that it's much more than a school project.

It's actually another important explanation of who and what the Outfit is, and someday, when I'm done with it, I'll include it where it belongs—in the notebook.

I used to study Italian in order to prepare for the trip my parents promised me if I graduate from Fep Prep with honors. Now I study it as a survival course, since so much of the notebook is written in Italian. Somewhere in that collection of tattered and worn pages stuffed between old leather is a secret that tops all others—the ultimate secret that I hope will help me find and free my family.

Especially the last chapter, "*Volta*."

I knew that it meant "time."

Once I looked deeper into my Italian dictionary, I realized that it has another meaning too. So, for tonight, my three new words are:

potere—power

interno—inside

volta—vault

I removed the brass key from the back cover, thumbed away tarnish, and saw "001" engraved on its face below three letters—UNB.

It hadn't occurred to me until now that the key to ultimate power may actually be a key, and that it would open a vault.

Now, all I have to do is find it.

ACKNOWLEDGMENTS

I would like to start by thanking Jason Anthony at LMQ for encouraging me to write this book, and for continuously making a good story even better. I'm indebted to my editor, Stacey Barney, for her insight, patience, big brain, and deft touch. A sincere thank you to Sylvie Rabineau at RWSG for getting behind the book so enthusiastically. I owe a pair of overdue thanks to Dan Smetanka, for teaching me important stuff, and Will Klein, for fanning a flame that burns cold and blue. Michael Goeglein and Dora Goeglein, my two little tornadoes of love, inspired me each day with their displays of adrenaline and natural hugability. Finally, and always, endless love to Laura Goeglein, who reads like a fan and critiques like a friend.

KEEP READING FOR A PEEK AT SARA JANE'S NEXT PULSE-RACING ADVENTURE!